THE DARNALAY CASTLE SERIES BOOK FOUR

The Song of the Magpie

LOUISE MAYBERRY

THE SONG OF THE MAGPIE
BY LOUISE MAYBERRY

First Edition, September, 2024

Copyright © 2024 by Louise Mayberry
Edited by Amber Night
Cover design by Dee Dee Book Design

Ebook ISBN: 979-8-9876378-7-6
Paperback ISBN: 979-8-9876378-8-3

This is a work of fiction. Any resemblance to specific events or persons, living or dead, is entirely coincidental.

Author's note

The importance of landownership, and what it means for one's personal autonomy, is a central theme of this story. However, there is a deep and tragic irony that must be acknowledged—an irony that none of the European characters (as well-meaning as they may be), have the perspective to truly understand. In truth, the farm near Windsor, New South Wales that Caitlin so cherishes is located on stolen land. Land that rightfully belongs to its original inhabitants: the Darug and Tharawal Aboriginal people.

PROLOGUE

SYDNEY, NEW SOUTH WALES. APRIL 1825

"THEY'RE GETTIN' READY TO put out the plank." Davey had been taut with excitement for the last half hour, anxiously tapping his boot against the wagon's toe board as he and Michael watched the brig, *Jupiter*, make its way to the wharf. Now he sprang into motion. Without a backward glance, he jumped down from the bench and forged his way through the melee of carts, people, and cargo that stood between them and King's Wharf.

Michael watched him disappear into the crowd.

For a moment, he contemplated following his friend. But for what? The scene at the public wharf was raucous, as usual. The stink of old fish and unwashed men stagnated in the heavy, hot air. Burly stevedores toted barrels and crates, shouting as they made their way through the crowd. An old mule waited patiently as three native laborers unloaded a mountain of baled wool from its wagon. Half-drunk and newly shaven, a pair of sailors on shore leave weaved across the dusty street, eyes bright with anticipation as they gazed up the hill toward the pubs and whorehouses of The Rocks.

As Michael watched, two street urchins and a dog scampered in front of a dockworker lugging a crate. The man teetered, cursing at the waifs, then righted himself and carried on. The children ran away laughing, one of them stuffing the contents of the man's pockets into his own.

Michael had no desire to wade through all that. Besides, Davey didn't care about his absence. Why would he? The man's wife and two boys were on that boat, and he hadn't seen them in five years. The only reason Michael was here was to lend his friend the wagon and an extra set of hands to bring the family's belongings back to the house.

He'd just get in the way of their reunion, anyway.

He pulled out his tobacco pouch and pipe, stuffed it full, then held his magnifying glass to the sun, focusing the white patch of light on the bowl until little curls of smoke began to rise. One puff, two, then a thick exhalation of billowing white smoke. He settled in for the wait.

After a time, Davey reemerged on the other side of George Street. He strode quickly toward the wharf, eyes never leaving the deck of the *Jupiter*. Michael took another pull on his pipe, but the sweet smoke turned bitter in his mouth. He was pleased for his friend, of course, but he didn't relish the idea of sharing the house, especially with a woman and children. He and Davey had settled into a routine, one that suited Michael just fine.

And yet, he'd promised Davey he'd give family life a try, as unpalatable as it sounded.

A grimy pair of stevedores began securing the gangplank, and Michael forced his attention away from his friend. He didn't come down here often, but the public wharf held memories—of that day, just over four years ago, when the *Speke* had docked in the same exact spot where the *Jupiter* now sat. The day he, Davey, and the rest of the men had been marched out of the darkness of its hold into the hot sun. Most of the people on this ship were convicts too, of course, still chained belowdecks. Once all the free passengers had disembarked, they'd be brought up the hill and mustered at the barracks, then sent to whatever fate awaited them. Poor bastards.

Michael had been one of the lucky ones. His education as a gentleman had paid off, though certainly not how Father ever intended. He'd been given a position at Cowper's warehouse, and, along with Davey, the privilege to live outside the barracks. He'd started as a bookkeeper, then risen through the ranks until he now oversaw all the goods coming in and out of the place. A fine assignment for a convict—and a rare, salaried one.

But it didn't feel like much.

In his mind's eye, Michael watched his old self emerge from that black hole of the ship, blinking into the dust and swelter of Sydney, irons biting his ankles with each step. One might think that four years in this miserable place would make a man wiser, more certain of the world. But the truth was, Michael felt no different from that lad coming off the ship. Older, perhaps, and harder. But just as worthless.

Finally, the dockhands stood clear, and the free passengers began to disembark.

First came a military man in a crisp, clean uniform, boots shining. He was holding tight to his young wife, who looked both frightened and intrigued by the scene before her. A few well-dressed gents, wide-eyed and pale, were next. Settlers come in the hope of acquiring land and finding riches. Michael's lips tightened. Good luck.

Then a dark-haired woman appeared, the same woman who'd been waving at Davey from the rail as the ship approached. Two boys stood tight behind her. She shaded her eyes with her hand and peered into the bright sun.

"Emily!" Davey's shout echoed above the din. He waved frantically.

The woman's head swiveled toward the sound, and even at a distance, Michael could see her face light up. In two strides, she was clear of the gangway, her feet safely on the wooden planks of the wharf. Gripping her children's hands, one on each side, she broke into a run.

She didn't have far to go. Davey rushed forward, and there was a collision of sorts. Davey's arms wrapped around his wife as he kissed her long and hard.

Michael's hand tightened on his pipe. The sight repelled him somehow, yet he couldn't look away.

It struck him suddenly that he'd never seen Davey with a woman. Perhaps that's why it galled him. Michael had been with plenty. The salary he took at Cowper's gave him access to the best whores in the colony. Now he even kept a woman of his own, Lucy, in a small room behind *The Black Dog*, one of the grog houses in The Rocks. Davey could have afforded the same with his clerking position in the secretary's office, but he'd always elected to stay home alone, sober and chaste. When Michael turned up in the wee hours, stumbling drunk, he'd find Davey waiting for him, ready to help him to bed.

The younger of the two boys squirmed up between his parents, wedging them apart. The lad was blond like his father. It must be Ewan, the one who'd been just a babe when Davey had been transported. Davey lifted him and tossed him in the air, and the boy's shrill laughter wafted in on the sea breeze. The older lad, dark-haired like his mother, stood awkwardly to one side until she pushed him forward. Davey embraced him, too, then pulled back to look at his face. That would be Luke, Michael supposed. Nine years old now.

Davey held fast to his wife's hand while the family stood talking for what felt an eternity. About the voyage, no doubt. Four months at sea seemed an eternity when you were in the middle of it, though in Michael's experience, it wasn't much to remember. Just day after day of the same, broken up only by a few stops at foreign ports. Of course, Davey and Michael hadn't had the satisfaction of getting off the ship at Madeira or Rio. They'd hardly seen the light of day even when they were out at sea, as they'd been stuck in the hold with all the other prisoners. Even now, Michael shuddered at the memory: the rank smell of the men and their waste, the endless dark, the clanking of chains, and the feeling of crawling out of one's skin. Davey's hammock had hung next to his, and the man had taken ill at the start of the voyage, the roll of the waves too much for him. Michael had made sure he got his share of food and water, though he kept precious little down. And somehow, in all of it, they'd become mates. The fact that he didn't deserve such a friendship still nagged at Michael. But the truth was, he'd have gone mad without it.

After a time, Davey's illness improved, and over many games of whist, he'd told Michael his story. Like Michael, he'd been sentenced to seven years in New South Wales, but that was where the similarities between them ended.

Davey was unlike anyone Michael had ever met—the kind of man Father had taught him to despise, to fear, even. He'd been convicted of sedition, a radical. But as he told Michael of how he'd devoted years to the fighting in France, only to come home to Glasgow to find his livelihood as a weaver destroyed by the factories and his family in poverty, Michael had found himself wondering how he'd ever accepted the view that radicals were a scourge to be stamped out by whatever means necessary. Davey had only wanted what was his due. The right to vote and provide for his family, to give his children a future worth living. Where was the evil in that?

And then came the realization that nearly shattered Michael completely. The unavoidable fact that the man his father had been, the man Michael had strived his whole life to become—a gentleman so concerned with privilege and wealth and maintaining the order of things—was nothing but a damn fool.

Worse than a fool, really. A villain.

He hadn't given Davey his real story. Just a garbled lie about a wealthy farmer's son and a forged banknote. Thankfully, his friend hadn't pressed for details.

Michael's eyes darted down the cove to Cowper's store, where a merchant ship was docked. The men would finish unloading her soon, and Michael would be needed to check their work and tally up the cargo. The bloke he'd left in charge, Bixby, was the best of the lot, but Michael didn't trust him. And Cowper had been in a foul mood lately. The construction of his newest warehouse was behind schedule. It had been hard enough to convince the old man to loan him the wagon and grant him a few hours' leave. To be late would do Michael no good.

He turned back to the ongoing reunion and willed Davey to snap out of his trance. To get moving.

Thankfully, just then a sailor emerged from the ship, a trunk balanced on his shoulders. He dumped it at Davey's feet, then Davey nodded and handed the man a coin. He motioned toward Michael and the wagon, explaining things to his wife.

That trunk looked heavy. Michael should help. That was what he was here for, after all. He set his pipe aside and forced himself to stand, but before he'd even jumped to the ground, Davey and Luke had each taken up one side of the trunk and were forging ahead, both of them grinning broadly.

Michael sat back down, mutely watching as father and son made their way toward the wagon. They hoisted the trunk high, then dropped it onto the bed, and the conveyance shuddered under the weight.

"You're strong, lad." Davey tousled his son's hair, and Luke beamed. Then they turned toward Michael. "Mikey, meet Luke. And Emily—Mrs. Flemming." He drew his wife close, his arm circling her waist. "This is Michael Dunn," he told her.

Michael nodded. "Mrs. Flemming. A pleasure." She was pretty. Not what he'd imagined somehow. Though now that he thought of it, he wasn't sure what he'd imagined.

The woman wiped her eyes. "Mr. Dunn, I've heard so much about you. We're to be house-mates, I understand?"

"Aye, madam."

As Michael spoke, Mrs. Flemming's eye caught her husband's, and a flicker of concern crossed her face.

She didn't want to live with him. Why would she?

"Ewan." she shouted to her youngest son, who stood a few paces away, eagerly watching the traffic on George Street. The boy ambled over reluctantly. "This"—she caught hold of him by his shirt collar—"is Ewan."

"You're Michael?" Ewan Flemming peered up at him, eyes wide with wonder. "You're a convict too, like Da, right? And we're to live with you? What did you do to—"

"Ewan!" Mrs. Flemming rebuffed. "Mr. Dunn is your father's friend. And a gentleman."

"He's a toff, all right," Davey agreed, a twinkle in his eye. "But a good sort. You'll get along just fine." The last was directed toward his wife.

Michael ignored them and took up the reins. "We'd best be off. I've work to attend to."

Michael rolled over, pulled the blanket over his head, pressed his pillow tight against his ears. It did no good. Nothing could block out the rhythmic thumping and the low, guttural groans that filtered through the thin wall between his and Davey's bedrooms.

Of course Davey would be making love to his wife. He hadn't seen her in four bloody years. Five if you counted the time he'd spent in prison. And he'd managed to keep himself chaste all that time. Michael couldn't imagine that kind of pent-up need.

But it wasn't just rutting, was it? There'd been that look—the look they'd been giving each other all day, as if, at long last, they'd both been made whole again. It was a look Michael had never before seen on Davey's face. And he'd be quite content if he never saw it again.

He'd hoped to avoid this. He'd not gone home at dinnertime, opting instead to meet Lucy at the *Dog*. He'd come home late, spinning with drink.

But not late, nor drunk enough.

"Uhh. Uhh. Uhh." The noise grew louder as the rhythm sped up, now accompanied by the sharp knocking of the bedstead against the wall.

Bah. Couldn't they just finish already? Michael squeezed the pillow hard against his ears. He had to be up early, otherwise he'd be back at the grog shop now, or, even better, sleeping soundly in Lucy's bed.

"Uhh. Uhh." With each second, his anger grew, the blunt frustration bashing him over the skull again and again and again.

Then, finally, one last moan, louder than the rest, and all was still.

Michael exhaled and released the pillow, but his ears were still ringing. That look between Davey and his wife continued to stick in his mind.

He couldn't do this. Promises be damned, he had to leave. The room he rented for Lucy was small and dirty. But it was better than this.

He'd tell them tomorrow.

Mrs. Flemming prepared breakfast the next morning, which, on the face of it, shouldn't have been a problem. It meant less work for Michael. Davey liked to sleep until the last possible minute, so Michael had taken up the habit of building the fire and setting the kettle to boil, then putting a pot of porridge on to cook.

But not today.

He lay in bed, listening to the sounds of the woman cooking, of the boys and Davey waking, while in his mind he rehearsed the upcoming conversation. *No offense intended, ma'am, but it's high time I get a place of my own.*

The family was already eating by the time he came into the kitchen. He paused in the doorway, feeling like an intruder to the cozy scene.

"I dinna understand," Mrs. Flemming was saying. "You can be *assigned* to me? Like my servant?"

"Aye." Davey chuckled. "'Tis common enough for a married man. I'd be able to find a position that pays more, or even open up a shop of our own." He grinned at his wife. "*If* you allow it."

Mrs. Flemming blushed. "I might." Her lips tightened into a coy smile.

"I've a salary now at the office, but 'tisn't enough," Davey went on, serious again. "Not to send the boys to school and feed us all."

"I could take in laundry until then, if you think it would help— Good morning, Mr. Dunn." She smiled brightly at Michael. "Do sit down."

Michael sat, and Mrs. Flemming poured him a cup of tea. "Davey tells me you've been doin' the all the cooking 'til now."

"Yes."

"Where did you learn?"

"I . . ." Michael hesitated. He'd not been taught to cook, if that's what one called boiling porridge or stew in a pot. The only thing he'd been taught to do was be a gentleman—an earl. "I picked it up. It's not that difficult."

Mrs. Flemming shot him an amused smile. "Well, the kitchen is spotless and well organized. I'm impressed." Her tone was sweetly condescending, as if she were trying to coax a grin from a child. "You'll be glad to be done with all that now, though, I'd expect."

"Yes."

A long silence followed. Mrs. Flemming stole a worried glance at her husband, but he just smiled back at her. Michael hadn't seen Davey so carefree in . . . well, ever.

He'd just opened his mouth to make his announcement when Mrs. Flemming finally spoke. "I've been meaning to ask you . . . your surname. *Dunn.*"

"Yes?" Michael stiffened.

"Do you know Lord Banton, by chance? *Cameron* Dunn? Or his sister, Jane? They're Scottish, and you're—well, I believe you're English. But you're a gentleman, and I thought perhaps—"

"No," Michael choked out. How did this woman know his cousins? She was a weaver's wife from Glasgow, and Cameron—Cameron was the bloody Earl of Banton.

"Who's Lord Banton?" Davey's interest perked up. "I've not heard of him."

"A friend of Will's," Mrs. Flemming replied. "He was one of the group who found him that day, after your arrest."

"Of course." Davey nodded. "I remember Will sayin'. I dinna recall any Dunn though . . . and certainly no lord. The man was a doctor, wasna he? And there was another man, I think . . ."

"He wasna a lord then," Luke took up the conversation. "Mr. Sommerbell told us about it. Lord Banton himself didna even know he was an earl. He was in trainin' to be a doctor, but he had an evil cousin who tried to steal his title."

"An evil cousin?" Davey smiled in amusement, obviously assuming his son was exaggerating.

"Aye. He locked Mr. Sommerbell in a *dungeon.* A real one. For weeks."

"'Tis true," Mrs. Flemming confirmed. "But that was years ago now. All's well that ends well. I'm sure—"

"I'm going to be leaving." Michael's heart was pounding so hard in his throat he was amazed he'd managed to speak. "Moving to new rooms."

Mrs. Flemming's eyes widened. "Oh, but Mr. Dunn. There's plenty of room for us all, and it's no trouble to cook your meals. I'm sure there's no need—"

"No offense intended, ma'am," Michael parroted the words he'd rehearsed, forcing himself to sound calm. "I've a place in mind. And you—you all deserve a home of your own."

ONE

EIGHTEEN MONTHS LATER

CAITLIN STARED AT THE chaotic, curving lines that crowded the dirty paper. Her jaw clenched so hard it seemed her teeth might crack. Of course, she could make neither heads nor tails of any of it, but the trader didn't know that. And it was a good thing, too. That look she'd glimpsed on his face just now, like a sly cat licking cream off his whiskers . . .

It wouldn't do to show any weakness.

She set her face into what she hoped was an intimidating look—pursed lips, arched brow—then raised her gaze from the contract and met Mr. Staples's beady black eyes. "Thirteen shillings a bushel? John told me you'd promised 'im fourteen."

The man shrugged. "That was six months ago. Crop's better than expected." He reached his finger deep into his ear and scratched.

Caitlin swallowed back the wave of revulsion. She narrowed her gaze. "And how'll I be paid?"

"Well, that's right here, innit?" He used the finger that had just been in his ear to point at a spot near the bottom of the page. "Payment will be made in ready money," he read aloud slowly, as if to a child, "when the wheat's sold."

"And when'll that be?"

He shrugged again, and that oily smirk spread back over his face. "Hard to say. Four months? Five? It'll need to be milled first, o' course. That could take anywhere from a few weeks to a—"

An idea struck. "May I have this?" She grasped the paper between her thumb and index finger and slowly lifted it from the desk, not taking her eyes off the man's face.

"Have. It?" Mr. Staples's smile wavered.

"I'd like to show it to a friend before I sign. Make sure all's fair."

The trader's eyes narrowed. He breathed out heavily through his teeth, and Caitlin winced at the smell—stale grog and rancid meat.

She'd dragged herself out of bed before dawn this morning so she'd have time to bathe in preparation for this meeting. What a waste.

And yet, here she was. Perhaps the deal could still be salvaged.

She kept hold of the paper, her eyes locked on the man behind the desk. Would he chase her if she turned tail and ran out with his contract? The Flemmings' store was just down the street. If she could get it there, Emily could read it, and at least Caitlin would know what it said.

"Nah." The trader closed his mouth and loudly sucked the snot into his throat, then swallowed. "I need this business finished by the end o' the week. I've limited space in my store, you see, and other sellers wantin' to—"

"I'll have it back within the hour." She retreated a step.

Mr. Staples leaned forward in his chair. "I'm afraid I can not allow it, madam." His voice rose. "I can't risk any fraud."

Fraud? Caitlin's cheeks heated, and she bit down hard to keep the angry words from flying out. There was only one person attempting fraud here, and it wasn't her.

She shot him a tight smile. "What are you afraid of, Mr. Staples?" She backed up another step toward the door, her jaw almost too tight to get the words out. "I simply want some time to look it over."

"I said *no*." Mr. Staples stood abruptly. His chair scraped loudly against the floor.

He really didn't want her taking it. The bloody cheat.

She wheeled around and darted for the open door, but he was too quick. He dashed around the desk, put his back to the threshold, and spread his arms wide to prevent her escape. His face had darkened, and his chest heaved.

Caitlin steadied her breath, but her heart was beating like a rabbit trying to break loose, and she knew her cheeks were flaming red. The insults were itching at her tongue.

She wanted nothing more than to tell him off. Or force her way past him and make her escape, but—Mr. Staples had been John's chief trading partner. He was the only wheat buyer she knew in Sydney, and on top of that, he still owed her for the hogs they'd sold him last fall. She needed that debt paid if she were to settle the bill with the man she'd bought the hogs from.

If she knew what was good for her, she'd just sign his filthy contract, whatever it said.

But before she could force herself to admit defeat, the corners of Mr. Staples's lips curled upward. His eyes took on an ominous gleam. "Yer a sassy one, ain't ye?" He spoke quietly, as if to himself. His eyes slid to her breasts, her hips, then back to her face.

Caitlin's skin crawled. Contract be damned, she had to get out of here.

She darted forward, ducked under his arm, and practically ran through the passage to the outer door.

"Wait!" Mr. Staples's heavy footfalls thudded after her. Just before she reached the door, he reappeared, blocking her way once more. "Mrs. Blackwell." He flashed a lewd grin, showing his tobacco-stained teeth. "I hadn't thought o' it before, but now that yer husband's gone . . ." He wrung one grubby hand with the other, a red flush spreading up his neck. "I—I wondered if perhaps you'd consider an . . . *arrangement*?" His brows rose. "I've been thinkin' o' taking on a woman, ye see, and you . . . well . . ." He flinched. "Yer Irish, but . . ." Tentatively, as if trying to tame a wild dog, he reached a hand toward her.

"But what, Mr. Staples?" The heat in Caitlin's cheeks flared. She backed away, clutching the paper to her chest like a shield. "I'm fuckable, am I?" Then another thought. Of course. "Or is it me farm you want?"

"I—well—The thing is, if you agree . . ." He took a step forward, his arm still reaching for her. She retreated further until she hit the wall beside the office door. "You wouldn't have to worry about the price o' wheat, now, would you? Or what's written in any contract."

The grinder. She should have guessed this would happen. A wave of revulsion swept over her, and she pressed her back against the wall. She was trapped, the man's hand mere inches from her face. A slow smile spread over his pudgy lips as his dirty palm made contact with her cheek. Then, slowly, his eyes lost focus, and he leaned in. "I'm a well-off man, Mrs. Blackwell." His head tilted, his fleshy lips pursed in anticipation. "I'd be honored to—"

She slapped him.

She didn't intend to. It happened with the speed of lightning, quicker than thought could form.

Staples's eyes widened as her palm met his skin.

Then time seemed to slow . . . Caitlin's hand fell way. Four white stripes marred his cheek where her fingers had landed. The streaks turned pink as, finally, he backed away.

His mouth hung open with shock, but that lecherous gleam still lurked in his eyes.

At the sight of it, the bile rose, and Caitlin's rage finally broke free. "Honored? To steal me farm? To shag an Irish strap like me?" She advanced on him. "You'll not set foot on any part of Swindale. And if you touch me again—"

"But you could move off the farm," he pleaded. "I'd find an overseer. You could come into town. Have a servant or two. I'd—"

"Never." It took every bit of her willpower to resist spitting on the man, but that's what an Irish street wench might do, or a convict fresh off the ship. Caitlin was neither one of those. Not any longer.

She pushed past him and pried the door open, then stepped out into the blinding sun.

It was only after the door had slammed behind her that she realized she was still holding the man's contract. The foul thing.

Scorching anger still burned through her as she stomped through the dust and the heat to the waiting dray, but as she untied the mare from the post and met the animal's gentle, trusting eyes, her sense returned. She sagged against the wagon's bed, staring up at the bulging bags of wheat.

She'd come all this way—a full day's drive—for nothing. Less than nothing. She had a dray full of wheat and no buyer. Not to mention the rest of the crop, for this was only the beginning. This year's wheat was only half in, and already it looked to be the best harvest she'd had since the flood years. Then there was the money she'd been counting on from the hogs. John's name was on that contract, not hers. There was no way Staples would pay her now.

Melia murder. What had got into her? Even if he was cheating her a shilling or two, what did it matter? It would be better than turning around home with a load of unsold wheat.

If she'd only kept her temper in check and signed the cursed thing . . .

John had always taken care of this kind of business. Caitlin had thought—hoped—she'd be able to muddle her way through, but that had been foolish.

She couldn't even read the man's contract.

Shakily, she climbed up to the wagon box and gripped the reins, then sat, watching the traffic pass by. It hadn't rained in weeks, and the dust rose in great clouds. It mixed with the steam in the air and the smells of people and animals and their waste, all of it baking under the hot sun.

The mare looked back at her questioningly.

All Caitlin wanted was to turn north toward home, to the sweet green fields and fresh air of Swindale. To get away from the stink and the crowd. But—

Her jaw tightened. She couldn't. Couldn't go home with a full dray. She must find a way.

But how? It wasn't as if she could sell her wheat on the street like a bagman.

Her eyes settled on a shopfront just down the way. *Flemming's.*

She no longer needed someone to read the contract. That was a lost cause. And of course, the Flemmings would have no interest in buying the thirty-five bushels of unmilled wheat Caitlin had in her dray, but they did purchase flour to sell in their store. Perhaps they knew of a trustworthy buyer she could call on.

Caitlin had known Mr. and Mrs. Flemming for less than a year. The last time she'd been in Sydney with John, only a few weeks before he'd died, the grocer she regularly sold candles to had been boarded up. There was a new shop next door though, the dry goods displayed in the window and the wheel of cheese on the sign clearly marking it as a grocer's. Not knowing what else to do, she'd poked her head in and been met by Mr. Flemming at the counter. He'd been happy to pay a good price for the gallon of honey and two dozen tapers she'd brought. He and his wife had just opened up shop, he'd explained, and they had no suppliers for such fine things.

The next time she'd come to town, just after she'd learned of John's death, Mr. Flemming had been away. But his wife had been there and purchased more candles. After doing business, Mrs. Flemming—Emily, she'd told Caitlin to call her—had offered her a cup of tea. They'd talked of John's death and Emily's children, and of how the family had come to be in the colony. They were Scots from near Glasgow. The husband had been convicted of some political offense, and Emily had followed with the children.

They were kind, fair people. It was worth a try.

Caitlin squared her shoulders and gently slapped the reins. "Giddyap." Then she maneuvered the heavy wagon onto the street and toward the Flemmings' store.

Two

CAITLIN STEPPED INTO THE shop to find a line of customers snaking its way through the maze of barrels and crates that cluttered the floor. Mr. Flemming was at the counter, sweat dripping down his face as he helped each person in turn. When he finally spotted her, she hastily explained her errand, and he waved her into the back where the family lived. Emily knew as much as he did about wheat buyers, he said, and she'd be happy for a visitor anyhow.

Emily greeted her with a warm smile, her infant daughter, Margaret, perched on her hip. She ushered Caitlin into the kitchen, then put the kettle on and excused herself to go lay the child down for a nap.

Caitlin waited. After a few minutes, the other woman emerged, poured tea, then sank into her chair, wincing as if in pain.

"Are you hurt?" Cailin asked.

"My back. 'Tis nothing new." Emily waved her hand, bringing air to her heated face. "That lass is getting too big, is all."

"She's a pretty little lump." Caitlin couldn't keep the wistfulness from her tone. Emily's daughter reminded her so much of Mary, her own youngest sister, toddling about the farm in Goleen, teasing the pig and making all kinds of mischief. She'd run Ma ragged. "She'll be walking soon."

Emily chuckled. "And then we'll have a new host of problems, willna we?" She took a sip of tea. "So. You're in need of a buyer for your wheat?"

"I am." Caitlin exhaled. "I—the man John used is no longer available, and I'm afeared I don't know anyone else. I thought you might."

"I know of several." Emily rose, bracing her back with her hand. "I'll just fetch paper and pencil and give you the addresses—"

"Oh, that's not—" Caitlin broke off, not knowing how to finish. She'd not told Emily, had she?

Emily stopped and cocked her head in confusion. "But I thought you needed a buyer."

"I do. It's just . . ." Caitlin hesitated. "Perhaps you could *tell* me the addresses. I've a crack memory. I'll remember." She felt the heat creep up her cheeks.

"Of course." Understanding dawned on Emily's face, along with a bit of pity. But she was too kind to say anything. She sat back down and began speaking slowly. "There's Mr. Campbell on York Street, just two blocks down, across from the blacksmith's. He's the one we buy our flour from, when he has it. He's fair, though I'm not sure how much room he'll have at the moment."

Caitlin nodded, committing the name to memory. *Campbell. York Street. Across from the blacksmith's.*

"Then, there's Mr. Gordon up on Clarance."

"Where's—"

"Two streets north, then three to the west. Right before the military barracks. Gordon's just recently emancipated, and keen for new business, I've heard. He may be a good one."

Gordon. Clarance Street. Military barracks.

"Why dinna you try those two, and if you need more, you can come back? I'll ask around, if need be, or Davey may know some I don't." Emily set her empty cup down and sat back in her chair. "I do wish you luck. 'Tisn't easy being a woman alone, I can imagine."

Caitlin lifted her chin. Of course the other woman meant well. But somehow, the way she said it, as if Caitlin were to be pitied, it felt like an insult. Being a woman alone was exactly what Caitlin wanted to be. No men telling her what to do.

"I'm unfamiliar, is all." Emily's head tipped to one side, eyes widening at the clip of Caitlin's words. Caitlin softened her tone. "I—I'm much happier to stay at Swindale, if you want the truth."

"Oh, I understand that." Emily crossed her arms, and a wry smile played on her lips. "Once Davey gets his pardon, we'll be leaving. We'll set up shop in Parramatta, or farther out in one of the new towns. This is no place to raise a family." She set her hands on her knees and levered herself up. "Now then, Luke and Ewan will be home soon. I'll just—"

"One more thing, if you don't mind." Caitlin fished the now-folded contract from her pocket. "I wondered if you'd read this to me?" She held out the creased page.

"Of course." Emily accepted the paper. She squinted as she read the messy hand. "'Tis a contract." Her gaze rose to meet Caitlin's. "For wheat."

"It is. And what's the price?"

Emily scanned the page. "Ten shillings a bushel." She exhaled softly. "That's awfully low, isna it? I heard 'tis going for at least fourteen this year, maybe more."

"That *nipper*." The anger from earlier started to rise again, and Caitlin forced a long exhale. "He told me it said thirteen. Same as John got last year. But John said he'd been promised fourteen."

"Oh . . ."

"What's it say about payment?"

Emily read silently until she found the place. "'Twelve months. . .'" She let the paper fall. "I'm so glad you didna sign this."

Caitlin drew a breath. How on earth could she run the farm if men like this could take such advantage? She couldn't, that's what.

"How did you know?" Emily handed the contract back.

Caitlin shook herself. Such thoughts did no one any good. "I had a feeling, is all. I didn't know if I was right or not." She pressed her lips together. "John did all the—all the business for the farm. 'Tisn't easy without him." She wished she could eat the words as soon as they were out. The way she'd said them—it sounded as if she'd liked the man.

Emily's gaze softened. "You must miss him dreadfully."

"Nah." Caitlin snorted. Emily gave her a look, and she thought a moment, searching for the right words. "I miss his abilities. Not his company."

"Ah. Did he come as a bonded man, then?"

"Not him. Came as a purser on an East India ship. Governor King gave him the grant to Swindale in turn for—" She shrugged. "Some favor." She still didn't know what John had done to get such a plum, though she suspected it was a settlement of a gambling debt. "He wasn't a farmer."

"But *you* are," Emily observed.

Caitlin nodded. "I grew up on a dairy. In County Cork." Not that life there had prepared her for farming here. It had taken her years to learn the cycles of this strange land. "John wanted to go back to sea and needed someone to look after the farm. He picked me from a lineup."

Emily nodded her understanding. It was a common enough story. A free settler could have his pick of convict wives, and it was in his favor to do so. A wife's term of service didn't run out like a male convict's would.

And at least until he tired of her, Caitlin had been a warm body in John's bed whenever he did return to the colony.

But now she was a widow. Free of him and all other men. She'd just have to find a means to keep it that way.

"I'm surprised he didna teach you to read." Emily's head cocked to one side.

Caitlin shrugged, doing her best not to let the loathing soak into her words. "He never saw the need." She finished her tea in one gulp, then rose. "I'm off, then. Thank you."

Emily smiled. "You're most welcome."

An hour later, Caitlin stood with Mr. Gordon, a kindly old man with watery eyes and a warm smile, watching his laborer unload the wheat from her dray. Just as Emily had predicted, the trader was keen to fill up his almost empty warehouse. He'd readily agreed to pay fourteen shillings a bushel, and he'd promised to buy all Caitlin could sell him over the coming months, the quality being so good.

Just as the worker hefted the last bag, a grand carriage rumbled by, drawing his eyes, and those of everyone else in the vicinity—the street urchin lingering nearby, the two ladies coming out of a shop. The coach was sleek and black and pulled by two beautifully matched horses. A rare sight indeed in the colony. Caitlin caught a quick glimpse of an old woman's weathered face within.

She looked to Mr. Gordon, who was gazing at the retreating coach. "Who was that?"

The carriage disappeared around a corner, and Mr. Gordon grinned at her. "Mrs. Johnstone, of course." He spoke the name as if she should recognize it.

She didn't. "Mrs. Johnstone?"

"Aye. Used to be Abrams. Esther Abrams, Johnstone's mistress. Macquarie forced them into respectability a while back, though the old man's dead now."

"Oh." Caitlin looked back up the street, suddenly wishing the coach would come back. She *did* know of Esther Abrams. Like Caitlin, Esther had been sent to New South Wales as a convict, and had become an officer's mistress during the crossing. Except in Esther's case, that officer had been Lieutenant George Johnstone, a prominent member of the New South Wales Corps and a giant in the colony. For a brief period, he'd even served as governor. By all accounts, they'd fallen in love. They'd had children together, and while Johnstone dithered in politics in Sydney and England, Esther had raised their brood and run their farm—quite profitably, if what Caitlin had heard was true.

"Well, good day to ye, Mrs. Blackwell," Mr. Gordon's voice filtered through her thoughts. "It's been a pleasure."

She smiled at the old man. "Good day, Mr. Gordon. I'll be back with more in a week or so."

The trader went back inside, and Caitlin hummed a happy tune, a bounce in her step as she climbed up to the driver's box. Mr. Staples could go hang. Just like Esther Abrams, Caitlin would prove to them all what a lowly woman could do.

She'd just lifted the reins when Emily's oldest son, Luke, came bounding up the busy street.

"Mrs. Blackwell," he gasped, out of breath. "Ma and Da want a word with ye. Back at the shop."

Caitlin's good humor dimmed. She scanned the sky. It was well past noon. If she hoped to make home before nightfall, she must be off. She opened her mouth to give her regrets, then met the boy's bright eyes and closed it again. The Flemmings had shown her nothing but kindness. The least she could do was give them a few minutes of her time.

"All right, but it must be quick."

The shop was empty, save for Mr. and Mrs. Flemming, who were waiting for her behind the counter.

"Oh, Mrs. Blackwell." Emily bustled around, leading her husband by the hand. "Thank you for coming. I know it's late, but we've had an idea." She beamed, clearly excited.

"An . . . idea?" Caitlin struggled to return the woman's smile. "Everything is well. I've sold the wheat to Mr. Gordon, and I'm—"

Emily lifted a hand. "Just hear us out. If you dinna agree, we willna be offended. We just—we've a friend in need, you see, and I thought . . . Well, you might be able to help *each other*. Luke." Emily turned to her son. "See to the shop while we talk to Mrs. Blackwell."

Luke took up his post as Emily ushered Caitlin through the back door into the kitchen. Mr. Flemming followed, pulling the door closed behind him.

The hopeful look on Emily's face made Caitlin's skin prickle. She was in no position to help anyone. It would be all she could do to hold on to the farm.

"Tea?" Emily asked brightly.

"I can not, thank you." Caitlin did her best to hide her impatience. "I must be leaving soon."

"Of course." The other woman smoothed her skirts. "You want to be home before dark."

"I do."

"Well then, I'll get to it." Emily took a step closer. "You see, our friend—Davey's, to be precise," her eyes darted to her husband, still lurking by the door, then back to Caitlin, "is due to come back from Moreton Bay next week. We've been told he'll be assigned to a building crew or some other government work, but we thought—he can *read*, you see. He's educated. He ran Cowper's warehouses for a time. He may be able to help you with contracts and the like. If he were assigned to you, it would be a much better position for him, and . . . it would benefit *you*." Emily stopped, her face expectant and hopeful, her eyes never leaving Caitlin's.

Caitlin had no idea what to say. She didn't want to disappoint—Emily had been nothing but kind—but there were a hundred reasons this plan wouldn't work.

"He's a good man." Mr. Flemming strode forward and stood next to his wife. "Loyal and dependable."

"He's . . . at Moreton Bay?" Caitlin asked. Only the worst convicts got sent there. Men who had reoffended during their sentence, murderers, thieves, the ones that couldn't be controlled and weren't fit to work in the colony.

Mr. Flemming's shoulders sank a bit. "Not by his own fault. Though, to tell ye the truth, he can be a bit of a drinker."

"Tell her how he came to be there," Emily prodded.

"Aye." Mr. Flemming heaved a sigh. "Mikey and I stayed together when we first came here. And before that, on the ship, he cared for me when I was ill. Saved my life, I do believe." He put his arm around his wife. "But after Emily and the boys came out, he left, and . . . went to live in The Rocks." He shook his head. "We didna see much of him. I believe he lost himself a bit to the grog houses. Then one night, he—"

Mr. Flemming stopped, obviously uncomfortable, but his wife elbowed him. "Go on. I'm sure Mrs. Blackwell's heard worse."

"He came across a man takin' advantage of a lady, in the wee wynd behind *The Black Dog*. According to Mikey, the lady was cryin' out and tryin' to get away, but the man—he struck her. Wouldna let her go."

Caitlin shuddered, and despite the heat, a wave of cold washed over her. She'd known such alleys in Cork. Though, after that first time, she herself hadn't tried to get away. After Ma and Da had died, such encounters had become her only means of feeding her younger siblings.

"Mikey got the polecat off and left him in a sorry state," Mr. Flemming continued, "but in the dark, he didna see who the man was."

"Who was it, then?" Caitlin held her breath.

"George Phelps."

"Who's—"

"First clerk to the superintendent of police." Mr. Flemming shook his head as Caitlin stifled a gasp. "He was doomed, Mikey was. There was a sham of a trial. Phelps denied any lady existed. Said Mikey was roarin' drunk—which I dinna doubt was true—and attacked him, meanin' to rob 'im."

"But didn't the woman vouch for him?"

"She ran away as soon as Mikey got her free." Mr. Flemming shrugged. "Disappeared. Can hardly blame her." He pulled his wife closer. "He's an honest man, Mrs. Blackwell. And after all that's happened, I believe some peace would do him good. He willna get that as a government man."

Caitlin gazed at the couple. Clearly, they cared about this man. And what Mr. Flemming said was quite true. Life as a government laborer in Sydney would mean backbreaking work, poor rations, and—for a man with a weakness for drink—constant temptation. Such a life would do *nobody* any good.

But Moreton Bay. It changed men. What if Dunn had become the thieving sort, or worse? What if he tried to come at her?

"Is he violent when he drinks?" Caitlin was surprised at her own boldness, but she must know.

"Heavens, no." Mr. Flemming chuckled. "I was shocked to know he had it in 'im. He's a bit gruff and stiff. He's a toff. A gentleman." He rolled his eyes and gave a small affected bow. "But he's not violent. Ye'd be safe with him."

A gentleman.

Caitlin's mind was racing. To have a man who could read and write at her disposal . . . If he'd run a warehouse, he must know how to keep ledgers too.

And there was that pile of letters on John's desk. She had no idea what any of them said.

Perhaps she could even have this man teach her to read.

"And you're sure he could be assigned to me?" she asked. "I've got three men already, and I've not a right to more than that. One of them's due for his ticket though, so perhaps—"

Davey waved away her concern. "I used to work in the secretary's office. I've friends there still."

"How long does he have on his sentence?"

"Just one year more. 'Tisn't long, but I do think he could be a help to you, Mrs. Blackwell."

It was a risk, but she'd had plenty of rough men on her field crew over the years, and the Flemmings were vouching for him. That meant something.

"You can always return him to the barracks if he proves unsuitable," Mrs. Flemming added, her face taking on that hopeful look again.

Caitlin bit the inside of her lip. It sounded like nothing but trouble. But if she was to be an independent woman . . . and the idea of learning to read . . . "Very well. If you can secure the assignment, I'll take him on. Or I'll try."

Emily's face lit up like a match on tinder. "Oh, thank you. Thank you."

A shiver crawled down Caitlin's spine. She tried to smile, but her lips felt stiff and tight. What was she getting herself into? "You're quite welcome." She turned toward the door. "Now I really must be going."

The smile faded from Emily's face. "Of course. Have a safe journey home."

THREE

"YOU. DUNN. YOU'RE TO come with me." The redcoat bent and unlocked Michael's leg irons from the chain that connected him to the five other men in line. It fell slack with an empty clink. One of the two guards marching the gang to the worksite barked an order, and the long line of men moved away.

The soldier who'd unlocked Michael rose and grasped his arm roughly, pushing him back down the road the way they'd come.

Michael stumbled, free of the gang now, but nearly losing his balance as the irons on his ankles jerked taut. He'd been certain the redcoat—Grigsby was his name, the one with the mustache and the taunting glare—had come for Whit, the man behind him in line. Whit was a fool. He'd openly stared at one of the officer's wives working in the garden while they'd been marched past yesterday. The woman had noticed, and of course she'd reported it. It was a surefire ticket to the whipping post.

But the man had not come for Whit. He'd come for Michael.

"What did *I* do?" He looked over his shoulder and glowered at the guard.

In answer, Grigsby raised his rifle and poked the cold steel into Michael's back. "Move."

And so they went, down the road and away from the worksite where the gang was building a new stone barracks for future unfortunates. Back toward the rough, slab huts, where Michael and the others had just finished their meager breakfast.

"Get a move on." The metal dug deeper into Michael's back.

When Michael had first arrived in this hell, months ago—he'd lost count of how many—he would have argued with the man. He'd have pressed to know why he was being singled out and made the point that he couldn't very well walk quickly with chains shortening his every stride. But that had been before. Before the hunger, the solitary confinements, the floggings. Now, he just shuffled along, head down as he examined the rutted, muddy road and the tips of his worn-out shoes.

Why was a pointless question. It didn't matter why. The punishments were unavoidable, like the sun coming up each day or the river flowing out to sea.

At least he was accustomed to them by now. He no longer flinched at the smarting pain of his ever-healing back. Nor did he notice the bite of the irons around his ankles, the gnawing hunger in his gut, the burning of the sun on his neck, or the press of the hot air in his lungs. The smell of his own stench.

His gaze fell on the whipping post in the distance, the buffed wood shone evil in the morning sun, ready for its next victim. They were going to flog him again. For nothing. Maybe the wounds would fester this time, and he'd die.

Grigsby jabbed him in the back, and Michael lost his balance. He fell to his knees, bracing himself with his hands to keep his face out of the dirt.

"What the devil are you up to? Get up, man." the soldier barked, as if he hadn't been the one to push Michael to the ground.

Michael scrambled to his feet and stumbled forward, showing only placid obedience. The soldiers of Moreton Bay were just as miserable as the prisoners. That was a fact. Just as isolated, nearly as hungry. Some had their wives with them, but not Grigsby. Tormenting a man like Michael was the only pleasure this swad ever got, along with his daily allotment of rum.

Michael expected to be marched toward the store and the whipping post. But instead, Grigsby stopped at the dilapidated slab hut Michael shared with six other men.

"Get your things."

Michael looked back at the man. "What—"

"Get. Your. Things." The soldier glanced over his shoulder.

Michael followed the redcoat's gaze. A sloop was tied to the dock. He could see the new prisoners being marched off it, with a few others standing to the side, waiting to embark to be brought back to Sydney.

Back to Sydney.

He looked at Grigsby, searching the man's face, but the soldier was expressionless.

Could six months really have passed?

Sydney—the color, the bustle, the people. The smells of good food and the taste of rum. The feel of a woman's skin—

The cold iron of Grigsby's gun jammed between Michael's shoulder blades, nearly knocking him down again. "Have you gone daft, man? The ship won't wait." The extra bit of loathing in the redcoat's voice and the sharp jabs of the gun made sense now. He was jealous.

Michael grunted and stumbled through the low doorway. It was too dark to see anything, but he walked the three paces to the dirty straw he'd slept on for the last six months by rote. His hand trembled as he slipped it underneath to collect the few things he'd managed to bring with him.

A comb. His pipe and tobacco pouch—empty these last six months—an extra shirt that had once been clean, and a rough linen sack to carry it all in.

All his worldly possessions in hand, Michael straightened. The chains of his leg irons clanged as he shuffled into the light.

FOUR

AFTER FOUR INTERMINABLE DAYS on the water, the ship from Moreton Bay cleared The Heads and docked at King's Wharf. It was a gloomy afternoon, the sky a slate gray mass hanging low over the town, threatening rain. A hard wind blew at their backs. Besides his time at Moreton Bay, Michael had worked every day of the last five years on this waterfront, and as the sailors secured the sloop, he stood at the rail and scanned the port, searching for familiar faces. But there were only strangers. A few peered warily at the ragged group of convicts as they shuffled down the gangway in their chains. Most tried not to look.

Not that anyone who'd known Michael Dunn would recognize the pitiful sod who stepped off that sloop. His skin was reddened by the sun and darkened with dirt, his hair matted and greasy, and he was stones lighter than he'd been. He hadn't shaved in weeks. His jacket had been stolen months ago, and he no longer owned a hat—only a grimy pair of trousers with holes at the knees, a ripped government-issue shirt, and shoes worn through at the soles.

But it wasn't just his appearance that had changed. Michael looked at the scene on the wharf through different eyes than the man who'd left six months ago. That man had belonged here, at least to a point. He'd had a place. A use. A sense of rightness, and a burning outrage at his conviction. But now, he had nothing. Less than nothing.

The rain began to fall as he was marched across George Street alongside the other convicts. It started as a heavy mist, but between one stride and the next, the skies opened to release a torrent. It hammered down as they slogged up the hill, muffling the sights and sounds of the town, turning the streets to mud and plastering Michael's shirt to his back.

And yet, he felt nothing. Only a simmering sense of loathing.

This absence, the dearth of feeling was beginning to unnerve him. He'd expected it on the journey. The dark hold of a ship always felt like a place between, not quite real. But here—here he ought to begin to feel more normal, oughtn't he?

The group was brought to the grounds of the prisoners' barracks, to the blacksmith, where one by one the irons were cleaved off. It hurt like the devil when the smith hammered the rivets that held Michael's shackles in place. Then all at once they fell away and . . . He'd expected relief at finally being free of the irons, but oddly enough, as he took his first few steps, he felt only their loss, unstable, like a ship without an anchor.

And what lay beneath the shackles . . . the raw, exposed flesh. It was repulsive. He couldn't bear to look at it.

They were brought into the barracks proper, to the mess hall. The government men who lived there had already had their noon meal and returned to work in the city. There was no end-of-day meal on offer, so Michael and the others from Moreton Bay were given bread and water, separated so as to not get into any trouble, and sent to one of the twelve sleeping wards.

The ward was eerily quiet as Michael and his guard entered, their footsteps echoing in the great yawning space of shadow and silence. There must have been a hundred flaxen hammocks strung neatly from great beams of eucalyptus wood.

The guard assigned him one, then left without a word.

Alone, Michael stood for a moment, feeling the quiet, the beating of his own heart. And for the first time since they'd landed, he felt almost himself. The space was clean, cleaner than anywhere he'd been in months, with the minty, lemony sharpness of the eucalyptus wood permeating each breath he took. The paned windows gave a clear, if distorted, view of the rain and gloom. The wood floors shone in the dim light, the walls were newly whitewashed.

There were no more orders, so not knowing what else to do, he lay in his hammock and stared at the cavernous ceiling, listening to the rain.

Where would he be assigned? A government crew of some kind, no doubt. No respectable master would accept a man so fresh from Moreton Bay.

They'd taken his irons off, so it wouldn't be a chain gang. Probably, it would be something in the city, a building crew or the brick works. He could only hope the labor would be tolerable, whatever it was. With a decent overseer.

Anyway, it was out of his hands.

He was just drifting off to sleep when the working men came in, weary from their day's labor. The space filled with their rough voices. They brought out whatever scrapings of food they'd been able to stash away in their pockets and ate, laughing and talking. Some played cards.

Michael didn't move.

A man from the group nearest to him approached his hammock and peered down at him warily. "You're one of the lot from Moreton Bay, then?" His tone was cautious but good-natured.

Michael growled, and the intruder quickly backed away to the safety of his mates.

At last, the warden called lights out, and the men climbed into their hammocks. Gradually, the talking was replaced by whispers, then snores. Michael slept.

And by the grace of God, he didn't dream.

The next morning dawned clear. He didn't dare leave his few possessions in the sleeping quarters—they'd be stolen for sure—so he took his things with him as he fell in with the crowd of men shuffling through the muddy yard to the privy and then to the mess. The meat stew the cook's boy slopped into his bowl was salty and thin, but it seemed a king's ration after the allotment at Moreton Bay. He'd forgotten what a full belly felt like.

When they'd finished eating, the men around him got up and went off to whatever work they'd been assigned. Michael was left sitting alone, staring at his empty tin bowl.

The dull sense of panic grew as silence settled back over the room. What was he to do next? Where were the others from Moreton Bay? They weren't here. But he'd been given no instruction. Perhaps he was supposed to know what to do. Perhaps they'd discipline him if—

"Dunn?" a gruff voice sounded. Relief coursed through Michael as he looked up to see a redcoat staring at him expectantly.

"Aye." This was it.

"Come on, then." The man motioned for him to get up.

Obediently, Michael rose, slung his sack over his shoulder, and followed the guard into the courtyard.

Bah. He squinted into the light. The orange brick of the barracks building blazed bright in the morning sun, blinding him. It was already hot. A thin mist rose from the cobblestones—yesterday's rain, steaming off.

"This way." He'd expected the soldier to lead him to the court rooms where he'd be assigned to a gang, but instead they moved toward the front gate.

A man stood just inside the courtyard, leaning against the wall. The sun reflected off the light-colored stone, making it almost as painful to look at as the brick. Michael's eyes were dazzled. It was hard to tell, but from the way the man was positioned, he appeared to be waiting for something.

The man came away from the wall and walked toward them. He was dressed well—a jacket, waistcoat, and clean linen beneath. Slight build with pale hair under a tall hat—

Jesus. It was Davey.

"Mikey?" Davey squinted, craning his neck. The rising sun was behind Michael, and it seemed Davey was having just as much trouble seeing anything. Or perhaps he simply didn't believe the man walking toward him was, in fact, his old friend. What the devil was he doing here?

"You're David Flemming?" the soldier asked.

"Aye." Davey's eyes never left Michael.

The redcoat handed him a folded piece of paper. "His pass. It's only good for today. See he's delivered by nightfall."

Davey finally looked from Michael to the guard. "Do you have clothes for 'im? He's hardly—"

"Clothing is the responsibility of the master," the soldier recited in a bored tone.

Davey knew better than to argue. "Of course."

His task complete, the redcoat nodded, then turned and quickly walked away.

As soon as the guard was out of earshot, Davey leaned toward Michael, pitching his voice low. "Yer a sight for sore eyes." He grinned. "I've got ye a place, a good one."

Michael stared at him. "A—a place?"

The dumb confusion in his words hung between them, and Davey's face fell, his eyes darkening with concern. "Aye. A *place*. Of employment."

Michael blinked. What did he mean, *employment*? What was this?

"What have they done to ye, man?" Davey spoke softly, gazing at Michael with narrowed eyes. Then, louder, "I'll tell ye more on the way." He turned and started toward the gate where another guard was waiting to search them on their way out. "We'll stop back home before we go," he called over his shoulder. "I've a suit of clothes ye can have."

Davey's place was a quick drive from the prisoners' barracks. It wasn't the small house they'd once shared, but a new shop, the one Davey had taken up since his wife and children had come to Sydney. He didn't say so, but Michael knew he wouldn't be welcome inside. Not in his current state. He'd scare customers away. So he waited in the wagon, watching the bustle of the street while Davey ducked into the shop, then reemerged with a rucksack stuffed full and pulling at the seams.

He tossed it to Michael, and Michael opened it, shaking out the contents. A shaving kit and a comb, a copy of *The Australian*, and a new set of clothes. Fine ones. Much too fine for a road gang or a field crew.

What kind of position was he going to?

His friend heaved himself up to the box, then fished in his pocket and threw a short piece of twisted tobacco into Michael's lap. "You still have a pipe?"

Michael grunted. "But—"

"Ye can pay me back." The firmness in Davey's tone broached no argument.

Michael used his friend's pocket knife to cut the twist as Davey maneuvered the wagon north out of the city. "I suppose you'll want to know where we're goin'?" He shot Michael a sly grin, clearly pleased with whatever this scheme was.

Why did Davey's good humor feel so ominous? As if it were a trick. "Yes."

That searching, pitying concern fell back onto his friend's face. That, too, put Michael on edge. As if he were being inspected, and failing. But thankfully, Davey quickly looked away and began to speak.

"We're off to the Hawkesbury, to a farm there."

So it was farm work? That was hardly any better than a chain gang.

"But you willna be doin' field work," Davey added quickly. "Or not much of it. The owner makes candles and sells 'em to us at the shop. Her husband died four months ago, and she's got possession of his farm. She wants to make a go of it, to keep a hold of the land. But she canna read, you see, and that's not makin' things any easier for her. We thought—Emily and me—we thought you could help. Read contracts for her, help her with runnin' things, like ... like a secretary mi—"

A kangaroo hopped across their path, startling the horse, and the wagon swayed dangerously. "Whoa, now." Davey pulled on the reins, bringing them to a halt. Then he clucked to the nag, and they continued.

"Anyway. We thought you could help, and it's a sight better than government work, so I called in a favor from my old mate at the office, and he got ye the assignment. Wasna easy to do." Davey looked over at him, brows raised, as if expecting a thank you.

Michael stared at him, but the words wouldn't come. He nodded woodenly, then looked away.

For a while they sat in awkward silence, listening to the plodding of the horse's feet and the creaking of the wheels as they jounced over the rutted road.

A secretary. He was to be the secretary of a widow farmer. The words played over and over in Michael's head, but they didn't make any sense.

It wouldn't work.

It was a good assignment, that was true, but he couldn't be a widow's secretary. Not in this state. He could barely speak to his best friend.

And if he failed, she would send him back. With that mark against him, he'd be clapped back in irons for sure, sent to a road gang, finally worked to death—

A bird squawked loudly in the trees overhead, and Michael jumped.

What the devil was wrong with him?

He forced a long, slow breath. He should be happy. The sun shone brightly, though the heat was tempered by the dappled shade. A warm breeze blew through his hair, bringing with it the perfumy smell of acacia blooms. He pulled at his pipe, drawing the smoke into his lungs, then exhaled slowly.

Nothing changed. That acrid sense of distrustful revulsion still simmered inside him.

There was no guard searching for an excuse to flog him. No threatening word or glowering look from another prisoner. Nothing at all to be afraid of. Even if this new position was tenuous, in *this* moment he should be enjoying himself, and yet . . .

He couldn't. He just . . . couldn't.

He closed his eyes and rubbed them hard.

Davey shifted beside him on the bench. "I think you'll like it there, on a farm. It'll be peaceful."

Peaceful. How could his friend be so daft? So blind? A widow's secretary. Peace. Bah. Michael would ruin it, just as he'd ruined everything else in his bloody life.

But then, Davey didn't really know him, did he? It was all lies and deceit. Further evidence of Michael's villainy.

When the sun reached its zenith, they stopped and sat under a towering lemon gum tree, allowing the horse to drink from a stream as they ate the meal Mrs. Flemming had packed: dark wheaten bread with butter, boiled eggs, and spring radishes. After six months of plain hominy with the occasional half-rotten bit of meat, it seemed unfathomable that food could taste so good. And for a moment, when Davey got up to take a piss and Michael was alone, reclined against the white, papery bark of the tree, his nostrils full of its fresh earthy scent, he almost felt the pleasure of it.

But then Davey returned and stood over him with a raised brow and a look of pitying disapproval. "Do you want to change before we get there?"

"No." Michael's answer was partly because he knew better than to put himself, as dirty as he was, into clean clothes, and partly out of foolish spite. He didn't want Davey's pity.

They climbed back into the wagon. Heavy silence settled between them once more as Michael packed another bowl, smoked, and glared at the pretty day.

What an ass he was being. Davey deserved better. Michael pulled on his pipe and racked his mind for something to say—anything to break this intolerable tension.

"What's she like?" His voice sounded coarse and sour in the sweet air.

Davey looked at him blankly.

"The widow," Michael clarified. "Mrs. . . ."

"Blackwell." Davey brightened up, clearly pleased that Michael had asked. "I dinna ken her well. 'Twas by chance she wandered into the store lookin' to sell her candles and honey." He paused, thinking. "She's Irish. Came a convict, though I dinna ken what she did to get here." That was no surprise. People rarely spoke of such things in the colony. "I believe she came from Cork, from the city. But she knows farming. She must have had a farm before that. Or her family did."

Candles and honey. Michael hadn't tasted honey in . . . years. Since Darnalay.

"She's companionable, though a bit . . ." Davey searched for the word. "*Wary*. I dinna get the impression she's lived an easy life."

Michael grunted. People who came to New South Wales had never lived an easy life. If they had, they wouldn't be here. "How old?"

"How old is she?" Davey clarified. Michael nodded. "Older than us, I'd think. 'Tis hard to know." His friend was quiet for a moment. Then he turned his head to look at Michael, and his blue eyes took on an intensity Michael knew all too well. A scolding was coming. "I told her you were a good man, loyal and hard workin'. And I still believe it. But you must stay away from the drink, Mikey. It does ye no good."

Michael grunted. As irritating as it was, his friend wasn't wrong. If he hadn't been drunk, he might have recognized the man in the alley. Thought better of his idiot impulse to go after him . . .

"Promise me? Mrs. Blackwell's a good woman. She needs a steady hand."

Michael opened his mouth, then closed it again. He couldn't lie. He *wasn't* a good man, and he had very little will when it came to drink, no matter how hard he tried. So he didn't answer at all. He only glared at the road ahead and said nothing.

After another half hour of oppressive silence, the wagon finally turned onto a dirt drive lined by gum trees.

"This is it." Davey forced his lips into a false smile.

A modest brick and clapboard cottage came into view, surrounded by a garden flush with spring vegetables. Chickens scratched in the yard. A barn stood to the side, and further back lay an orchard, with a cow grazing on pasture nearby. Fields sprawled in the distance, with some convict huts just beyond, and a line of trees that marked some kind of creek, or river—the Hawkesbury, most likely.

It looked like some damn painting Father would hang in his library, then never look at again. The dull simmer of panic that had been roiling in his veins ever since Michael got off the ship swelled into a rushing torrent.

He did not belong here.

FIVE

CAITLIN PULLED BACK THE curtain and peered out of her bedroom window.

Beyond the smudged pane, there was still just the empty road leading out through the tunnel of gum trees, muddy from yesterday's rain.

Good. She was behind. Adding new frames to the hives had taken more time than she'd expected, and she'd only just come in to change into a clean dress and finish with the candles.

She glanced at the clock. Half past one. If they'd left Sydney early as Mr. Flemming had planned, they'd arrive any minute now. She must be quick.

She let the curtain fall, then hurried to the kitchen, tying on an apron as she went. She quickly stoked the fire, put the kettle on, then began carefully pulling the tapers out of the molds. Mr. Flemming had ordered eight dozen to bring back with him, and she hadn't enough made to allow for any mistakes.

It was warm in the kitchen. The sun had moved to the other side of the house, and a breeze filtered in through the open window, but it wasn't enough. A bead of sweat dripped between her shoulders.

Something about this day felt frenzied. As if there were too many things to do and not enough time. But everything was in order. She'd readied the new man's room, put the kettle on, changed her dress, almost finished with the candles. There was nothing to fret about—

Damn.

A wick broke, leaving the wax stuck in the brass. She'd have to melt it to get it out, and there was no time for that.

What was wrong with her? She usually had steadier hands.

Oh well. Seven dozen and eleven it would be.

Slowing down, she carefully pulled the rest of the candles, stacking them neatly on the table as she went.

A gentleman. A toff. Mr. Flemming's account of Michael Dunn had been stirring in her mind all day.

Was he the kind of swell who'd turn his nose up at the room she'd prepared for him? It was meant for a dairy just off the kitchen, and she used it to press honey as well . . . it was a lot to give up. But it wasn't large, and it was sunken into the ground, a bit musty. The bed was only straw. Not the kind of place a gentleman would be accustomed too.

But he'd been at Moreton Bay. Hardly a place of luxury.

Finally finished, she lifted an empty crate onto the table and began setting the candles in, counting as she went.

Two, four, six. A full row. *Eight, ten, twelve.* Another.

Something about the scent of the candles mixed with the sharp camphor of the gum tree leaves she used to pack them in settled her mind. And the counting. She liked this task, the way the smooth tapers fit together when she stacked them, one layer nested perfectly on the last.

Fourteen, sixteen, eighteen. Her hands were sure at this task and quick, and the counting became a song, a lilting tune sung under her breath. *Twenty, twenty-two, twenty-four.*

There. The crate was full.

She pivoted to take up the next one—

A knock sounded on the front door. *Bugger.* She'd almost finished.

Caitlin eyed the pile of candles waiting to be packaged. Another knock came, more insistent this time.

She heaved a sigh, untied her apron, and hurried toward the door.

"I'm on me way," she called. She took a moment to straighten her dress, smooth her hair, and school her face into that of Mrs. Blackwell, the employer.

This new man might be a gentleman, and he might be educated, but *she* was in charge. She'd learned from experience that it was necessary to make that clear from the start.

She pulled open the heavy wooden door to reveal Mr. Flemming, hat in hand. His fist was poised as if he'd been about to knock again. Behind him stood a man.

But that couldn't be—could it?

Dunn, if that's who he was, was older than Caitlin had supposed, or he *looked* older. It was sometimes hard to tell with men who'd lived hard. His face was turned toward the ground, but she could make out his tan and the thick stubble of white blond whiskers covering his cheeks and neck. He wore dirt-streaked trousers with holes at the knees, the kind that buttoned up at the side to allow for shackles, a ripped, blue-striped shirt, and flimsy shoes that his big toe had poked a hole through. He clutched a small sack.

Melia murder, what had she got herself into?

He wore no hat. His hair was a pale yellow, almost white. Its fine, curly strands blew gently in the breeze, reminding Caitlin, oddly, of a little boy. It looked just like her brother's hair—wee Gerry, the youngest of the four she'd left behind on the streets of Cork—

"Mrs. Blackwell." Mr. Flemming cleared his throat. "'Tis a pleasure to see you again." His words sounded forced, overly polite.

Caitlin started. She'd been staring at the stranger. She nodded at the shop-keep. "And to you, Mr. Flemming."

"I . . ." Mr. Flemming moved his gaze to the man standing behind him, as if inviting him into the conversation, but the convict ignored him. After an awkward pause, the shopkeep cleared his throat and looked apologetically at Catlin. "This is Mikey—Michael Dunn. He's not had a chance to clean up yet, I'm afraid."

Mr. Flemming nudged the man, and he finally raised his gaze. Caitlin caught her first look at his face, and her heart sank.

This would never work.

Worn, ruddy skin obscured by dirt and whiskers. A hard line of a mouth. Piercing blue eyes. They met hers and flashed with a lightning strike of anger and fear—as if he were a wild animal, ready to lash out at the slightest provocation.

Caitlin had known men like this before, so hardened by life in the colony that they'd turned feral. They could rarely be tamed.

She pinched her lips together and gave him a tight nod. Then she brought her eyes back to Mr. Flemming and forced a smile. "Do come in. I was just packing up your candles."

She led the two men into the sitting room, her mind racing.

She could send him away. He could go back to Sydney and be the government's problem. They'd made him into what he was, anyhow. 'Twas only fair for them to deal with the consequences.

But Mr. Flemming was her buyer for candles and honey. Her only real contact in Sydney. And this man was his friend. If she sent him back, she'd be jeopardizing all of that.

Perhaps he wasn't as bad as he appeared?

The sitting room felt airless and hot. Sunlight poured through the windows.

She closed the curtains, trying to bring some relief from the heat. "I'll just go finish up. May I bring you some tea?" She kept her attention pointedly on Mr. Flemming and away from Dunn, though an odor wafted to her in the heavy air. The pungent smell of a man gone far too long without a bath.

"I'd love to stay, but I canna," Mr. Flemming replied, fanning himself with his hat. "I promised Emily I'd be home for a late dinner, and she doesna like to be kept waiting." He winked.

Caitlin smiled politely at her guest, then allowed herself another quick glance at Dunn. His blank, angry expression hadn't changed from the moment she'd opened the door. His gaze stayed trained on the cold hearth.

Could he even talk?

And again, that smell.

Caitlin smoothed her hair. "I'll just be a minute, then." She tied her apron back on, strode back to the kitchen, and hurriedly packed the rest of the candles.

How stupid she'd been. She'd been so excited by the idea of learning to read that she hadn't given weight to the facts. The man was fresh from Moreton Bay. Mr. Flemming could say what he liked, but even if Dunn had been an angel before, that place would have changed him. Men committed murder at Moreton Bay, just for the chance to be shipped back to Sydney and hanged for their crime.

She should have known better.

"Mrs. Blackwell?" Mr. Flemming's head poked into the room. "May I have a word?"

"Of course." She offered him a strained smile and a nod.

"I—" He broke off, then came in, quietly closing the door behind him. He took off his hat, clutching it nervously. "I ken he's a bit rough. He only got back to Sydney yesterday, ye see, and the pass I got was only for today. There was no time to—"

"It's no matter." Caitlin's voice sounded shrill. "I'm sure he'll—"

"*No*. It *does* matter." He shook his head, as if in disbelief. "To be quite honest, he's in much worse shape than I ever imagined. I dinna ken what they did to him. He willna talk to me. But he—he doesna seem himself."

Caitlin turned her attention back to the candles. "I suspected as much."

"With a little time and *kindness* . . ." He paused, and Caitlin glanced up to meet his gaze. "I believe he'll come 'round. But—" Again, he hesitated. "But if he doesna, of course you must send him back to the barracks. I would never want you to keep him here on my accord if he isna any use to you."

"I do appreciate that, Mr. Flemming." Caitlin shot him another smile, a real one this time, a relieved one. "I shall do me best with him, but . . . but I do appreciate that."

The shopkeep nodded quickly, then edged toward the door. "I'll be gettin' back to him, then." He opened the door and paused. "Thank you, Mrs. Blackwell. It means a lot to Emily and me. We're in your debt." He turned and disappeared into the dark of the hallway.

Caitlin carefully placed the lid over the first crate, positioned a small nail, and began lightly tapping it in.

Michael Dunn was done for. She'd put a wager on it. And, anyway, she hadn't the time to waste on him. She'd have to send him back.

It was too bad. Mr. Flemming obviously cared for the man. But such was the way of this place . . . it was everyone for himself. It had to be. Mr. Flemming knew that as much as she did.

But she wouldn't send him back today. That would be too much of a slap in the face—and it wasn't as if she had anything to fear from the man. He was sullen, to be sure, but she could see nothing dangerous about him. She needed to bring another load of wheat in next week, anyway. She'd bring him along then, and at least she could say she'd tried.

"Eight dozen?" Mr. Flemming sprang up from where he was perched on the settee.

Caitlin carefully set the two crates down onto the floor. "Almost . . . One stuck in the mold, I'm afraid." She smiled wanly at the shopkeep, hoping he'd understand. "Seven dozen and eleven. There's two more crates in the kitchen."

"Close enough." Mr. Flemming grinned. "You can take payment in credit at the shop, or ready money next time you're in town if you like."

"Credit would be lovely."

Mr. Flemming turned toward Dunn, as if expecting the convict to say something, but Dunn still hadn't moved. Caitlin suspected he hadn't spoken a word in all the time she'd been in the kitchen.

"Just let me know if any are damaged on the drive." Caitlin said. "I'll replace them and the missing one when I come in next week."

Mr. Flemming chuckled. "If they break, it's because I'm a lousy driver. I canna ask you to pay for that, now, can I?"

He might be in her debt, but she wouldn't stand for poor business. "If they break," she said sternly, "it'll be because I didn't pack 'em tight enough. Just let me know."

"I'll send a note." Mr. Flemming grinned at her again.

A note. A spark of something akin to excitement rose in her chest. Caitlin's inability to read had meant that, until today, Mr. Flemming had to rely on a messenger boy to bring news. But now . . .

Her eyes swung again to Michael, who was still glowering at the hearth, ignoring them.

The spark died.

She swallowed. It would be a long week. "I'll just fetch the rest, and you can be off."

Michael helped Davey load the crates. Then he stood silently beside the widow and watched his friend drive away. He didn't say anything. He didn't have to. It wasn't his place, and she'd made it clear with her stern glances and clipped words that she expected him to stay in his place.

Somehow his uneasiness dimmed a little as the wagon juddered down the long drive. The widow had no ideas that he should be a man of his own. Her only concern was that he follow orders. He could do that. Or he could try, at least.

She was an angular woman, that was sure. Younger than Michael had supposed, but older than him, tall and thin with a flat chest and an oval-shaped face. Her dark hair was streaked with silver and pulled into a tight bun, though a few curls sprang loose. Her clothes were plain but clean, and an Irish lilt clung to her speech. Not the thick brogue of an Irish right off the boat, but of someone who'd been in the colony for a time. She had the air of a woman accustomed to hard work and authority.

The wagon grew smaller and smaller, then finally turned the bend and disappeared behind the trees.

The widow cleared her throat and turned to him. She spoke in that same stern voice she'd used earlier—so different from the tone she'd taken with Davey. "Come. I'll tell you of your duties."

He followed her through the front door, down a dark corridor and into the kitchen.

The sitting room had been bright, hot and tidy but layered in dust. A room rarely used. In comparison, the kitchen was dark, airy, and positively filthy. The floor was littered with candle wax, dried bits of food and dust. The windows were grimed with dirt. The hearth was cluttered, and a heap of old ash sat before it.

"Sit." She nodded to a chair.

Keeping his eyes on the gray boards of the worn wooden table, he obeyed. The table was covered in candle molds and wax. Clearly, she'd just finished making Davey's tapers.

The widow ignored the mess. She sat across from him and poured herself a cup of tea—without offering him one. "Mr. Flemming said you can read and write." She arched a disbelieving brow.

Was he really so depraved looking that she couldn't believe he could read?

Yes, he probably was.

"I can."

"And where did you learn?"

He stared at her. What was he supposed to say? "M-my tutor Mr. Lance taught me."

"In England?"

"Yes."

The widow took a sip of her tea. "And can you do ciphers as well?"

"Yes."

"Complex ones? I've many different crops here, as well as livestock and the candles, and honey, of course. All at different prices with different buyers. 'Tis a lot to keep track of."

An indignant heat rose in Michael's chest. *A lot to keep track of*? This was a farm, and not a large one. He'd achieved high honors on the Tripos at Cambridge. Run Cowper's warehouses for years. But as soon as it flared, the anger dimmed. She clearly didn't believe he was capable, and she had good reason. "I—I believe I can, ma'am." He spoke slowly, each word even with the last.

Despite his effort, the widow's cheeks flushed. "Are you mocking me?"

Michael froze. Two minutes in her company, and he'd already made a mess of things. "N-no. I . . ." He lowered his gaze. "I'm sorry, Mrs. Blackwell." He kept his eyes trained on the tabletop, tracing the lines between the boards, waiting for her to reprimand him.

She would send him back. If not now, then eventually.

There was a long pause before she spoke again, sternly. "Look at me, Dunn." Here it came. Michael held his breath as he raised his gaze to meet hers. Her eyes narrowed at him. "I'm not certain you will stay here, and that's the truth. But Mr. Flemming has vouched for you, and I owe it to *him* to give you a chance." She paused, tilting her head in emphasis. "If you *do* stay, your duties will be as follows." She ticked the items off on her fingers. "You will take dictation and read things to me. You will keep the ledger books up to date."

That would be easy enough, though it would hardly keep him occupied—

"And you will teach me to read and write."

Michael felt his brows raise.

"Can you do that, Dunn?" The heat of her attention burned into him.

"I—uh." His tongue felt thick and clumsy. "Do you have a reader, Mrs. Blackwell?"

"A reader?" She scowled.

"A book that lists the alphabet and simple words and rhymes. It . . . it could help."

"I do not," she snapped, and for the first time, Michael spied something behind her tight demeanor. A fear, or nervousness. "Do I need one?"

"No."

She took another sip of her tea. "I understand you took a salary at Cowper's. I have no money for such things, you know that?" She shot him another severe look, but now that he'd seen it, he couldn't ignore that unease behind her eyes.

She was as uncomfortable as he was.

"Of course."

"As long as you do well, you'll have a supply of tobacco and tea, and you'll eat well. We've fresh meat regularly, honey, and vegetables." She rose and began clearing the table, placing the candle molds into a basket before sweeping the excess wax into a pile and off the table into her hand. She ignored Michael, as if he'd been dismissed.

"Mrs. Blackwell," he began. "Where will I—"

"You will sleep in the dairy." She didn't look up as she spoke, and her cheeks turned vaguely pink. It was a brave thing for her to do, to let him stay in the house and trust that he wouldn't come at her. And beyond that, such an arrangement would make people talk, even out here. Though Michael had no illusions that this stern, thorny woman would take him into her bed. "Just through there." She pointed with her chin to a door leading off from the kitchen. Then she dropped the bits of wax into her basket, picked it up, and started toward another door in the back that must lead to the yard. "We'll eat dinner at half five," she called over her shoulder, balancing the basket on her hip as she pulled the door open.

She disappeared, only to poke her head back in a few seconds later.

"You'll be needing a bath, I should think." Michael winced. He must stink to high heaven. "There's a tub in the back pantry and soap"—she pointed to a door—"and the well's just out here." She motioned toward the yard, then turned and shut the door behind her.

A bath. That would be good.

Michael rose and got to work.

SIX

CAITLIN CLOSED THE BACK door with authority, but her confidence ended there.

She stood on the brick path, her gaze wandering across the farm, her mind grasping for what to do next. She'd finished the work she'd planned for today. It was too late to start any big projects and too early for the milking. The cows and the mare were grazing in the far pasture, the pigs snoring away in the hot sun. Hud and Greg were harvesting and stooking in the field, while Finn saw to the threshing and winnowing. She could hear the dull thud of the flail as he pounded it into the barn floor. None of them had need of her help.

On any other day, she'd go back into the house, melt the wax that had stuck in the mold, and press the honey from the combs she'd collected last week. But with Dunn bathing, that was out of the question.

The sound of something heavy scraping against the floor came from behind her. He was pulling the metal tub out of its nook in the pantry.

He'd be out any minute to collect water. And wouldn't she look the fool, just standing here? The last thing she wanted was to face that blank expression of his again so soon, his surly silence. The hopelessness of it, and the awkwardness.

A sudden flush of anger rose, but not at Dunn. This wasn't his fault. It was hers. What had she been thinking, to take a man into her house? Even if he'd turned out the perfect secretary, it was *her* house. The one place in the world she could simply be, without pretense. And here she was, locked out of it, fretting and antsy on her own back stoop. Perhaps it was for the best that he was unsuitable. Just a few more days, and he'd be gone.

Her gaze fell on the garden, the patch of lush green fenced in by woven sticks. The turnips could use a thinning, especially after the rains yesterday. She'd eat the greens for her evening meal—or *they* would. Dunn would be there too, wouldn't he?

Gor.

She set her basket down then pushed away from the house, passing through the yard and letting herself through the gate. Indeed, the bright green turnip leaves grew thick in their rows, crowding in on each other. The carrots and leeks too. She hunkered down and began the work.

A small breeze had picked up, a balm to her heated skin. The damp black earth cooled her fingers, and the small plants slid from the ground without any resistance at all. The ease of it, and the peace, was soothing. Her hands fell into a rhythm. Pull this one, leave that one. Pull these two, leave this one . . .

A bee buzzed by, landed on a melon blossom and began its busy dance, filling its legs with powdery, bright orange pollen.

Caitlin smiled at it working away. How happy it seemed in the usefulness of its simple labor.

It flew off again.

The sound of the back door opening and closing floated past on the wind. Caitlin held her breath. He'd never see her, stooped low as she was, and she had no desire to be seen. Next came the creak of the pulley at the well, the splash of water pouring into a bucket. Then the opening and closing of the door once again.

She exhaled and tossed an uprooted turnip onto the growing pile.

She'd given him the impression that there was a chance he might stay, hadn't she? Selfishly, so at least it would seem to Mr. Flemming that she'd tried. But it was a cruel thing to do to a man like that . . . to give him hope. She had no choice, of course. She couldn't afford to take on a charity case, nor could she afford to offend her buyer for candles. But still . . . 'Twas such a shame, what this place did to a person. And she had so wanted to learn to read.

The bee returned, or perhaps this was a different one. It buzzed about aimlessly, then zoomed away.

What would she do now? She wasn't any worse off than she'd been before all this. Yet somehow it felt that way, now that the notion of learning had seeded itself.

Perhaps she might find someone else to teach her. Her assigned men knew a bit more than she did, but not by much. Mr. and Mrs. Flemming were too far away, and her neighbors were less than friendly. None of them had called when John had died, nor spoken with her at his funeral. Except for one—the new owner of the farm just to the east, who'd introduced himself only to tell her how delighted he'd be to acquire Swindale.

There was no one. And that was the truth.

The only real friend Caitlin had known in her years here was Jedda, the native woman whose family camped nearby and who'd sometimes brought her baby to play in the yard. Caitlin had been new to the farm, then, and new to the colony, too. They'd barely understood one another at first. Yet they'd spent hours under the gum trees, trading songs and playing silly games with the child. . . But, of course, Jedda and her family had left years ago.

Or they'd been driven out, was more like it. Caitlin only hoped they were alive. If they were, that baby girl would be a full-grown woman by now.

The door opened again. Then the sound of the pulley. The bucket. The door.

She inhaled the scent of the damp earth, the richness in the air. There was a sense of things growing—she could hear it, almost, feel it in her bones.

The strong, sure line of plants that she'd left in the ground extended behind her. Even, neat, and tidy.

And next to it lay the heap of discarded turnips, the filaments of immature roots and the thin green leaves already wilting under the sun. Just a moment ago they'd been thriving, vibrant and full of health.

How quickly life could change. For better or worse.

She turned back to her task, firmly pulling out the small plants and leaving only the large, the dominant, the strong.

She would at least have Dunn read John's letters and look over the ledger books before he went. Surely, he could accomplish that. And perhaps there was someone in Windsor, someone who might agree to teach her in trade for vegetables or milk or eggs ... the smith's daughter, perhaps? She'd gone to school ...

Caitlin worked and waited for what seemed a very long time. At last, when she was certain the new man would be finished with his bath, she made her way back to the house.

Dunn was sitting at the table reading a newspaper. He looked up as the door opened, and Caitlin froze on the threshold. The transformation was remarkable.

Without the thick layers of dirt and whiskers, he wasn't a bad-looking man. His thick brows curved over high cheekbones and full, well-formed lips. His damp hair curled nicely, dark gold with little wisps of light where it had started to dry. He'd changed into clean, respectable clothes—crisp white linens, wool trousers, and a coat with a light blue waistcoat underneath.

Studying him now, she could well believe he was educated, and even that he'd once been a gentleman.

Except that his eyes still gave him away. His sharp blue gaze lanced her with that scared, wild desperation. And his expression—set, and rigid. As if he'd forgotten how to smile or frown.

He glanced away quickly. The way he sat there, so expectant and nervous and lost ... Caitlin wanted nothing more than to turn around, to go back to the peace of the garden.

She set her jaw. Just a few days.

"You have a paper with you." She pitched her tone somewhere between polite and exacting.

"Yes. Davey—Mr. Flemming gave it to me." Dunn sounded defensive, though it had hardly been an accusation.

Caitlin took a few steps into the room and softened her tone. "I'd like you to read it to me later. I so rarely get any news."

Dunn nodded quickly. "Of course."

Caitlin held up the basket she carried. "I thought we could have boiled turnip greens for our dinner. I've a pork bone to cook it with, and some new potatoes."

Without warning, Dunn sprang forward as if to take the basket, and Caitlin impulsively drew back.

"What—"

"Oh—"

They spoke at the same time. Then they froze, eyeing one another.

"I—I'm sorry," Dunn stuttered. "I thought you wanted me to cook—"

"*Cook?*" Caitlin raised her eyebrows. "You know how to cook?"

"I cooked for Mr. Flemming and me, when we lived together." Dunn's speech took on that rigid, defensive tone once more. His blue eyes, darker now that he stood in shadow, flicked to her, then away.

The man was nervous as a hen on a hot griddle. She'd only meant to tell him what she planned to make for the evening meal, but it had sounded like a directive, hadn't it?

"No need to be sorry." She walked past him to set the basket on the table and caught a whiff of lavender on the way—the same soap she made and used herself. "I'd be glad for your help. Why don't you ready these for the pot?"

Dunn seemed relieved to have something to do. Or perhaps it was Caitlin who was relieved. He folded his paper and set it aside, then began tearing the turnip roots from the leaves while Caitlin put the pot on to boil with the bone and fetched the potatoes and a knife.

She sat across from him and began to cut. "Tomorrow morning I'll show you the ledgers." She cleared her throat. "And there are some letters I'd like you to read."

Dunn looked up, only for a fraction of a second, but enough for the biting pain in his eyes to lash at her one more. He nodded quickly, then dipped his head back down.

Michael was falling. Falling and falling through endless blackness. He flailed his limbs, desperately reaching for something, anything to hold on to, but only smooth, wet stone slipped past his fingers, evading his grasp. He screamed, but there was no sound, only a raw strangling pain in his throat.

Then a sudden jerk, and all was still. He lay on his back, breathless, his blood pounding horror through his veins, the floor cold as ice beneath him.

It was dark. Silent like a grave.

No. This couldn't be happening.

He struggled to his feet, extended his arms before him, feeling for a way out. A door. He reached a wall, the same stone, great blocks of it, slick and clammy to the touch. He followed it, hands desperately searching and searching and searching for a way out . . . fingernails scraping against stone . . . but there was none.

He was trapped.

He blinked, but he couldn't see. He screamed, but there was no answer. The darkness was moving in. Cold terror crushed him. He would die—

Michael awoke with a start.

Shit. That goddamned nightmare. It was a wonder none of the other men had clouted him awake to shut him up.

As the terror of the dream faded, another kind of fear took its place. The sky outside was streaked with light, and it was eerily quiet. He could hear his own heartbeat, fast and loud. There were no snores coming from the other men beside him. In fact, he couldn't hear them at all. They'd left already.

A cold sweat broke out on his brow.

Why had they not woken him? Any minute now, the guard would come and kick him in the gut.

Panicked, he rolled himself over, carefully keeping his feet together so the irons wouldn't bite into his flesh as he stood—

Irons. He wasn't wearing leg irons.

He froze, half sitting, and slowly took in the room around him.

There was a paned window open to the morning air, whitewashed board walls, and a sloping, low ceiling with a tin roof above. He was lying on a straw tick. A real bed.

He practically sobbed in relief. The widow. He was at the widow's house. Mrs. Blackwell's.

Suddenly weak, he sank back onto the mattress and lay still, allowing his pulse to slow.

A magpie began to sing outside the window, a bubbling, throaty air, as if the creature hadn't a care in the world. Only a bright, wondering joy at the day to come.

He'd never heard bird song in Moreton Bay. Or *had* he? He couldn't remember. Perhaps it had simply been drowned out by the crack of the whip and the clanking of chains.

A gentle wind filtered in through the window, drying his sweat and sending a chill through him. He couldn't go back there. Not to Moreton Bay, nor to Sydney, nor to the grog houses or the barracks or Davey's pitying looks . . . to the constant fear of being clapped back in irons.

Somehow it hadn't dawned on him yesterday, in the confusion of everything that had happened, but the truth came rushing in on him now. He wanted to stay here. More than anything in the world, he wanted to stay here.

A door opened, then slammed shut. He could hear footfalls in the kitchen.

His employer. The woman knew nothing of him and cared even less. All she expected was that he be useful. Teach her to read and write—something he'd learned as a child. It seemed such a simple thing, yet he'd made a terrible impression yesterday. Today, things must be better.

He got out of bed and dressed quickly, taking the time to comb his hair before leaving the small room.

She was standing by the hearth, dipping a spoon into a steaming pot. Porridge, it must be. She'd cinched an apron around her waist, and her black hair hung down in a long plait. Seeing her from behind, he realized she wasn't all angles as he'd thought yesterday. There was a graceful, long curve to her figure, pleasing to the eye . . .

She glanced over her shoulder. "Good morning." All thoughts of softness were lost to her cold expression and curt tone.

"Good morning." Michael edged toward the door that led to the yard and the privy, suddenly conscious of the fact that she was a woman. He couldn't just announce the need to piss. "I'll just—I'll be right back."

A look flitted across her face. Almost an amused one, but . . . no. "Breakfast'll be ready when you get back."

It was a relief to be outside, alone again. The sun had just crested the horizon, painting the wispy clouds in pale pinks and purples. The air was cool, the breeze sweet and fresh. The magpie still sang, as if in ode to the rising sun, joined now by the cackling laugh of kookaburra.

He relieved himself, then stopped by the well pump to wash. The cold water stung his cheeks, waking him fully.

When he came back in, two bowls sat on the table, full of yellow mash. An earthenware honeypot sat between them, and a pitcher of cream rested alongside a steaming pot of tea.

"It's only maize," Mrs. Blackwell said, sitting down. "I've not had any of this year's wheat milled yet, and even then, I only keep enough for a bit of bread."

"It's fine." In fact, the maize porridge looked almost *too* good. Michael didn't trust it to be real—so fresh and golden, and as much as he could eat. He poured cream in, then reached for the honey and drizzled some on top. It flowed in a shining column, dark and rich, then disappeared into the thick yellow cream.

His stomach growled.

Feeling his ears grow warm, he slowly twirled the honey stick to catch all the drips before returning it to the pot. Then he nervously glanced at his employer.

Sure enough, she was watching him, elbows on the table, fingers interlaced, brows raised in disapproval.

He looked down quickly, summoning the kind of words that used to come so naturally. The polite nonsense that had been drilled into him as a child. "Pardon me, Mrs. Blackwell." He attempted a smile in her direction. "The porridge looks so delicious my stomach can't seem to wait. Thank you."

Her eyes widened. "So, you *do* know how to talk, then?"

Again, he forced what he hoped was a smile, though his face felt stiff with it. "I once did."

Her brows lowered at this, as if in confusion. And for a moment, Michael was sure she'd speak. But she simply readied her own breakfast and began to eat.

Michael picked up the spoon, scooped up some cream and honey and maize, and brought it to his lips.

Sweet. Rich. Hearty. Like heaven and earth combined. He swallowed, and the food traced a path of comfort down his throat to his belly.

It *was* too good to be real, but in this moment, he didn't care.

They ate the rest of their meal in silence.

"I'll show you John's study now." Caitlin turned away from the basin where she'd just piled the breakfast dishes and wiped her hands on a towel. Then she led Dunn into the corridor.

What to make of this man? There'd been a flash of something different at breakfast. Something more like the person he used to be, most likely . . . But now he was back to that sullen silence, avoiding her gaze.

She led him into John's study, a small closet attached to her bedroom—the bedroom she had supposedly shared with John, though she could count on one hand the number of nights her husband had spent here in recent years. He preferred to stay in Sydney between voyages and had only come to the farm to take care of necessary business.

That had been fine with her. It was bad enough dealing with him when he was here, bossing her about like some scullery maid, acting as if he knew better than her how to run a farm, and expecting her to put up with it like an obedient cur, dependent on its master for food and shelter.

And she *had* put up with it, hadn't she? Just like a stinking dog, she'd had no choice.

She tightened her jaw. No, she did not need another man here, not even if Dunn recovered himself somehow. She'd been foolish to even consider it.

"You'll get more light in here." She stopped short of the door and waved Dunn inside the small room. "But if you prefer, you could bring it all to the sitting room or the kitchen. There's more space out there."

He stepped past, then surveyed the room, John's desk, the sideboard. "This'll do."

As soon as he'd said it, Caitlin wished she'd insisted they bring the books into the kitchen. This room was entirely too small for two people.

Never mind. She'd be gone in a minute. She pushed past him, doing her best to ignore the brush of her shoulder against his coat. Then she opened the desk drawer and pulled out the books. "Here are the ledgers. This one's the most recent." She handed him the book with the bright red cover, and he accepted it without comment. Then he stepped back, holding it to his chest as if it might put more distance between them. He too, must have been feeling the closeness of the room. "And these are the others." She set them on the desk. Ledger books going back twenty-two years, to when John had first been granted the farm.

There was an awkward pause. Caitlin felt a flush creep up her neck. It truly was hot in here. She turned and opened the window.

"What would you like me to . . ." Dunn spoke to her back.

"Just look them over." She straightened up. "Acquaint yourself."

He nodded.

"And those"—she gestured to the small pile of sealed papers on the desk—"are the letters I spoke of. They've all arrived since John died, and I have no idea what they say. Perhaps they're important."

She stepped back, expecting Michael to take her place by the desk, but he just looked at the letters, then back at her. They were close enough now to touch, and there was something about him . . . the way the sun shone on his fine golden hair . . . Just as when he'd arrived on her doorstep, she was reminded of a young boy. A boy who'd been hurt and was trying desparately to hide it.

Or a man. Caitlin swallowed. She'd never be so rattled by the presence of a boy.

She cleared her throat and edged toward the door. "I must go see to the chores. I'll be back in an hour or so, and you can read to me then."

"Of course." His mouth did that thing again, just as it had at breakfast. The corners turned up into what looked like a sarcastic, bitter kind of smile. Caitlin was starting to suspect it was the closest he could come to a real one.

She returned his look with a tight smile of her own, then held her breath and ducked past. He squeezed himself against the wall, the book still clutched to his chest, and this time she managed to avoid brushing against him.

But when she finally reached the cool dark of the corridor, her cheeks were still burning.

SEVEN

THE BACK DOOR SLAMMED shut, and stillness settled over the house. A clock
ticked in the adjoining room—Mrs. Blackwell's bed chamber. Warm air blew in
through the open window, ruffling the plain white curtains. Michael was alone.

He exhaled and let himself drop into the chair that sat before the dead man's
desk.

He could do better than this. He *had* done better than this, at Cowper's.
He knew how to act like a dutiful, polite servant. Hadn't he grown up around
enough of them? But every time he opened his mouth, the only thing he could
get out were thick grunts and stumbling, short words.

It hadn't helped that she'd brushed up so close to him in the enclosed study,
and he'd noticed, really *noticed*, her breasts for the first time. They were small
but pert, shoved up by her stays, and swelling just below her neckline. The smell
of her, clean like the lavender soap he'd found in the pantry with a hint of the
outdoors and woodsmoke . . . it clung to him, and made his head spin. It had
been so long since he'd been near a woman. It didn't matter that her hair was
streaked with gray, or that her eyes had creases at the edges. Indeed, those things
only made her *more* appealing somehow. She'd lived and lost the softness of
youth, just as he had.

And she needed him. To read to her, to teach her. That thought warmed him, more than anything had since he'd come back from Moreton Bay. Almost as if there was something to look forward to.

The kookaburra began to sing again, its loud, grating laughter breaking the stillness and jarring Michal's thoughts. It was mocking him. Of course it was. This warmth, it was ass-headed. He must snuff it out like a wayward flame before it spread and he began to believe his own foolishness. She didn't need him. Anyone could teach her to read. And she wasn't *like* him either. She was his master. A good woman. No matter what she might have lived through, she would never, *could* never be the evil he was.

If he had any hope of staying here, he must focus on his job, maintain the detached relationship of servant and master. Anything else, even the thought of it, would only lead to trouble.

Never mind.

He turned to the ledgers. It was a bit much, to give him so much time to glance through a few record books. It would take fifteen minutes at most. But if he was going to do the job, he might as well do it justice.

He flipped through the first book, the most recent one. It was written with a flowing, practiced hand, rather than the disjointed one of most of the men in the colony—convicts, sailors, and soldiers alike. It must have been penned by her husband. John, she'd called him.

Michael scanned the entries. There wasn't much to it. The purchase of seed and livestock in the spring. The sale of wheat in the summer, to Staples. Michael knew the man—a weasel if there ever was one. The entries stopped abruptly in the fall, five months ago.

Michael closed the book. The sun was shining on him fully now, erasing any coolness the breeze had brought. He took off his coat and draped it over the back of the chair.

What had happened to John Blackwell? Davey had said he'd died recently, but he hadn't mentioned how. Was it a long illness? An accident? Mrs. Blackwell wasn't in mourning, or at least she didn't dress that way. But such things as mourning and half mourning were rarely practiced in the colony, except by the highest of society. And, of course, most marriages were based on convenience, not love.

What had her marriage been like?

His thoughts wandered to the bed he'd seen when they'd passed through Mrs. Blackwell's room, with its tarnished brass headboard and wide mattress . . .

It was none of his business. He had a job to do.

He scooted the chair out of the sun and looked through the other books. They spanned back more than twenty years, all the way to 1804. And the longer he looked, the clearer the story became. There were far more negative entries than positive, especially in recent years. Supplies purchased on credit. Crops—a good amount—sold, but no record of debts paid.

Either the man was a lousy bookkeeper, or he'd used the money in other ways.

Did Mrs. Blackwell know of the debts? He hoped so. They were considerable, and they were her debts now. He didn't relish the idea of giving her the news.

Michael glanced at the clock, barely visible through the doorway. Only twenty minutes had passed.

He eyed the pile of letters on the desk. The red wax seal on the top one shone in the sunlight. He could open them and read them so he'd have an idea of what was important and what wasn't. That's what a true secretary would do . . . No. She'd not directed him to. It was better to wait.

He sat a few minutes, baking in the sun, listening to the tick of the clock. Waiting.

Bah. This was ridiculous. Surely there was something else he could do. In the kitchen perhaps. That room did need a good cleaning, and it might help him prove his worth.

He rose and left the small study, taking his coat with him. Passing through Mrs. Blackwell's chamber had felt oddly intimate when they'd come together, and now by himself, it did even more so. There was nothing off about the room itself. It was exactly what one would expect for a widowed farmer of the middling class. The bedstead, made up with a white sheet and light cotton blanket . . . Michael quickly looked away. A chest of drawers. A small dressing table by the window with a bowl and pitcher, a hairbrush and a small hand mirror sat discarded beside. A clean white apron hung from a hook on the wall, next to a plain cotton dress. There was nothing outwardly personal about this room. And yet, it was a place Michael distinctly did not belong. He hurried through and to the kitchen.

He was just finishing wiping the windows when the door opened and Mrs. Blackwell appeared. The sunlight poured in around her, wreathing her in light. She'd pinned her hair up, but it was coming loose, and her cheeks were pink with exertion. She held a basket of green peas in one hand, and a full milk pail in the other. She reminded Michael of a portrait of a dairy maid he'd once seen in London. So healthy and pure.

She walked in a few paces, then stopped short, her eyes widening as she took in the room.

Michael held his breath as her gaze slowly tracked from where he stood by the window, cloth in hand, to the freshly swept hearth, the neatly stacked wood, the clean floor, the basin, empty of the dirty dishes she'd stacked there.

"Wh-what have you done?" She set the milk pail down and shut the door behind her.

Shit. Michael's stomach clenched. Clearly, he'd overstepped. "I thought—" he started.

"It's so clean . . ." Her hand rose to her cheek, as if to test the temperature. Then she smiled. A wondering, sweet curve of her lips.

And Michael remembered how to breathe again.

She stepped further into the room, scrutinizing him as if she'd never seen him before. Michael felt the urge to back away, but at the same time, that warm feeling welled again in his chest. He didn't trust it, not one bit. But it pulled at him nonetheless . . .

She was pleased with him.

"I'm surprised." She exhaled a chuckle, then met his eye. "Thank you."

The warmth grew, the heat spreading up his neck and his ears. Michael couldn't take it any longer. He broke eye contact and went back to wiping the pane.

There was a long silence. He could feel her eyes on him.

When she spoke, it was with that brisk, employerly tone again. "I thought we'd have peas for our midday meal, along with maize bread and milk. I'll just fetch those letters, and you can read while I shell them."

She left the room, and Michael put all his focus on wiping the last of the grime off the window.

When they were settled at the table, he slit open the first letter in the pile. It was postmarked Sydney, from a creditor looking for payment for seed that Mr. Blackwell had purchased last spring. She nodded after he'd read it out, her eyes never leaving her hands, which were busy with the rhythmic task of breaking the pods open, extracting the peas into one bowl, then discarding the empty pods into another.

Her fingers were work-roughened and coarse, though her fingernails were immaculately clean. A long scar lined her left palm.

What would they feel like, the hands of such a woman?

She glanced up at him, shooting him a severe look. "There'll be plenty of those, I'm afraid."

Right. The letter.

"Did you look at the money book?"

"Yes."

"I'd like you to total the debts there. They're considerable, I've no doubt."

So she knew. One could only hope she had an idea of the scope. "Very well."

The second letter was a note from Mr. Whiteford, the magistrate in Windsor. Peter Gregory, one of her assigned men, had applied for a ticket of leave, and it had been granted. The recommendation had been forwarded to the secretary's office in Sydney for processing, and Mrs. Blackwell was to inform Mr. Gregory of the news and allow him to travel to the city and collect it.

Michael looked up when he'd finished reading to find the widow staring at him across the table, her jaw set and her hands still. A ticket meant she was losing the man, and he was gaining his freedom, or at least a bit of it. She sighed. "I'll tell him this afternoon."

"How many do you have?" The question crossed Michael's lips before he could think better of it. He was not meant to ask questions. It was none of his business.

But she replied without hesitation. "Men?"

He nodded.

"Three."

Now two. With Michael here, there was little chance of her getting a replacement for the ticketed man.

He looked down, studying the weathered table. She *should* send him back. That would be the prudent thing to do. She was in much greater need of an experienced field hand than someone like him. All the reading in the world would do her no good if she hadn't the means to run her farm.

The next letter was from London, postmarked six months before and with an official-looking seal. Michael picked it up and turned it over. From a solicitor or a barrister?

He broke the wax and unfolded the missive. A piece of thin notepaper slipped out, a list of some sort. He set it aside and began to read the main portion of the letter.

London, May 10, 1826

Mr. John Blackwell,

Dear Sir,
It is my most solemn duty to inform you of the death of your late brother, Mr. Benjamin Blackwell, who departed this earthly plane two weeks ago, on April 24,

after a long illness. I have been managing his London accounts for some years, and I have been given the task of executing his estate.

As you may know, your brother had no issue, and as there are no other surviving siblings, you are the sole beneficiary to the property and accounts of which I have enclosed a full accounting.

Given your remote location, I've no doubt you will need a man in London to manage your new interests. I served your brother faithfully & I would be most obliged to continue in that role for yourself if it so pleases you. I await your reply.

With deepest condolences and regards,

MR. GORDON JAMES, ESQUIRE.

Silence fell like a heavy woolen blanket. Michael waited, his eyes tracking the looping letters of the solicitor's signature. Mrs. Blackwell said nothing.

Finally, he allowed his gaze to rise from the paper, unsure of what he'd find. Certainly, the death of her husband's brother would come as a shock. Though she'd likely be due at least some of the money.

But he couldn't read her expression at all. Her eyes were wide, staring into space, her lips pressed together. When she noticed him looking, a tremor ran through her, as if she were shaking something off. Then she began shelling the peas again, more quickly than before.

"That's the list of accounts, I gather?" She pointed with her chin to the note paper.

"It would seem so." Michael picked up the slip and read it off. "An account at Goslings and Sharpe for £50,000, and one at Cunliffe's for £10,000, both earning four percent. A country house in Norfolk valued at £2,000." A buzzing sensation crept up his spine as he read. It was a fortune. "A Scottish estate, rather large, valued at £4,500. Investments in coal and shipping." He totaled the percentages in his head. "They're considerable. At least another £40,000 worth."

His words hung in the air, and he had the urge to glance behind him, as if the ghost of John Blackwell was looking over his shoulder. The man had inherited all this . . . after he died.

"Fifty—thousand *pounds*?" Mrs. Blackwell's voice was a squeak.

"Yes."

Her breath whooshed out of her, and her hands stilled, her work once again forgotten. She blinked rapidly.

Michael didn't know what to say or do. Clearly, she'd had no idea her husband was due to inherit such a sum. Was she pleased? Upset? Whatever she was feeling, it was wrong of him to stare, so he averted his eyes, letting his gaze fall back to the table and the next letter in the pile.

It was also postmarked London, written with a shaky hand. Michael turned it over. It was sealed with a signet. An ornate letter B.

An ominous weight settled in his gut.

"And what's that one, then?" Mrs. Blackwell's voice wavered. She was trying to regain her composure, so Michael didn't look up as he unfolded the letter and began to read.

April 12, 1820

Dear John,

You are, perhaps, wondering why, after so many years of silence, I am finally writing. I will get to the point. I am ill, and the doctors say I do not have long to wait before I am bereft of life. Given this, I feel it necessary to do what I can to mend the rift that has separated us for so long.

Forgive me, brother, for the wrongs I have done to you. I was a heedless, jealous youth, and the lengths to which I went to keep you and Elizabeth apart were neither right nor fair. She was never happy as my wife. Though I gave her every luxury money could buy and often reminded her that she'd never have enjoyed the same with you, she loved you to the end. It was your name she uttered on her deathbed all those years ago.

Since her passing, I have dwelt in our parents' house alone, bitter with regret and guilt. Not only did I make Elizabeth's days a trial, but my selfish jealousy pushed you, my only kin, away and deprived you of the life you were born into. I should have written to you years ago, but I have been too proud to make amends. I only hope this letter reaches you, as I have no address other than the distant colony where I have learned you now reside.

When I am gone, you will inherit all our family's wealth as well as the few investments I have interest in. Nothing will make up for the years lost to us, but knowing that you will live out your days in comfort will ease the suffering of the time that remains to me.

Farewell brother. Deepest regards,

BENJAMIN

Caitlin stared at the paper in Dunn's grasp.

He set the letter down between them. Then his hand retreated, slowly, as if backing away from something dangerous.

She broke out of her trance and looked at him. He stared back, his face an impassive mask. "I—I had no idea. He never spoke of a brother or . . . of anyone." She reached for the letter, picked it up. The paper felt weighty, but the writing was unsteady and thin. "John came as a purser on an East India ship. Not an officer or . . . anything of consequence." Again, she met Dunn's gaze, doing her best to keep her tone even. "He never spoke of England or his life there. I assumed—" What had she assumed? Nothing. She'd not ever thought of John's past.

Dunn's eyes darkened. They bored into her, asking questions she should know the answers to.

She averted her eyes and began working again, forcing her movements to be smooth and controlled. "Would you fetch water, please? And build up the fire?" She spoke to the peas, not the man.

"Of course." Michael rose and left through the back door. As soon as it shut behind him, Caitlin let her hands fall to the table, her shoulders droop, her eyes close.

It all made sense now—John's lack of attention, his distance. They'd been husband and wife for twenty years; yet she'd never got to know the man. He was so often at sea or in Sydney . . . and there was always that feeling, even the few times he'd taken his pleasure of her, that she was distasteful to him. That he wished he were somewhere else, *with* someone else. She'd always thought it was because of her Irishness, or her Catholic upbringing, or her looks. But it wasn't.

Elizabeth.

He was heart-scalded. He'd been in love with this Elizabeth, and his elder brother had stolen her from him.

Caitlin had rarely found reason to miss her husband or to feel anything resembling tenderness for him. But there was a tendril of remorse at this news. She wished he could have lived to know of this woman's love.

She uprooted the thought.

It made no difference now. And certainly, Caitlin herself gained nothing from all this. John was dead. Some other distant relative would inherit the fortune listed out on that slip of paper, and Caitlin's life would continue on as it always had. She'd still have to pay the debts her husband had left her—through her own hard work.

The door opened, and she jerked herself back into motion, broke open the next pod, slid her nail down the middle, popping each pea off its tether and watching as it tumbled, pell-mell into the bowl. Then on to the next.

"You want this in the kettle?" Michael grunted as he lowered the full bucket of water to the floor.

"I do. And the pot. We'll need water for these." She gestured to the peas.

Michael didn't answer, but he moved to the wood box and began picking out kindling.

Caitlin watched his practiced, easy movements out of the corner of her eye. John had never done such tasks. He'd always accused her of being a piss-poor housekeeper. And he wasn't wrong. She'd never liked such work, nor did she have the time for it. She much preferred being outside, working with the animals or crops.

But Dunn almost seemed to be enjoying himself.

Apparently satisfied with his armful of wood, he rose and moved toward the hearth, scooping up the water bucket as he went. He'd taken off the jacket he'd worn this morning, and she could see the outline of taut muscle, lean and strong, against the thin linen of his shirt.

He turned toward her as he set the bucket down, and their eyes met.

"I'll write a letter to that man in London." She quickly brought her gaze back to her work. Michael didn't answer. He crouched by the hearth and began arranging the kindling. "To tell him of John's death," she clarified. Still, no answer. He blew on the coals. "Do you think—" Once again, she stopped herself. She was master here. "I'll dictate it this afternoon."

"Very good." Michael stood back from the flames he'd just made and moved to fill the kettle.

They ate in silence, though Michael's thoughts were anything but peaceful.

That look she'd given him as he was building the fire. Almost as if—

No. That wasn't why he was here. Such thoughts would only muck things up. Hadn't he just resolved to remain her servant and nothing more? And anyway, women had only ever desired him if he had something to offer them. Money or power. He had nothing in that regard now. She was probably thinking of how useful he'd be as a house maid.

Which was exactly what he wanted her to think, wasn't it?

Yet, he couldn't deny the letch *he'd* felt when he caught her looking. *Faugh.* It had been ages since he'd had the desire to take himself in hand, but now he found himself anticipating the night when he'd be alone in that little straw bed.

After they'd finished eating, Mrs. Blackwell sent him back to the study to fetch pen and paper, and they settled again at the kitchen table. Michael dipped the quill in ink, then held it over the paper, waiting for the dictation.

Mrs. Blackwell opened her mouth, but nothing came out.

He cleared his throat.

She closed her mouth, looked at him, then opened it again, but she didn't utter the dictation. Instead, she addressed Michael. "You were a gentleman once, were you not?"

"Something like that."

"Then you must know something of these things. How would you begin?"

"I—" He hesitated. "I suppose I'd write something like, *Dear Mr. James.*"

She raised her chin. "That's good. Write that."

He did, then looked up to find her watching him intently. "I sincerely regret," she began, "that—to tell you—or *inform*?" Her brows knitted together, and she bit her bottom lip. She was entirely lost but doing everything she could not to show it.

He tried a smile, though it still felt wrong. "Perhaps if you give me the gist of what you mean to say," he prompted, "I could write it up."

She nodded, clearly relieved. "Just tell him John's dead. That's all he need know."

"I suppose so, but—" Michael hesitated. Really, it was none of his business.

"But what?" When he didn't answer, she repeated herself, more insistently. "But *what*, Dunn? Out with it."

Michael sighed. There could be no harm in asking the question. "Did your husband leave a will, Mrs. Blackwell?"

Her brows shot up. "No. His death was sudden. At sea."

"Then how did you—"

"Inherit the farm?"

"Yes."

"There were no other heirs." She shrugged.

"I see. And your husband died *after* this letter was written, correct? In April?"

"He did. It was early July, or that's what the ship's captain told me."

"Then I'd expect you'd be entitled to a dower at the very least."

"A dower?"

"A third of your husband's estate, for your use until your death. Or—" He paused, searching his memory for the knowledge of such things. "I believe it's half if there are no children. According to English law."

Her eyes widened as she registered the meaning of what he'd just said. "But I don't *want* half of all that." She gestured to the list of assets. "I'd have no idea how to . . ."

"Not the investments, I shouldn't think. Nor the accounts. But the land. The estates." He stopped. He'd reached the end of his knowledge of dower laws. He'd probably said too much already.

But then another thought snagged. If her husband had left no will, and heirs were found for the rest of his estate, could it be possible that the new heir might be entitled to *this* farm, as well?

"What else?" Mrs. Blackwell's voice cut through his thoughts. She sounded suspicious. "What are you thinking?"

His concern must have shown on this face. "I'm thinking—" He looked at her, not wanting to say it. It wasn't his place anyway. Nor his business. "Do you have a lawyer, Mrs. Blackwell?"

"A lawyer?" Her eyes widened. "Whyever for?"

Michael spoke slowly, choosing his words with care. "It may be prudent for you to speak to one. Before you send anything back to London."

"Just to tell him John's dead?"

"No. To ensure you're able to keep hold of your assets. Here."

She blinked at him. "You mean *Swindale*?"

He nodded.

"But—I own it. The title's in me name."

"Yes." He shouldn't have said anything. "I'm sure it's nothing. I'll just—" He lowered the quill to the paper.

"I do *not* have a lawyer." Her words, and the fearful worry behind them, cut him short. "Do you know of any?"

He looked into eyes clouded with fear, and every instinct told him to keep his mouth shut, to stay out of her affairs. He could be wrong, after all, and she'd be worried for nothing and think him a fool. But . . . what if he *wasn't* wrong? "I do know of one in Sydney," he heard himself say. "He worked for Cowper. A good man. Mr. Snodgrass."

A hint of relief gentled her face, and the same warmth as before pooled in his chest. "I've need to go to town with a load of wheat anyway. You'll come with. We'll go tomorrow." She folded the letter and set it aside. "And now"—she looked at him expectantly—"pour some tea, and we'll finish these letters. Then I'll go tell Greg his good news."

EIGHT

DUNN TOOK HIS TIME getting the tea, and Caitlin was glad. She needed a break from those eyes of his.

A lawyer? Lose Swindale?

What rubbish. She'd been granted the deed, fair and square. It had her name on it—that much she *could* read.

Clearly, Dunn didn't know what he was talking about, and the nonsense about a dower was proof of that. It was not possible that a woman like Caitlin—an Irish wench, a Catholic, a convict from the streets of Cork—could be entitled to a portion of any fancy Englishman's estate. Even if that's what the law said, they'd find a way around it.

But the farm, that was *hers*.

Even still, she couldn't stop remembering the man at the land office. He'd been quite clear with her when he'd handed her that deed. The only reason she'd inherited Swindale was that John had no will and no known male heirs. If there *were* an heir . . . and he *did* try to claim Swindale . . .

She bit down on the inside of her lip and snipped the thought before it could unravel any further. There was no sense in it. Surely this lawyer would clear things up.

Michael passed her a steaming cup. "Would you like me to read the rest?" He gestured to the letters.

"I would."

Wordlessly, he picked up the next letter in the pile, opened it, and began to read.

Happily, there were no more surprises. Mr. Umbrage was looking for payment for the hogs they'd purchased last year. She'd known of that debt, and it didn't worry her. What worried her were the debts she didn't know of. The total of them, from the ledgers.

But that was a concern for another time.

Then there was a note from a merchant ship's captain who was docked in Sydney, asking John to consider a position on his next voyage. The ship had left months ago, and either the captain had learned of John's death or he hadn't. There was nothing for Caitlin to do.

When the letters were all read, she began clearing the tea things.

Dunn remained at the table, staring blankly at the stack of opened letters as she collected the cups and crossed to the basin. He seemed lost and uncomfortable, as if he didn't know what to do next.

She took her time at the sink, trying to ignore the pricking sense of his gaze on her back. It was unnerving. She had nothing else for him to do, and she didn't need the bother of thinking of something.

She wiped her brow with the back of her hand. *Gad*, she'd be glad when he was gone—

Melia murder. Her hand stilled, then lowered slowly. When had she become so heartless? The poor man was only doing his best. He was quiet, surely, and nervous, but he'd improved since he'd arrived. That wild, dangerous look in his eye, the one that reminded her of a cornered animal, had disappeared. She couldn't quite remember when. Now he seemed only to want to make himself useful. He'd cleaned her kitchen, for heaven's sakes. And he seemed quite content to follow her every order. None of the convicts she'd been assigned over the years had shown quite this type of obedience. Like a true servant. Then again, none of her other assigned men had ever been in service, had they? They'd been pickpockets by trade or thieves or forgers—not professions where one learned any kind of deference. Dunn, on the other hand, had probably grown up with servants. He knew how they should act. And while it was true that Caitlin did not relish the intrusion of a man—any man—into her house, she did quite enjoy being obeyed in this way. Like a fine lady.

And now she needed him, didn't she? To introduce her to this lawyer, to help write the letter to the man in London. Of course, she would still send him back. There was no way she could tolerate a man like Dunn in her house for a full year, but . . . not yet.

And if he was to stay for a time, he should probably meet the other men.

She turned to face him. "I'd like you to come with me and meet the men. Then I'll need to prepare for leaving tomorrow . . ." She thought quickly. Of course, why hadn't she thought of it before? "You can total the debts while I do."

"Very good." He didn't smile, but he seemed to relax at the orders. And suddenly, looking at him, it dawned on her. She'd assumed that by commanding him in this way, she would be demeaning him somehow, that he would resist it, be shamed by it. That's how all her other men had been, and in truth, that's how Caitlin herself would feel in the same circumstance. But Dunn was different, wasn't he? His discomfort came from his own freedom, from having to speak up and think for himself. He enjoyed being ordered about; he really did. It was a relief to him.

She spoke again, testing the theory. "Do you really think it's a good idea? To visit a lawyer?" She deliberately left all the certainty out of her tone, as if she were lost and needed his affirmation.

Dunn's eyes widened, and that uncomfortable, almost panicked look came back over his face. "I—You certainly don't need—"

"Never mind." She shook her head, as if casting the doubt aside. "'Tis decided anyway." Then she put the command back in her voice. "They'll be thirsty out there. Get the bucket and fill it on the way. We'll bring it to them."

Without hesitation, he rose and crossed the room to fetch the bucket he'd brought in earlier.

Caitlin smiled to herself. She could put up with the discomfort of having him here for a week or two more.

Michael followed the widow out the back door. The midday sun was blinding after the dark of the kitchen, and the heat of it beat down on his bare head and shoulders, sending a trickle of sweat down the back of his neck. He wiped it away. What he wouldn't do for a hat.

They walked in silence, Michael trailing slightly behind Mrs. Blackwell, past the garden, through a barren field, recently planted—or ready for it—then finally to a wheat field where two men were bent double, swinging scythes. A third followed behind, tying the freshly cut stalks into tall sheaves. The golden waves of ripe wheat rippled in the breeze before them as if they were dancing, while, behind them, the neat sheaves marched away evenly to the end of the stubbled field.

They were a motley trio. One man looked at least ten years younger than Michael, with the dark skin and features of an African. The other two, one fair and one dark-haired, appeared older and more hardened. All were in their shirtsleeves and wide-brimmed straw hats, their faces grimed with sweat. Bits of golden chaff and dust stuck to their skin and clothes.

They stopped when Michael and the widow approached, then peered at Michael curiously between sips from the water dipper he offered.

Mrs. Blackwell ignored Michael as she told Greg, the younger man, of his ticket of leave. His smile grew wide at the news, revealing a thick gap between his front teeth. The other two eyed him, obviously jealous.

"You'll want to go to Sydney and collect your ticket, then," Mrs. Blackwell said. It wasn't so much a question as a statement of fact.

"Yes, ma'am." Greg bounced on his toes, as if he were holding himself back from setting off this very instant.

"If you like," she added, "you could come back here and stay at Swindale while you decide what's next. I've no money to pay you, of course, but you'd have a place and rations. And a portion of the harvest, as I promised."

Some masters made arrangements with their assigned men to receive a share of the profits of their labor. More than once, Michael had petitioned Cowper to do so, as it seemed a small price to pay to keep the men working hard. But Cowper, always shortsightedly focused on his bottom line, had only sniffed and grunted his dissent.

Michael hadn't seen any such entries in Mr. Blackwell's ledgers. It must have been something Mrs. Blackwell had instituted since her husband's death.

Greg scuffed the ground with his foot. "I do appreciate it, ma'am. But I've an idea to go to Sydney. To the docks. I've a friend there, ye see."

Mrs. Blackwell's chin rose. "Of course. I'm to Sydney meself tomorrow. I could take you." Her lips settled into a hard line, but she showed no other outward sign of disappointment. She gazed past the men to the half-cut field, lost in thought. Trying to figure out how she'd do everything with one less man, no doubt. Then, suddenly, she seemed to remember Michael. "This is Dunn." She jerked her head toward him. "He'll stay in the house and work as me secretary." She gestured to the older man with fair hair. "This is Finn." Then to the other, who'd been bundling the wheat. "And Hud." Then, finally to the younger man, "And Greg, of course."

All three sets of eyes fixed on him, looking him up and down. The older two met each other's gazes, and a flash of amusement passed between them.

Mrs. Blackwell stiffened. She had, no doubt, also noticed the men's unspoken judgment. "Back to work then," she told the older two. "Greg, you may take your leave now, if you wish."

Greg shrugged nonchalantly, though he couldn't seem to contain his grin. "No reason to knock off now, ma'am. I won't be goin' till mornin' anyway."

"Thank you." Mrs. Blackwell shot him a smile, and her eyes flicked to Michael. She nodded at him, directing him without words to follow, turned, and began walking toward the house.

Before Michael had taken two steps, the muted voice of one of the convicts sounded behind him in a thick Scottish brogue. "Ye take good care of the mistress now, mate."

Michael wheeled around. It was the one called Hud talking. His face was creased and weathered with a long scar running down one cheek, but his eyes twinkled with mischief. "She deserves a good bit a' action, after that husband o' hers." The man's friend, Finn, grinned knowingly from beside him. Greg, looking slightly embarrassed, took up his scythe and examined the handle.

Michael felt his face go hard. His own idiotic thoughts about her aside, it was clear she wasn't that kind of woman. He took a step toward the man, tightening his expression into the familiar, menacing glower.

Hud lifted his hands in mock apology. "Easy, there, mate. Just lookin' out for her, is all."

Mrs. Blackwell had noticed the exchange and was coming back toward them. Hud didn't move, but the other two jolted into motion, gripping their scythes and turning back to their work.

"What's this about, then?" the widow snapped, looking from Hud to Michael.

Michael didn't take his eyes off the other man as he spoke. "Nothing, Mrs. Blackwell. I was just coming." Meanwhile, Hud shrugged and turned away to take up his place behind the harvesters.

Michael followed Mrs. Blackwell back to the house, not giving in to the temptation to glance over his shoulder to see if the men were watching. They went through the back door, and in the sudden darkness of the kitchen, Michael nearly collided with her when she stopped suddenly and pivoted toward him.

"I'll not have you threatenin' me men." Her chin was raised, and her fists balled. She was angry. Angrier than he'd yet seen her. "They're good workers, and the only two I got left."

Damn. Was that how it had looked? "I—I'm sorry, Mrs. Blackwell." He stumbled over the words. "He insulted your virtue, and—"

"Insulted me . . . *what*?" Her eyes widened. "Hud?"

Michael didn't know how to respond. He swallowed.

Her eyes narrowed. "And what did he say, exactly?"

He felt his face flush.

"*What did he say?*" It was a clear question. He had no choice.

"He implied that I'm here to—to—" Michael stammered.

Understanding dawned on her face. "To bed me," she finished his sentence, her expression staying surprisingly calm.

"Yes." He closed his eyes in shame. "Or—sort of." His cheeks were burning. "He suggested that Mr. Blackwell had not been . . . *sufficient* in that area. Said you deserved better."

"Well." She sniffed, and an odd kind of grimace came over her face, almost as if she were in pain. Michael expected her to say more, to admonish him further, but she didn't. Instead, her hand came up to cover her mouth, and she quickly turned away.

She stared into the warm ashes for a moment, then turned back to him, that odd look erased from her face. "I've work to attend to. You'll stay here and total up the debts. Then . . ." she seemed to be searching for a command, "then get supper. There's maize for bread and some hard sausage in the larder."

"Yes ma'am."

She started toward the door. "Tomorrow, we're to Sydney. We'll start reading lessons the day after."

"Very good." So they *were* to start the lessons. She hadn't mentioned it since yesterday, and he was beginning to wonder.

"I'm off, then." Mrs. Blackwell nodded curtly and darted out through the back door.

Caitlin felt as if she might burst.

She walked to the barn, head down. As soon as she was inside, hidden from view of the house, she leaned against the wall and allowed the laughter that had been fighting its way to the surface to finally break loose.

Hud, bless him. He'd been righter than he could ever have dreamed. About John at least.

And that look on Dunn's face as he'd recounted Hud's words, red and stumbling, as if such talk would shock her. As if she were a lady.

He insulted your virtue.

She bent over, her stomach clenched with mirth.

What was *happening* today? It was one thing after another. The letters. John's lover. His inheritance. Losing Greg. The daft idea she'd lose the farm . . . and now Michael and Hud in a huff at each other over her virtue.

Her virtue.

She'd been a street whore. An officer's mistress . . . her *virtue*?

She lost herself to another fit of convulsive laughter. It hurt. She was barely able to breathe. Tears streaming down her face, she braced her hands on her thighs and drew a long, shaky breath, then another, smoothing out the giggles.

She shouldn't be laughing. It was serious, all of it. But what else was one to do?

Truth be told, none of it mattered. Not really. The lawyer would see to any worries about the farm. She'd already known she was losing Greg. It wouldn't be easy, but she'd run the farm with two hands before; she could make do. And John . . . What did it matter that he'd loved a girl so long ago? Or that he'd come into money two months too late? He was gone. It didn't change anything. Not now.

And her virtue . . . well. Virtue would have seen her dead two times over. If she'd clung to such notions, she'd have starved on the streets of Cork, then died of the sickness that swept through the hold of that convict ship during those endless months at sea. It was only as Lieutenant Smyth's mistress that she'd managed to find a place away from the pestilence and hunger the other women suffered.

Perhaps Hud had a point. It had been a long time since she'd known any pleasure in shagging . . . and even then, it had been rare. Whoring was hardly a pleasurable act. Dunn was far from perfect, but he was handsome. And he seemed happy to follow her orders . . .

Gor. She levered herself off the wall and strode toward the threshing floor. Those were the thoughts of a miserable, horn-mad master. One intent on taking advantage. The very thing she'd been on the receiving end of too many times.

Anyway, there were no men in her future. Not Dunn, nor anyone else. She'd had enough of them. And she'd only known him for two days. He could change. He *would* change. She'd put a wager on it.

Greg had left the flail propped against the weathered wooden wall. She picked it up, testing the weight in her hand. The heavy wood of the beater swung free, ready for its task.

The future—*Caitlin's* future—would be exactly as she'd dreamed. The fruits of her labor would belong to no one but herself. She'd settle the debts, and in a few years she'd be profitable enough to pay free men in ready money to work her land. Then she'd get a maid, someone to cook and clean while she tended to the animals and the fields. Even if he stayed for a time, Dunn wouldn't be here forever.

She chuckled at the memory of him, cloth in hand, so nervous he'd offended her by cleaning her kitchen.

Her fingers tightened around the wooden handle and she forced the mirth from her mind. She mustn't soften. Not too much. He was a tool, nothing more. Just like the flail in her hands. Something to use, then let go of.

Five years from now, Caitlin would ride into town, just like Esther Abrams, and people would watch as she passed, thinking, *There's that woman who surprised us.* The lowly Irish who took the luckless cards life had dealt her and turned them into gold.

A buoyant power welled inside of her, and she used it as she lifted the flail and brought it down on the wheat. *Thump.* The grains shook loose. Again. *Thump.* Again. *Thump.*

Michael reported the total of the debts over dinner. Two hundred forty-three pounds. That was the sum of it. More than she'd hoped, but not insurmountable. The wheat harvest would bring in at least half, and she had some money already set aside from the candles and the honey. There would be none left to buy piglets next spring, but with luck she'd be able to get them on credit and sell the excess meat for a profit. Perhaps by the end of next year, she could be free of John's debts.

Then a bitter thought took root. Had John lived just a few more months, he'd have been able to pay off this debt with his inheritance. It wouldn't have made so much as a dent in it.

Although, who knew if he actually would have? He never seemed to think much of the debts, had only paid them when absolutely necessary. A triviality . . . And now she knew why. He'd grown up with wealth. A few hundred pounds probably seemed a pittance.

Before she had a chance to rise from the table, Michael began clearing up, and by the time she'd come back from the barn with the evening's milk, he'd disappeared into his room.

The stillness of the night seemed heavier than usual as she went about her evening rituals. She covered the milk, poured her drop of rum, and stuffed her pipe, then sat on the verandah listening to the chirping insects, letting the drink and the smoke settle her body for sleep. Then she hoisted herself up and went out back to wash and visit the privy.

When she returned, there were noises coming from behind Dunn's door. Was he crying? She turned her head, listening.

Muffled shouts filtered through the thin wooden door. No words that she could make out, but he sounded scared. Terrified.

He must be dreaming. Poor man.

She stood there for what felt like a very long time, not sure what to do. Should she wake him? His cries were so pitiful, so agonized that it seemed the kind thing to do . . . but what if he attacked her? She was certain he wouldn't do such a thing in his waking hours, but if she startled him in his sleep . . .

In the end, the choice was made for her. The noises subsided, replaced by soft snores.

Relieved, Caitlin left the kitchen, padded down the hallway to her own room, and climbed into bed.

NINE

CAITLIN WAS UP EARLY the next day in preparation for the trip to Sydney. She did the milking by lantern light, then came in expecting to wake Dunn, only to find him up and breakfast on the table. They ate in silence, listening to the morning song of the magpie that nested in the eves. She wasn't nervous about the coming day, not exactly. But even still, something about the bird's haunting tune was a comfort. It always had been.

Then she left to ready the wagon while he cleared away their few dishes. It seemed some kind of miracle to have the kitchen tidied—and without even having to ask for it. Had it been her, she'd have had a cold breakfast of milk and stale bread, left everything, and come home to the morning's mess.

The sky to the east was awash in color as she brought the horse and dray round to collect the bags of finished wheat. Greg walked up just as she was climbing down, a huge smile on his face and a half empty rucksack slung over his shoulder. "Beautiful morning, ain't it, Mrs. Blackwell?"

"It is." She couldn't help but return his smile. The man looked positively radiant, and who could blame him? Today marked his first taste of freedom in six years. "I've something for you." She fished in her pocket for the coins she'd brought.

Greg accepted them, his eyes widening. "But I thought—"

"You were here for the planting and the harvesting. And I did get something for that first load. You deserve it." She caught his eye. "Just don't drink it all up. Use it well."

If it were possible, Greg's smile grew even wider. He tucked the pouch away. "You needn't worry about that, Mrs. Blackwell. Thank you."

Dunn came out of the house just as they had finished loading the dray. He must have stopped to wash, as his hair was damp and his face shining and freshly shaved. With a flash of guilt, Caitlin remembered what she'd noticed yesterday—he had a suitable set of clothes, given to him by Mr. Flemming, no doubt, but he was in need of a hat. His shoes, too, weren't whole enough to deserve the name. He could hardly go to town like that.

"I'll just be a minute." She left the men and ran into the house, then quickly rummaged through the chest in her room and came away with the straw hat John had kept here for his use, as well as a pair of boots. Both were too well made for a man of Dunn's standing, but it was what she had.

She walked briskly out to the dray, handed Dunn the things, and climbed up to the driver's seat.

There was a moment's hesitation, as there was only room for two on the bench. Dunn looked up at her questioningly, the hat and boots still clutched to his chest. "Shall I—?"

"I'll ride in back," Greg's cheerful voice interrupted him. "More comfy there, anyway."

Dunn nodded and hoisted himself up to sit beside Caitlin, then bent down to pull on the new boots.

An uncomfortable silence settled between them as Caitlin directed the dray down the drive and onto the road. It was another mild, sunny day, with fluffy white clouds moving lazily across the blue sky. The scent of acacia and things growing filled the air. Greg ignored them completely. He lay on his back, chewing absently on a grass stem and gazing at the sky.

Michael's thigh rested beside hers. He'd donned the hat she'd given him, and he wore it well—better than John ever did. It was cabbage fiber, trimmed by a sober black ribbon. The type of hat well-to-do men in Sydney wore when out and about during the day.

"Do the boots fit?" Her question was the first break in the quiet for at least half an hour.

"Yes. Thank you."

A brightly colored king parrot moved in the branches over their heads, squawking merrily. The wagon jounced in a rut.

She couldn't get but two words out of the man.

"There's a good bit more wheat still to come," she tried again. "I thought I'd send the rest down river instead of hauling it the whole way. Mr. Colfax in Windsor will take it on his barge if we get it to him." Silence. "'T'will be difficult for me to leave the farm during harvest, with Greg gone. I thought you might haul it for me. The wheat, I mean."

"Of course."

Her eyes drifted to his leg, clad in thin woolen trousers, right there beside the cotton of her skirts.

One didn't have to talk to shag, did one?

She allowed her eye to move up his thigh, his body, then sneaked a glance at his face. He appeared at ease. His gaze was fixed on the road ahead, his face relaxed. His flaxen hair, fine as spun gold, blew gently in the breeze.

He was like a shell. A handsome, useful shell. If she did request his . . . *services*, would he comply as simply and thoughtlessly as he did with every other command she gave?

Was that even what she wanted?

And what kind of lover would he be? Would he expect her to take charge of that too? It was hard to imagine him ordering her about in bed, but that's what men did, wasn't it? Certainly, John had only desired her as something to rut into, and then only rarely. Before him, on the ship from Cork, Smythe had wanted the same. He'd command her to lie down or suck, and then he'd quickly fallen asleep in the tiny cabin he'd kept her in. In both cases, the men's attention had been to her benefit. Worth it, to be sure, but it had hardly been pleasurable.

Even in Cork, most of the men who'd employed her services seemed to only require a wench to do their bidding, to woodenly stand or lie down while they pumped into her.

But there *had* been one man, different from the rest. She hadn't thought of him in years. He had been wealthier than most, old but still handsome enough. He'd brought her to a clean, warm room at an inn, fed her, and had a bath brought up—a luxury she hadn't known since she'd left the farm as a child. When she'd asked him what he wanted her to do, he'd just looked back at her, a lustful twinkle in his eye, then turned the question around.

"What would you have *me* do, Miss Caitlin?"

Remembering that moment, even all these years later, a shiver ran down her spine, and her cunt throbbed. She'd been truly clean for the first time in two years, her naked body wrapped in a soft towel and reclined on a bed of feathers. She'd hesitated, not knowing what to say, but he'd waited for her to speak, stacking more money on the dresser until, finally, she'd found the nerve.

"Come 'ere."

He did.

"Touch me cunt . . . No. There. That's it."

His hand had been gentle, almost tenuous, like he wanted her pleasure, not just her hole. It was so unlike the others who only took what they wanted, rough and quick, sometimes in a back alley, sometimes in a dark and dirty room. She'd been heady with the feeling—desire, she supposed. It wasn't something she'd ever before felt with a man, and she'd rarely felt it since.

"Take off your clothes," she'd commanded, her confidence growing along with that strange feeling of *wanting* a man to fuck her. Not for the money it would bring, but for the pleasure of it.

He'd obeyed without hesitation, dropping his coat and trousers like a shot off a shovel, then pulling his shirt over his head. She could still remember his cock—thick, but not long—standing at attention. And his eyes, waiting for her command.

"You may fuck me now." She'd said it like she imagined a lady might, and she chuckled to remember it. She'd been a sixteen-year-old street whore, fresh from the country. She hadn't even known what a lady was.

Perhaps that's what got him off?

The actual shagging had been a bit of a letdown. Nothing out of the ordinary.

And she'd never seen the man again. It wasn't long after that little Gerry'd got sick. She'd needed money to pay the doctor, and that fat old man's fine silk handkerchief had seemed such an easy thing to nick while he lolled, drunk and satisfied on the bed . . .

Michael shifted beside her, pulling her from her thoughts.

Goodness. Where had that come from? It was so long ago . . . the man, so handsome and fine in her memory, was just another grinder with a nasty imagination. It wasn't as if he'd actually thought she was special. He'd just got off on being bossed about by a dirty mot.

Dunn's elbow bumped against her arm as he reached into his pocket. Then came the sweet smell of tobacco as he cut off a plug and packed it in. He was as different from that far-away toff as could be. Not kind at all, and certainly not interested in her that way. Only obedient.

Yet, he had once been something different, hadn't he?

He lit the pipe, and puffed the bowl to life. A white cloud blew past her and the acrid, earthy aroma of the smoke filled her senses.

"What was it that got you sent here?" she asked before she could think better of it. It would only make him more uncomfortable, and it wasn't as if it mattered. "Never mind—"

"Forgery. I forged a document. Claimed to be someone I wasn't."

She glanced at him, waiting for him to say more, but he just pulled deeply on his pipe and stared at the road ahead. The skin on his neck was tanned and rugged, his fair hair ruffled in the breeze. What would it feel like to touch him?

She blinked the thought away. "Could I have a draw?" The tobacco would settle her mind and her body. With hours of driving still ahead of them and this handsome, silent man beside her, she'd need *something*.

He handed her the pipe. She pulled from it, held the smoke in her mouth, then breathed out slowly, allowing that weighty, rooted feeling to soak through her.

"Thank you." She handed it back, and he brought the pipe to his own lips, puffing on it in turn.

The damn pipe tasted of her. Her mouth, his mouth. Breathing the same air, the same smoke.

Michael should have sat in the back with Greg. It had been far too long since he'd been with a woman. He'd known that. And sitting so close to her . . . it brought out the animal in him. Not the vicious, snarling beast from Moreton Bay, but the rutting, vulgar one. The one ruled by his cock. The man known to many whores in London. The man who'd accidentally tried to bed his own cousin, thinking she was a housemaid. The man who'd allowed a woman in Sydney to keep him just drunk and satisfied enough for her to spend all his earnings.

He angled away from the widow and pretended to examine the trees as he smoked.

They reached Sydney at midday and left Greg by the police station, just a few blocks from the secretary's office where he'd get his ticket. The young man shouted a gleeful farewell as he leaped from the wagon bed. Then he disappeared down George Street and around a corner. Michael watched the spot where he'd vanished. He seemed a good sort, hopefully one to keep his wits about him. A ticket of leave meant freedom, but only to a point. Any infraction, even a small one, could see that freedom revoked and the man back in chains.

"I only hope he's got the sense to stay out of trouble." The widow spoke softly. "He's so young . . ."

Michael glanced at her, and their eyes snagged. A silent agreement. Then she quickly looked away and chirruped to the mare, directing her toward the warehouse where they'd drop the wheat.

Unloading the wheat was quick work. Mrs. Blackwell's buyer seemed an honest man, and he paid her in ready money.

All too soon, Michael was knocking on the door to Mr. Snodgrass's office. Mrs. Blackwell stood stiffly behind him, shoulders squared, back straight, and an expression of tight politeness plastered on her face. She'd donned a bonnet today as well as gloves, and she alternated between balling her hands into tight fists and stretching out her fingers.

It was the same kind of posture she'd greeted him and Davey with when they'd first arrived at her house. He was coming to recognize it.

Michael balled his own fists, as if the movement might give him some kind of assurance that this was a good idea. It wouldn't. The last time he'd met this lawyer, Michael had been in charge of Cowper's warehouses, a man of standing, albeit still a convict. Now, he was . . .

He didn't even know what he was.

Did Snodgrass know he'd been to Moreton Bay? Would he even agree to see them?

Mrs. Blackwell cleared her throat nervously.

Michael clenched his hands tighter, forcing his head up. He might be good for nothing, but he must pretend, for her. He straightened his back and arched his brow, summoning the manners and assurance of his youth.

The door opened to Snodgrass's clerk, a plump man of middling age. His eyes widened behind his spectacles. "Mr. D-Dunn?" Then his gaze moved to Mrs. Blackwell, standing tall and serious behind Michael.

"Is Mr. Snodgrass in? We'd like a word with him if we may." Michael managed to sound as if he expected to get what he wanted, and it worked. The man stood aside, motioning them in.

"He is here, but . . . he's not expecting you, I'm afraid. I'll—I'll just have to—" The clerk closed the door behind them, then motioned toward the inner door that Michael knew led to Snodgrass's office.

"This is my new employer, Mrs. Blackwell." Michael gestured toward her.

"Pleased to meet you, ma'am." The clerk bobbed his head in the widow's direction.

"An urgent legal matter has come up, and I recommended Mr. Snodgrass's services. If he's not available—" Michael turned as if to leave.

"Oh, no. He's here. I'll just—" The clerk knocked lightly on the interior door. A short, "Come," filtered through the wood, and the bespectacled man disappeared into the lawyer's office.

The door snicked shut behind him, and Mrs. Blackwell exhaled loudly. Michael turned to see her warily looking around. Clearly, she felt justs as out of place as he did. The antechamber was nothing special. A small desk for the clerk, some drawers. A half-drunk cup of tea sat next to a pen that had been hastily set down.

Michael felt the urge to reassure her, to smooth her shoulders and get rid of the stiff nervousness, though, in truth, his heart was hammering in his chest. It had been so long since he'd had to act with authority that it had taken far more effort than he'd anticipated. "It's—it's going to be all right, you know," he managed.

"Of course it is," she snapped.

The clerk reemerged, the surprised look he'd greeted them with banished from his face. He held the door open. "He'll see you, but you must be brief. He has another appointment in—" The man checked his fob. "Fifteen minutes."

"Of course." Michael didn't glance at the man as he passed into the room. Mrs. Blackwell followed at his heels.

Snodgrass greeted them with cautious curiosity. It was clear from the way he looked at Michael that he knew of Michael's removal to Moreton Bay. But as Michael had hoped, the lawyer's good nature overruled any trepidation he may have felt. Once Mrs. Blackwell had presented the letter from the solicitor in London, along with the outline of her predicament, Snodgrass seemed to forget Michael's presence altogether.

"Are you quite sure your husband died *after* his brother, Mrs. Blackwell?" The lawyer let the letter fall to his desk, though he still stared at it pensively, his brows drawn into a straight line.

"I am. John died in July. This letter is dated April." Mrs. Blackwell's tone was so confident even Michael would have been fooled into thinking she'd read the letter herself.

"And your marriage was legitimate and recorded?" Snodgrass looked up, one brow arching.

"It was—it *is*. He picked me out of—" She stopped, then restarted. "We were married in Sydney in aught-six. I have the document."

"And you hold the deed to your farm now? In your own name?"

"I do." She hesitated. Michael gave her what he hoped was an encouraging look. "But the man at the land office said it was only because John had no other heirs."

"I see . . ." Snodgrass's eyes had wandered to the window. Now they refocused onto Mrs. Blackwell. "And you want to keep your farm—Swindale—I suppose? Or would you rather go to England given the opportunity?"

She seemed surprised by the question, almost offended. "I'm Irish, sir. I've no desire to go to England. All I want's the farm." Her chin raised. "And to be left alone."

"Where is Swindale, Mrs. Blackwell?"

"Just west of Windsor."

"Is it on the Hawkesbury? Or near?"

"It is near. There's a creek that runs into it just past the fields."

"A valuable piece of property." The lawyer's gaze wandered back out the window.

"I suppose so," Mrs. Blackwell replied tightly.

Mr. Snodgrass nodded to himself, as if deciding something, then focused on the widow once again. "Would you like me to represent you in this case, Mrs. Blackwell, or simply advise you on a course of action?"

Her eyes widened almost imperceptibly. Then she looked to Michael, clearly unsure.

The lawyer's fees just for meeting with them would be enough of a financial burden. Representation would be far too dear. Michael knew that much. "Mrs. Blackwell is interested in your advice, sir. We'll handle the rest for now," he answered.

"Well, then." Snodgrass ignored Michael and continued to speak directly to Mrs. Blackwell. "In my opinion, ma'am, much depends on your late husband's heir. As his widow, you are entitled to a dower, which, given that you have no children, is one half of your husband's estate, devoted to your use for the rest of your natural life. But that is limited to real property, not investments or accounts. And *which* part of the estate is dependent entirely on the whims of the heir. He could decide to move you back to England if he wanted the property here for his own use."

"But sir, I hold the deed. Surely, he couldn't . . . "

Snodgrass shook his head. "In my experience, the courts in Sydney bow to England, ma'am. Again, it depends on the heir himself and his connections. But there's no guarantee that deed wouldn't be revoked in his favor, if he desired it. He will have a great deal of wealth, that much we know."

Mrs. Blackwell's hands tightened into fists again. The muscles of her jaw moved. "What should I do then, sir? In your opinion."

"If *I* were you," Snodgrass caught Michael's eye, making sure he was following before focusing his attention back on Mrs. Blackwell, "I'd write to this solicitor." He picked up the letter. "Tell him of your husband's death and the timing of it. He'll need to locate the next in line. You could also state your desire to stay in New South Wales on the land you currently occupy, in lieu of any claim of dower in England. Make it seem as if you're doing him a favor. With any luck, that will be enough, and the matter will be finished."

"But there's still a chance . . ." she prompted.

The lawyer nodded. "There's a chance, as slight as it may be, that he'll have an interest in the land here." The lawyer shrugged. "Only time will tell. Certainly, you are not required to give any detail of the property in question or its desirability." He arched his brow. "Not deception, per se. Simply choosing the right words."

Michael was already drafting the letter in his head. There would be no mention of access to the Hawkesbury or the newly constructed road to Sydney. Certainly no mention of the yields of crops. Probably even the creek on her property would be reduced to a mere muddy trickle, useless in the dry season, but liable to flood the fields in the wet.

Mrs. Blackwell drew a long breath, and if it were possible, sat up taller in her chair. "Very well. I will write to this solicitor right away."

Michael felt a swell of admiration for the woman.

The lawyer glanced at the clock. "Now, if there's nothing else, I believe I have an appointment due any minute." He stood, circling round the desk to usher them out.

He opened the door, and Michael left the room as any servant would, leaving Mrs. Blackwell to shake the man's hand and give her thanks. Then the two of them crossed to the front door.

Just as they were coming out of the shadow of the office into the bright sunlight and raucous noise of Sydney, the clerk's voice called after them.

"I'll send you a bill."

They rode home in silence, albeit a more comfortable one than on their way into town. Caitlin was so lost in her thoughts she forgot about Michael altogether.

Lose Swindale. Go to England. Everything the lawyer had said seemed impossible. And it was. It wouldn't happen; he had more or less assured them of that. They'd just have to write the letter in a certain way. But even still . . . it had turned up worries that she couldn't seem to bury.

This wasn't what she needed. Not now. There was wheat to harvest and thresh and winnow. A garden to weed. Candles to make. Honey to press. The bees were busy, and she'd have to add more frames to the hives soon. One of the cows was nearing her time; she would calve, and there would be more milk than they could use. Caitlin would have to churn butter and make cheese to sell in Windsor.

"What if we didn't tell him?" She didn't realize she'd spoken the words aloud until Michael answered.

"The solicitor, you mean? In London?"

She nodded, speaking slowly as she tested the idea in her own mind. "What would happen if we just ignored the letter? Didn't write him back to tell him John's dead?"

Michael was quiet for a minute. "If he didn't hear back . . . My guess is he'd inquire elsewhere. With the secretary's office. Or he'd put a notice in the paper. He'd find out somehow."

They'd reached an open part of the road. The rolling landscape stretched before them, the sun hanging low above it, a great fiery ball in the sky. A drip of sweat trickled down Caitlin's neck, tracing its way between her breasts. "I suppose we must, then. Tell him, I mean."

Michael didn't answer.

"You'll help me write it, won't you?" She hated how pathetic she sounded. But truth be told, she needed his help.

This time he was quick to speak. "Of course. I've had plenty of practice writing letters to solicitors." A bitterness permeated his words, though she knew better than to ask what he meant.

Instead, she turned her head to look at him, so near, yet not touching her. "Thank you."

He stared straight ahead. "It's nothing." The words were a low grumble.

A warm tingling spread across her chest, her belly. She opened her mouth to say more but closed it again before the thoughts could take form.

Ten

THEY ARRIVED HOME JUST after dark. Mrs. Blackwell saw to the horses and the evening chores while Michael went in to fix supper. He'd just set two plates laden with boiled eggs, green peas, and maize bread on the table when she came through the back door.

She seemed as lost in her thoughts as she had during the drive, so Michael let her be. Still, he couldn't help but sneak glances out of the corner of his eye. A single candle flickered between them—beeswax, a small bit of luxury in her otherwise sparse home, though he'd noticed the candles she burned were the odd ones, misshapen or with a scratch in the wax. Her fair skin glowed in the soft light, and he could just make out the shifting planes of muscle in her arms, strong and lean, shadow and light. Her hair had slipped from the tight bun she'd fixed it in this morning, and her black curls formed a halo around her face. But that face . . . It was creased with worry. She was still brooding about what Snodgrass had told her.

She caught his eye, and he quickly looked away, putting all his focus on buttering his bread. What could he say to help? "No one in London would want a farm out here," he managed. "Especially a rich man." It was true. There was shame attached to anything connected to New South Wales: the people, the land, all of it. The well-to-do in England avoided even mentioning the colony if they could.

She looked at him sharply, then shook her head. "I'm sure you're right." She took a bite of egg, chewed, swallowed, and curled her lips into a weary smile. "It'll be a year before we hear anything back anyway. There's no use in worrying now." But still, that troubled look clung to her face.

As soon as he'd finished his meal, Michael rose and cleared his dish, then hers. He carried them to the basin and poured in hot water from the kettle to wash them. He didn't hear her approach, but he smelled her and felt a soft brush of air on his cheek.

The hairs on the back of his neck rose.

"I often sit on the verandah this time of night, to smoke and take a nip of rum. You're welcome to come." Her tone was tenuous. Not the commanding mistress, but a woman inviting him to keep her company.

Michael didn't turn around. He couldn't. The warm water that surrounded his hands seemed to wash over his entire body. But his mouth—his mouth was dry as dust.

Did she mean . . .? He swallowed, casting the thought aside. "I don't drink."

"Fair enough." She chuckled. "You *do* smoke though. I've proof of that." A pause as she waited for him to speak. This would only lead to trouble. Women always led to trouble. She didn't mean it as that kind of invitation anyway. She probably felt sorry for him and was just trying to be kind. "It's been a day," she coaxed. "You'll sleep better for it."

Her words spiraled around him, along with her scent. Why not? He was her servant. She wanted company. It needn't turn into more than that. Surely even Michael had that much control. And she was right, a quick smoke before bed would help him sleep. Perhaps it would even ward off the nightmares.

"I'll be out when I'm done here."

The grinding chirrup of insects was almost deafening when Michael came out onto the verandah a few minutes later. The heat had lifted, and the stars shimmered above, alongside the near-full moon, illuminating the landscape and turning it almost as bright as day. In the shadow of the verandah, all was dark aside from a candle Mrs. Blackwell had brought out, which stood shrouded in a tin lantern. He might have missed her completely, had he not known she was there—and had the smell of pipe smoke not hung in the air.

She sat in shadow, still as a statue. The tin cup in her hand gleamed dully in the candlelight. Her pipe glowed faintly red.

"I brought you a chair." She gestured with her cup toward a straight-back chair that sat beside her. It must have come from the sitting room.

Feeling like an intruder, Michael perched uncomfortably on the edge of the chair and packed his pipe. He glanced up. The candle stood on Mrs. Blackwell's other side. He'd have to—

"Here." She set down her cup and took up a twisted, half-burnt piece of paper. Then she opened the lantern, held the spill to the candle until it ignited, and drew it slowly across herself, shielding the small flame as best as she could with the hand that held her pipe. It flickered but didn't go out. Smoothly, she maneuvered it so the flame pointed away from them and offered him the butt end.

The spill was short and growing shorter. There was no way to take it without touching her hand.

Unwittingly, Michael's eyes rose to her face. She was watching him, a tiny smile on her lips and a gleam in her eye.

Or perhaps it was only the flame's reflection.

"Are you going to light your pipe, Dunn?" She raised a brow.

"Hmph." Michael grunted, jerking his gaze away. Then, slowly, as to not put the fire out, he wrapped his hands around the paper, just above where she held it. As he'd known it would, his hand enveloped hers, his palm brushing the spot where her index finger met her thumb. The feel of it, of his skin over hers . . . it was—

Hot.

A tiny change in the breeze blew the flame his way, and it licked the backs of his fingers. Instinctively, he pulled the twisted paper toward his pipe. Mrs. Blackwell released it, and in the process, the flame sputtered out.

Of course it did.

She chuckled.

Of course she did.

Still holding the charred twist, Michael closed his eyes and tipped his head back. Bah. He was such a bloody idiot.

"Oh, now." The widow's tone was bemused. Condescending. As if he were a child. She began to rise. "Don't you worry, I'll just go get another—"

"No." Michael stood. "I'm tired. I'm to bed." He dropped the blasted paper on the table beside her and, cold pipe in hand, escaped back into the house.

He'd left. Without even lighting his pipe.

Caitlin shouldn't have laughed, but she'd done it before she could even think. And he'd taken offense.

"Well then, that was a smash," she muttered to herself. First the lawyer, and now this. She leaned over and blew out the candle, then closed the lantern. No use for it now.

The darkness spread out around her, and she felt herself growing smaller in it, merely a spectator to the grand stage of the world. The silvery light of the moon. The soft curve of the land, the deep shadows of the gum trees. The song of the crickets.

She should have known better than to invite him out here, into the time and space she usually took for herself. But he lived here now, at least temporarily. It had seemed the kind thing to do.

But no, it wasn't just kindness, was it? She desired him, and she'd not wanted to say goodnight so soon.

She took a drink of the rum, let it slide down her throat.

When she was a girl, before they'd been evicted from the farm, and even before her younger siblings were born, Ma had sometimes taken her to the shore to catch periwinkles. The little snails lived in the rocky pools at the edge of the sea, and they were as tasty as anything Caitlin could remember from those days of plenty. But it wasn't so much the eating that held the joy for her. It was the catching of them. Of being with Ma, away from the work of the farm, splashing in the sunshine, breathing in the salt air. The way the wind off the sea combed through her hair and cooled her cheeks. The smile on Ma's pretty face. Happy as larks, they'd been.

Caitlin had found that if she snuck up on the tiny snails, she could sometimes catch them out of their shells, their fleshy stalks exposed to the sky and their beady little eyes looking about. But as soon as they noticed her, they'd pull themselves back in, quick as a flash, and slam their little doors behind them.

Dunn was like that, wasn't he?

There were moments when she felt sure she was starting to see the man underneath the shell. His softness. His kindness. His desire, even. Then the next, he was jerking himself away.

Was he scared? Or ashamed? Did he think he was too good for her, perhaps?

Was *that* it? Did he think his upbringing as a gentleman made him superior? Was the servant act just that, an *act*? It was in his interest to please her, surely. He knew as well as she did that he'd be put to hard labor if she sent him back to Sydney.

But that look in his eye over supper as he'd watched her in the candlelight. And just now, as he contemplated taking the spill from her hand. Contemplated touching her.

Caitlin knew what it looked like when a man desired a woman. Knew it only too well. All the rest might be an act, but that, surely, was not.

She sipped the grog again, and the cool of the tin on her lips gave way to settled warmth spreading down her throat, her belly, lower. Her cunt throbbed dully at the memory of his large hand over hers on the spill.

His palms were calloused, but underneath his tough exterior was a softness, a vulnerability. Just like a periwinkle, he'd retreated as soon as she'd come too near. Back into his shell, slamming the door shut.

Afraid. That was it. He was *afraid* of touching her. Of offending her, perhaps, or of what might happen if they did take up together.

And it *would* be complicated, that was the truth. She, his master; he, her assigned man. It mustn't get in the way of anything. Even if she allowed him to stay—and that seemed more likely somehow, after today—he would only be here for a year. And they had much to accomplish in that time.

But if he *did* want her, she wouldn't be taking advantage, would she? The pleasure would be mutual. They could talk it out beforehand, smooth out all the complications . . .

And what would be the harm?

She'd have to be more direct the next time. Talk to him about it like two adults rather than two younglings awkward in their lust.

She took one last puff of her pipe and watched the smoke float up into the night air, curling little bits of moonlight into the stars above.

Tomorrow night. She'd get him back out here, light his damn pipe for him, and they'd talk.

Eleven

THE HARD FACT WAS, Michael had no idea how to teach someone to read.

He woke just before dawn with that thought stuck in his mind. His only experience of such things were the lessons he'd taken as a boy, and that ordeal had consisted mainly of repetition and pain, with great emphasis—in his memory at least—on the pain. His tutor, Mr. Lance, had been particularly fond of the ferrule, using it alternately on Michael's knuckles and palms when he stumbled or balked at a word.

Then there had been the time young Michael, not more than six years old, had been unable to recite the correct conjugation and mood of the verb *to be*. Mr. Lance's face had turned purple with rage. He'd forced Michael to extend his arms and hold three heavy tomes for a full half hour without flinching.

Michael could still see the man's ruddy countenance looming over him, could still feel the shaking and burning of the muscles in his arms as they threatened to give way. Though it was all overshadowed by the terror of what Father would say when he found out.

What *had* Father said? The memory was hazy, mixed up with all the other scenes of himself trembling before Father's big desk. Indeed, such interactions were all Michael had known of his father as a boy. He hadn't yelled, of that Michael was sure. He never yelled. He'd simply stared at his son, his blue eyes burning into him, and explained just how disappointing a son he had turned out to be . . .

"Do you want to be an even worse earl than your uncle, boy? Because that's where you're headed. A dimwit." Father's eyes narrowed. "An embarrassment."

The words landed on Michael's chest like blows, though somehow, even as a young boy he'd learned to hold himself stiff, to feign indifference.

Father pursed his lips in loathing. "Get out of my sight."

But Michael was already going, darting through the door into the corridor, his facade crumpling as the tears broke loose—

Bah. Michael pushed the thin blanket off. It would be a hot day, and he was already sweating.

No, there was nothing in his past he could use to teach Mrs. Blackwell. And anyway, what reason did she have to know the first perfect tense from the pluperfect? All she needed was to be able to read a contract, and to write passably.

If he only had a first reader. He should have thought of getting one when they were in town yesterday, but he'd been too preoccupied with the other business.

She had paper and ink in her husband's office, at least. He could write out the alphabet. That was a start.

But there was another problem. Mrs. Blackwell herself. As he'd proved quite deftly the night before, getting too close to her was a dangerous thing. He winced at the memory. What a beetle-headed fool he'd been. Not just the antics with the spill, but his pathetic retreat afterward.

The room was growing more stifling by the second. No air at all came through the open window.

Mrs. Blackwell was his employer. He must do right by her, and that meant teaching her to read. Not ogling her and fumbling about.

The magpie began to sing again just outside the window. So bloody loud—it must have a nest near the house. It sounded so pleased with itself. How could a dumb creature like that hold so much joy? What did it have to be so happy about? All it would do in its short life was eat, fuck, build a nest, and raise its brood. What sort of existence was that anyway?

It wasn't unlike the life Davey lived with Emily. So dashedly content.

Goddamn bird.

Michael growled into the gray light. There would be no more sleep this morning.

He rose and stalked into the kitchen. The room was still, the air already heavy and hot. He cocked his head, listening. Only the sound of the blasted bird filtering in from outside. Nothing from Mrs. Blackwell's chamber. She must still be asleep.

He might as well get breakfast.

Thankfully, the sound of the back door opening and closing sent the bird soaring away over the barn. Michael washed his hands and face with water from the well. It was blessedly cold, though he was hot again as soon as it dried. Then he drew a pail for the cooking. Back inside, he put the kettle on, poured a bit of maize and water into a pot, and set it over the cold hearth. Now to stoke the fire. It was an easy thing to do: dust off the white layer of ash that coated yesterday's coals, then feed a few twists of straw and dry sticks to the warm embers. A bit of breath, taking care not to blow ash everywhere, and the straw ignited. He stirred the pot a few times as the new flames licked around it, yellow and bright. When they began to die down, he added thicker sticks and a log, then left the lot to cook while he skimmed some cream off yesterday's milk and set the table—the honey pot, the pitcher, the teapot, two cups, bowls, and spoons.

He stood back, surveying his work. It would do. Then he returned to the hearth. The porridge was beginning to thicken, so he stirred it while adding a quick pinch of salt.

He breathed in the rich steam, and his stomach growled. There was something satisfying about the mindless routines of a kitchen. He'd discovered this when he'd lived with Davey in Sydney. Before *that*, back at home in London, he'd never even set foot in a kitchen. Why would he? The only reason Father would have tolerated was to annoy the maids, but Michael was never one for such things.

Except for that time in Darnalay . . .

Bah. That was a memory better left alone.

But in Sydney, with Davey, it was either live in a filthy house and eat the greasy meat pies sold in the tavern across the way or to learn to cook and clean. And so, as Davey had seemed quite content with the meat pies and the mess, Michael had learned.

He'd been surprised when he hadn't minded it. It wasn't merely the routine, but the contentment on his friend's face when he enjoyed a meal, the satisfaction that came from making something dirty clean again. Of doing something worthwhile. Something he could *see*.

Of course, Father would have hated knowing that he'd lowered himself to such tasks. That fact brought a certain kind of satisfaction in itself. The man hadn't spared a second thought for the servants, much less considered the worth of their labor . . . but then, Father had been wrong about a good many things. Everything, as far as Michael could tell.

If only he'd learned that sooner.

"Good morning."

Startled, Michael looked up from the pot. Mrs. Blackwell stood at the door, her elbows jutting back awkwardly as she tied her apron strings. She was the epitome of neat and tidy, her hair freshly pinned, her clothes clean—a sky blue dress Michael was coming to recognize—her face rosy and freshly washed. But her expression . . . it was undone somehow. Soft and open and unwary, eyes bright and still a bit puffy from sleep. She hadn't yet donned the mask she wore in her daily life.

He only stared a second or two, but Michael felt as if he'd been caught at something completely untoward. He grunted, then quickly looked back to the steaming pot.

All too soon, he felt her presence at his back. Close. "I'm never again goin' to cook breakfast in me own house, am I?" she teased.

He kept his eyes on the maize as it bubbled stiffly in its iron pot. "Do you want to?"

There was a pause. "I do not. I've never liked cooking much. Or cleaning. I'd rather be outside in the garden or in the barn."

Michael turned to collect the bowls from the table, only to find her halfway out the door.

"I'll be back in two shakes," she called over her shoulder.

And she was. He'd just finished spooning the porridge when she returned, clutching a handful of odd, bright yellow, orb-shaped flowers.

"Billy buttons." She held them up with a grin, then dipped a tin cup in the water bucket and stuffed them inside. "I don't grow flowers, but these come up each year by the back of the barn. Pretty, aren't they?" She set the bouquet on the table, then stood back and smiled approvingly. "There now. 'Tis perfect."

Michael felt the sudden urge to retreat, just as he had the previous night. But instead, he held his placid expression in place and passed her a warm bowl of porridge.

She accepted it, walked to the table, and sat down. Once she was settled, he moved to take the chair opposite, taking great care not to look her in the eye. A deferential servant. That's what he was. Nothing more.

She spooned in a mouthful, swallowed, and to his relief when she spoke again it was as a master to a servant. "I'd like you to write that letter this morning while I work with the men."

Michael nodded through his own mouthful of porridge.

"Then we'll have our first lesson. This afternoon." She smiled, clearly anticipating it.

"Of course," he managed. He'd never dreaded anything more.

"I thought we'd begin with the letters. Do you know any of them?" Dunn trained his gaze on the piece of paper between them, which he'd covered in script.

Caitlin squinted at the marks he'd drawn out, but they meant nothing to her, so she focused on his bowed head instead. She'd decided to take her lessons in the sitting room. It was brighter here than in the kitchen, and with the windows open and the front door propped, the heat was bearable. They sat in chairs on opposite sides of the small end table. Dunn's fine curls shone in the early afternoon light. So soft . . . She yearned to touch them, to run her fingers through them, to feel the stark contrast between his locks and his cheek with its stubbly shadow of beard. From this angle, she had a view of his lashes, which she'd never noticed before. They were as blond as the rest of him, fanned out thick against his cheek as he cast his eyes down.

She stared intently at them, willing him to raise his gaze. She counted in her head. One. Two. Three. *Look at me, Dunn.*

But he just sat there, head down, waiting for her to answer.

Caitlin exhaled and looked away. She was beginning to doubt this plan. Dunn had been the perfect servant all day. He'd made her breakfast and written the letter to London as she'd asked. He'd done a good job of it, from what she could tell. He'd made the farm sound like an inhospitable backwater, not worth anything. Still . . . There was no sign of the man who'd looked at her over dinner yesterday. He'd retreated into his hard shell. Perhaps she'd imagined his interest, after all?

Anyway, bedding this man—or any man—wasn't the important thing, was it? Learning to read was. She was being incurably silly.

She pressed her lips together and forced herself to focus on the page. He'd asked her a question. About her letters.

"I don't know any of these, but I know a few," she offered. "The ones in me name."

Still not looking at her, Dunn took up the quill from the ink pot at his elbow, tapped it against the edge with a practiced motion, then began to scratch something out on a fresh sheet of paper. When he was finished, he blew lightly on the page and turned it so she could see. "You can tell me what these are, then?"

Caitlin stared at the unrecognizable marks. "I—" She looked up, finally meeting the blue of his gaze, but not in the way she'd hoped. She felt anything but desirable. She was a clod. "That's not me name. Is it?" She despised the weakness in her voice.

Dunn's eyes flicked down to the paper. "Blackwell. B-L-A-C-K-W-E-L-L. Have I misspelled it?"

"Oh." Of course. She felt her lips curve into a smile. "Not Blackwell. O'Keefe. That was me name before. There were papers to sign in court, you see, in Cork. And the matron at the gaol taught me. I believe she hoped I'd learn to read the bible, but I shipped out before we got that far."

"I see." Dunn cleared his throat. "O'Keefe, then." He turned the paper back to face him and once again poised the pen above the page.

"*Caitlin*. O'Keefe." She watched his hand intently, anticipating the familiar letters.

"Caht-leenn." Dunn spoke slowly, drawing the sound out as his quill flowed across the page. Caitlin's scalp tightened at the sound of her name on his lips. Gruff, yet somehow tender. John had called her by her given name, but he'd intentionally said it wrong—using the sharp, grating English pronunciation rather than the Irish, as if she and her Irishness weren't worth anything. But Dunn drew out the soft, lilting Irish sounds as if they were treasures.

She felt herself relax as she recognized the marks.

He looked up to see if she was following, and their eyes met for a second. Then his gaze darted away again.

But not fast enough. She'd seen it, that flash of desire behind the hard shell.

He cleared his throat as he finished writing her surname and turned the page around to face her. "Now, tell me. What letters do you see?"

She glanced up, but his eyes stuck steadfastly to the paper once more. Better to try a different tack. She moved her hand to point at the letters he'd written, intentionally brushing her knuckles across his, gentle as a feather.

He stiffened at the touch, then quickly jerked his hand away. The paper dropped to the table.

Caitlin felt her cheeks heat. *For shame.* What was she doing? Trying to seduce a man who clearly did not want to be seduced, that's what. Even if, deep down, he *did* want her, he obviously had no intention of acting on it.

And that was his choice, was it not?

She forced her attention to the page, grinding her back teeth together. *Concentrate, Caitlin.* You're here to learn, not to lure a man into bed.

The letters he'd written were smoother and more graceful than the ones the matron had scratched out for her, but she could recognize them. The old woman had made her repeat them over and over again until she knew them by rote.

"C." She pointed to the elegantly curved letter he'd penned. He'd put a little loop at the top and bottom, a luxury of ink. "A - I - T - L - I - N."

"Very good. Let's ignore the surname for now." Dunn seemed to have regained his composure. He spoke as a tutor might, brisk and authoritative. He turned the paper around, wrote something beneath her name, and presented it to her. "And what do you suppose *this* word might be?"

She glanced at the page, then back up at him. "I've no idea. I—"

"Look at it." His blue eyes met hers, and this time, there was no heat at all, only a raised brow and a command. "What are the letters?"

She looked. Squinted. "Well, that's a C, surely. Then A and T. She pointed to each in turn. But I don't know what—"

"In your name." He interrupted. "What sound does the C make?"

She hesitated. It seemed too easy an answer. "*Kuh.*"

"Yes." He nodded approvingly, then pointed to the A. "Now, A can make several sounds, depending on the word, either *ay*, as one might say with the English pronunciation of Caitlin, or *ah*, as you say it in Irish, or *a*, as in *apple*. Does that make sense?"

"I—I think so."

"In this particular word," he pointed to the word he'd written, "it uses the *a* sound, like *apple* or *fan*." His cheeks were flushed. It was a hot afternoon, and the breeze seemed to have died. "Then this last letter—"

"T," she finished.

"Yes. T. What sound does that make, in your name?"

"Cai-t-lin." she recited under her breath, then gave him her answer. "*Tuh.*"

"Precisely." He raised a brow in challenge. "So, what's the word? String the sounds together."

Caitlin drew a breath. "C-ay-t—"

"No. This is *a*, as in apple, remember? Or *after*."

"Right." She shook her head and turned back to the page. "Cuh-a-tuh. C-a-t." She blinked up at him. "Cat?"

A grin, a real grin that lit up his eyes and yielded a sunburst of creases in their corners spread across his face. "That's it exactly. *Cat*."

His smile and her own satisfaction . . . a sudden flutter of happiness rose in her chest. Seduction be damned. This was better. She'd just read a word.

"Give me another." She flipped the paper back toward him.

Somehow, without much prompting on Caitlin's part, Dunn agreed to join her on the verandah again that evening. Perhaps it was the coolness of the night air after the suffocating heat, or perhaps it was the success of their first reading lesson—Caitlin had read every word he'd made from the letters in her name, and each had come quicker than the last. *Cat. It. At. Tin. Lit. Ill. Nail. Tail.* Then they'd moved on to the letters in O'Keefe. Tomorrow, they'd start on the alphabet proper.

She couldn't wait. The excitement of making sense of letters on a page, paired with that smile he'd given her each time she worked out a word . . . It was like the buzzy warmth one got from just the right amount of grog. But better.

She had planned to speak to him of an affair tonight, but as she sat in the dark and waited for him to appear, she found herself doubting the idea. Attraction aside, he was obviously not interested. If she'd held any doubt, it had been banished when she'd stupidly tried to caress his hand. He'd recoiled faster than a scared rabbit. The rest of the lesson had gone so well, though. To push him into a conversation he so clearly did not want to have . . . it wouldn't be right.

It was better to leave things as they were. He, the servant and tutor. She, the master and pupil. To add lover to that list would only complicate things.

At last, Dunn appeared at the door. He stopped just inside the threshold and peered out warily.

No. There would be no talk of bedding tonight. She'd be lucky if she could get him onto the verandah at all.

"I moved your chair." She spoke as carelessly as possible, waving a hand toward the second chair, which she'd put on the other side of the table to give him just as much access to the flame as she had.

He nodded almost imperceptibly, then pulled a folded newspaper out from under his arm. "I thought I might read to you. If you'd still like me to."

"Of course. Come. Sit."

Silently, he went about the business of lighting his pipe. She couldn't see much of him in the darkness, but she smelled the smoke as he puffed the clay to life, then came the stiff sound of the paper being unfolded. He moved the lantern to reflect light on the print.

"Anything in particular you want to hear about?"

"I don't think so." Caitlin had never read a paper, nor had one read to her. "Just start from the beginning, I'd expect."

"Very well." Dunn was quiet a moment, then he began. "It's the *Australian*, from a week ago—Friday, November the third, 1826." He cleared his throat. "Enquiry *de lunatico*. An inquisition took place on Tuesday in the court house, King Street, in pursuance of a *writ de lunatico inquirendum*, in the case of Mrs. Johnstone of Annandale. The enquiry was commenced on—"

"Johnstone," Caitlin couldn't help but interrupt. "That's Esther Abrams, is it not? Johnstone's mistress."

"His wife now, or widow, I suppose," Dunn confirmed.

"Please, continue."

Dunn began reading again, and with each word the excitement she'd felt at hearing Esther's name dropped farther into the floor. Mrs. Johnstone was accused of lunacy by her own son, it seemed, in an attempt to divest her of her farm. Annandale, the place she'd called home for over thirty years, and which her late husband had lawfully bequeathed to her. The article laid out these facts, then recounted a series of witnesses brought against her.

"Dr. Bland, cross-examined by Mr. S. Stephen," Dunn read, "has known Mrs. J. upwards of twelve years, a great part of that time intimately so. She is a woman of rather eccentric habits, hasty in her temper, and has an abrupt mode of expressing herself. He does not ascribe this to want of education, but allows that she is an illiterate woman. He does not consider such mode of expression to be the effect of insanity, but that such habits would be very likely to merge into insanity. And he admits the justice of the adage that passion is a temporary madness—"

"Enough." Caitlin couldn't listen to any more of this. "Skip to the end. What happened? Did she win?"

Dunn hesitated, and Caitlin was just about to repeat the command when he looked back down and skimmed ahead with his eyes. "Her lawyer called several witnesses in her defense, then . . . Ah, here." He began reading again. "The jury retired at a quarter to five o'clock, and after a lapse of one hour, during which much anxiety pervaded the auditors, returned into court, finding that Mrs. Esther Johnstone is not of sound mind, nor capable of managing her affairs."

Dunn stopped, and a deafening silence filled the void as his words reverberated in Caitlin's mind, drowning out even the grating din of the crickets. *Eccentric habits. Illiterate. Not of sound mind, nor capable of managing her affairs.* "So—she's lost Annandale then?"

"W-well—" Dunn stuttered. "It doesn't say exactly, but it seems so, yes."

"Even though her husband, one of the most powerful men in the colony in his day, gave it to her. In his will?" Caitlin swallowed. A bitter film coated the inside of her mouth. She took a quick drink of the rum to wash it away, but she could barely taste it.

"Yes," Dunn answered in a whisper.

"The poor woman." But that wasn't it, was it? Sympathy for Esther Abrams—or Johnstone—wasn't the cause of the dread that tugged at Caitlin's thoughts. For at least Esther had other children and some standing. She'd get by. But Caitlin—Lord help her. If she lost the farm . . . what else would there be? Brothel work? Service? Marriage to a sod like that dirty trader, Staples? And if Esther could lose it all so easily . . . What chance did Caitlin have?

All she could do was pray that the heir in London wouldn't want her farm. And wait.

She clenched her teeth hard, but it wasn't enough. She needed to get up. To move. "I—that's enough for now. I'm tired." She rose and tapped out her pipe.

"Mrs. Blackwell." Michael stood, concern creasing his face. "Just because Annandale was lost doesn't mean—"

"Please, Dunn." Caitlin held up a hand to stop him talking. "I know." And she *did* know. Chances were, everything would be fine. But . . . it wasn't impossible that she'd be turned out. Not impossible at all. "I'll see you in the morning."

And this time, instead of Dunn making his escape, Caitlin did.

TWELVE

CAITLIN COULDN'T SLEEP. THE scene in the courtroom, of Esther Abrams—the same proud woman she'd seen in that gleaming carriage in Sydney—despairing and defeated. And her son, a boy she'd carried in her own womb, who she'd raised up and loved . . . gleeful in his mother's defeat. It circled round and round in Caitlin's mind despite all her efforts to banish it.

This place, this *world* was so stacked against them. Against Caitlin and Esther and so many others like them. Anyone who hadn't the luck to be born into the very upper crust. Of course, Caitlin knew that. She'd known it her whole life, made peace with it. Orchids and turnips, Da used to say. The O'Keefe's were turnips and proud of it—so much sturdier and stronger than the vain, flimsy orchids of the world. They knew how to endure. But sometimes . . . sometimes there was a pain to it that couldn't be shrugged away. The unfairness of this life.

Perhaps it was the hope that made it worse. The prospect of learning to read and of a future on her own terms. It was within her grasp, her ability. But it could still so easily be wrested away by the whims of some rich man she'd never met.

And there wasn't a damn thing she could do about it.

Bugger. She tossed and turned for what felt like hours, then finally kicked the coverlet off and sat up.

She needed to move. To exert herself and distract her mind.

She pulled on her dressing gown. She'd go out to the barn to check on the pregnant cow. The poor thing was huge. Her udders had swollen, and Caitlin had noticed her standing away from the others this morning. Her time was near.

The house was quiet as she slipped down the corridor and through the kitchen. She'd heard Dunn come through ages ago. He was surely asleep by now.

The yellow moon hung low, and a mist was rising off the fields, but the stars lent enough light that Caitlin didn't need the lantern. All was peaceful in the barn, the cow and her sisters sleeping contentedly in the straw.

Caitlin stood and watched them until, finally, a weight pulled at her eyelids. Then she turned and walked slowly back to the house.

A sound, very faint, distracted her from her thoughts. A crying, or moaning . . . At first, she thought it was an animal, a possum or a snake in the hen house, riling the chickens. She nearly turned around to check before she realized it was coming from the direction of the house. Dunn's window, to be exact. As she crept closer, she could make out that same nonsensical babbling she'd heard the first night he'd been here. She paused at the open window and listened. He was crying out as if someone were hurting him. And she could hear now that there were words strung into the terrified muttering.

Please. Don't. Let me go—

Her heart lurched to hear him so scared and desperate. So unlike the stoic man she knew in the day.

What had happened to him at Moreton Bay? He seemed to have begun to recover from it—whatever it was—while awake, but it obviously had not left his dreams. Perhaps it never would.

She moved away from the window. He wouldn't want her to listen, of that she was sure.

But she *could* try to help, couldn't she? To wake him and end the suffering, at least for now. She came in, slammed the back door with some force, and stomped loudly across the kitchen. The sound ceased.

Good then.

She'd almost reached her own room when a blood-curdling scream pierced through the darkness, followed by a series of loud, horrified whimpers.

Melia murder. She turned and walked back to his door, then knocked loudly. "Dunn? Are you all right?" He was quieter now, but she could still hear him pleading with whomever had him in the nightmare. "*Dunn!*" she tried, louder.

The noise continued.

Caitlin squinted at the rough wood and worried her bottom lip. Should she go in? She no longer feared what he might do to her. He would never hurt her, even in his half-dazed sleep, but would he want her to wake him? Likely not. He'd be embarrassed, certainly. But wouldn't that be better than whatever hell he was going through now? There was no way she'd be able to sleep if he screamed like that again, that was sure.

She took a long breath and opened the door.

He would never escape. The darkness closed in, pressing at his eyes, his chest. There were snakes in the pit. He could feel them slithering around his ankles, their tongues grazing his flesh. One crept slowly up his body, the icy damp of its skin encircling his leg.

His heart stopped. He was petrified. Turned to stone. He could only stand and feel the cold of the serpent's scales as it coiled itself around him, pinning his arms to his side, tightening over his stomach. His chest. His neck. Tighter still.

He couldn't breathe.

Michael screamed, but no sound came. There was no air. No breath—

"Dunn."

It called to him. It would take him. It already had. It was too late—

"Dunn."

It was crushing him, breaking him apart. Fracturing the stone he'd become into a thousand pieces—

"DUNN. Wake up."

Michael came to with a start, his heart pounding, his limbs trembling, every muscle tensed. Damn. It had been some time since the nightmare had taken him like that. He was covered in sweat. Exhausted.

Exhaling, he let himself sink back onto the bed, willing his body to relax, his pulse to slow—

"Are you awake, then?" Mrs. Blackwell's voice, very near.

Shit.

Michael's eyes flew open. Sure enough, there she was, a silhouette sitting beside him on the bed. Her eyes reflected the starlight that filtered through the window, wide and concerned. Her hand hovered above him, as if she—

She'd shaken him awake, hadn't she? That voice and the tremor he'd felt . . .

He'd woken her.

Shame rose hot on his cheeks, and Michael reached a hand up to scrub his face. What could he say?

"I—"

"Good." She lowered her arm, satisfied that he was, indeed, awake. "No need to explain. You were having a nightmare, that was clear." She cocked her head. "You're hardly the first man from Moreton Bay to be plagued by such things, you know."

Ha. She thought it was Moreton Bay he was reliving in that dream. If only it were that simple.

"Do you—are you all right now?" She looked down at him, the concern still etched on her face.

"Yes," Michael managed. He closed his eyes, as if that would do anything to make this less humiliating. But it worked. With the sight of her gone, she became distant, unreal, another dream, perhaps . . . albeit not a nightmare.

"Do you want me to stay?" He felt her voice, the whisper of it, almost like a touch. "'Til you fall asleep again?"

There was a part of him, the weak, pitiful man who hid inside, that wanted to give in and say yes. *Yes, please. Stay with me.* He exhaled, pushing that man away. Then he drew a breath, intending to say no. But before the word could come, something brushed across his cheek, light as a feather. Her thumb. Stroking him.

All his strength left him with that touch. He leaned into it, then opened his eyes—helpless as a babe—and met hers just in time for her to speak again. "I don't mind." Her thumb settled on his jaw, and she looked at him. Just looked. Then, slowly, ever so slowly, her head dipped toward his. All Michael could hear was his heartbeat pounding in his ears as she drew closer and closer.

When she was so near that he could feel her breath on his lips, she opened her own. "Can I kiss you?" She bit her bottom lip as soon as the words were out, as if she'd meant to catch them on their way and just missed. But they'd escaped, and there was no taking them back now.

It *was* a dream. But goddamn, Michael did not want to wake up.

"Yes," he whispered.

A luminous smile lit her face. Then, like the sun disappearing behind a cloud, it dimmed. Her eyes searched his face. "Are you sure?"

"Yes." And to show her he meant it he reached both hands up and drew her down to him.

She hadn't been expecting it. She gave a little shriek, and she lost her balance for a moment, but it quickly turned into a sweet, giggling kind of laugh as she allowed Michael to pull her on top of him.

Then their lips met, and all sound, all thought vanished.

It was unlike any kiss Michael had ever known. Not hard and desperate, nor soft and tentative. Only solid and flowing and sure. As if they'd done this their whole lives. As if they'd been born to it, like two parts of a well-matched team. Their mouths opened as one, then their tongues met, twining and dancing, giving and taking, generous and bountiful. Not holding back, nor forcing. Just being. Mouth on mouth. Breath with breath.

Her fingers threaded through his hair, pulling him closer as his hands wandered lower, to her shoulders, down her back, settling on the curve of her waist before burrowing into the soft fabric of her dressing gown.

The kiss went on for what seemed like hours. Or minutes. Or seconds of effortless, mindless bliss.

But at last, Mrs. Blackwell seemed to come to her senses. She straightened back up to sitting, then peered down at him. In the starlight, he could see her chest heaving, the dark smudge of her lips where they'd melded with his own. "I—I'd thought of this," she whispered. "Of talking with you about this, I mean—" She screwed her eyes shut, then opened them again, and this time her words sounded more sure. "Of talking to you of an affair. While you're here. But I didn't think—I don't want to press it on you and take advantage. You mustn't do it because I'm your master and you think—" She took another long breath. "I'm sorry. This isn't how I'd thought—"

"I'm not doing this because you're my master." Michael couldn't allow her to keep on like that, so flustered about what he wanted. Wasn't what he wanted clear? "I'm—I'm a man, Mrs. Blackwell. I assumed *you* wouldn't be interested in such a thing. But if you are . . . well . . ." He looked down to where his cockstand was making an obvious tent of the sheets.

Her gaze followed his. Then a slow, sly smile started in her eyes, spreading to her lips. "It's Caitlin to you."

"Caitlin." Michael repeated. "I can't promise I'll be a—"

She brought her finger to his lips, and the smile vanished. "I don't want your promises. There's no future in it, you understand. Just . . . now. While you're here."

Michael nodded. He had no future anyway. It hardly mattered to him. "Of course."

"Well, then." She rose and smoothed out her dressing gown, no longer the eager wanton he'd just kissed, but the brisk woman she showed to the rest of the world. "'Tis late now. I'd say we both get some sleep and start tomorrow night. If you agree?"

Michael stared at her, her mussed hair, her pink cheeks, the way her lips pursed with authority. Those lips had been so soft when they'd kissed. Yielding and pillowy . . .

"Dunn?"

He started. He hadn't answered her question. His throat was suddenly parched, and his cock pulsed with need. He swallowed. "Yes. I mean. If you'd like to begin tomorrow, I see no reason why not."

Her lips relaxed into a smile before she seemed to remember herself and pulled them back into their tight line. She nodded curtly. "Good night, then."

And she turned and left the room.

Thirteen

EVERYTHING ABOUT THE FOLLOWING day was distorted by a swirl of raw lust. It muddled Michael's mind and foiled his every attempt at rational thought. His cockstand just wouldn't go away.

Neither he nor Mrs. Blackwell spoke of the night to come, nor of what had happened between them the night before. He could almost believe he'd imagined their kiss and the conversation that followed, but then he'd accidentally brush against her or meet her eye, and she'd flush and look away . . . and, of course, his cock would stir once more.

And so the cycle continued.

They kept to the routine they'd begun to establish. A silent breakfast, accompanied by the song of that blasted magpie. Mrs. Blackwell went out while Michael saw to the dishes. Once the kitchen was in order, he dusted and swept the sitting room, then sat for a bit and prepared for the afternoon's lesson. It wasn't enough. He felt useless and idle, so over their midday meal, he asked her if there were any further duties she'd like him to attend to. She brightened at the question and promised to teach him to churn butter.

Then they moved to the sitting room and talked through the rest of the alphabet. As had happened yesterday, they both lost themselves in the lesson—a welcome relief from the tension between them. She was a bright pupil, eager to learn, and Michael found himself enjoying the process of watching her discover new words and letters. Each time she sounded out something new, her whole face lit up, radiant with pleasure. He had no doubt she'd be reading the paper within a few months.

Afterward, she demonstrated the butter churn, then left him alone with it. He finished the chore with plenty of time to fix supper. They ate and retired once more to the verandah where he read her the rest of the *Australian* which, mercifully, held only shipping reports and an account of Mr. Wilton's recent exploration of a volcanic mountain to the north. Nothing more about women losing their farms. Thank God.

"The writer has taken leave, for the present, of the mountain and its phenomenon, but proposes at some future period to pay it another visit," Michael finished.

That was the end. There was nothing else to read. Nothing more to say. All was quiet except for the racket of the crickets. His pipe had burned out. His stomach felt light, yet heavy at the same time. Every muscle was tensed, waiting for her move.

At last, she rose, her empty rum cup in hand. "Well, then. I'll just take this back to the kitchen—"

"I'll take it." Michael shot to his feet. Before she could object, he stuffed his pipe into his pocket, took the tin cup from her hand, and picked up the lantern.

"If you still wish to—"

"You'll come to me—"

They'd spoken over one another.

Mrs. Blackwell broke into a grin and started again. "You'll come to me room after, then? You haven't changed your mind?"

"Yes—I mean, *no*. I haven't changed my mind." Why must this be so bloody awkward? "I'll come to your room after."

"That's grand." In the light of the lantern, her eyes twinkled like stars. "I'll see you there." She turned and disappeared into the house.

He tried to take his time. Really, he did. He brought her cup to the kitchen, set it in the basin to wash in the morning, hung the lantern on its hook beside the hearth, emptied his pipe, and put it away in his room. Took off his boots and stockings and laid them neatly by his bed.

When he came back into the kitchen, he could hear muffled sounds coming from her room. Water splashing. She was washing.

A tidal wave of lust nearly overpowered him, threatening to lift him up and sweep him into her room, but then a thought occurred.

He lifted his arm and sniffed under it. Winced. He couldn't go to her like this, with the stink and dust of the day still on him. So he collected a clean rag and the basin and went outside.

The rope was rough against his palms as he lowered the bucket down and pulled it back up. Was she naked? The nipples of her pert little breasts pebbled with the chill . . .

He poured the full bucket into the basin, then lifted his shirt over his head and began to wash.

Michael's body was a pale shade. He'd never been well muscled—the life of a London gentleman didn't demand any great strength, and Father had always frowned upon boxing or riding or other such indulgent pursuits. At Cowper's, Michael had only directed the laborers; he'd rarely joined them. He'd kept a decent appearance, but really, his status as heir to an earldom was all he needed in London to bed any wench he pleased. And his position at Cowper's had easily secured him a woman. Good looks were not needed.

But now he had no such position. No such status. The last six months, he'd worked harder than ever in his life, but he'd been half starved. He was rail thin.

And then there were his scars. The angry red ones, still festering around his ankles. And, worse, the mostly healed ones on his back. His tiger stripes, courtesy of the cat-o'-nine tails at Moreton Bay. The terrible pain of the first few weeks had abated, but they still ached and itched like the devil some days. He'd not got a good look in a mirror in months, but he'd felt them—deep welts in his flesh. Unless he managed to keep his shirt on the entire time, she was certain to notice.

What would she make of them?

She wouldn't be shocked, of that he was sure. But would she still want him in her bed once she saw the proof of what kind of man he really was? Would the truth finally come to her? Disgust her?

A sudden sense of foreboding washed over him, dimming the lust. If she did reject him, he wouldn't blame her of course, but what would he do? How would they get through the next year? After what had already transpired, it would be incredibly awkward.

He shrugged his shirt back on. There was nothing for it now. She was expecting him, and even if he stayed away tonight, he'd give in to temptation eventually. It had been too damn long since he'd been with a woman.

A woman. Waiting for him.

He came in through the dark, silent kitchen, then strode slowly down the corridor, finally coming to a stop before the hard wood of her door. Light shone from underneath it.

A woman. Naked and reclined. Skin smooth. Nipples pink and peaked. Dark hair between her legs, which were slightly parted, the pink folds of her cunny peeking through, glistening in the candlelight . . .

Michael raised his fist. Knocked.

An eternity passed. Finally, Mrs. Blackwell's authoritative voice sounded from within. "Come in."

Heart pounding, he pushed the door open.

The sweet smell of beeswax was the first thing he noticed. It seemed to permeate this house, but all the more so in here.

She was sitting at the dressing table brushing her hair, her back to him. She wasn't naked as he'd imagined, but she'd taken off her dress and was clothed only in a thin shift. He could just make out the long curve of her neck in the light of the one candle that burned beside her. The window by her bed was open, and a gust of cool air, scented with gum trees, wafted through it, making the candle dance.

There was no mirror before her, and she didn't turn, but the faint creaking of the floorboards must have told her he'd entered. "Close the door," she said. Then, as if on afterthought, "Please."

He couldn't take his eyes off her. Her hair, free of the tight bun she usually wore, cascaded down her back like a twisting black cloud. He kicked the door closed behind him, then stood beside it, watching her from a distance.

She finished, set the brush down, then turned to look at him.

He lost his breath, his entire world condensing into a monolith of need.

She looked so different with her hair down, younger and more feminine. Softer somehow, and vulnerable. Her cheeks and lips stood out pink against creamy skin. Her arms were tanned, strong, and smooth. He could just see the outline of her nipples through the shift—

"Dunn?" That same amused smile from earlier creased her face as she cocked her head to one side. "You haven't come to tell me you've changed your mind, have you?"

"No—I just . . . You look beautiful." He clamped his mouth shut, but it was too late. What a daft thing to say.

"Oh." The amusement left her face, replaced by a sweet, bashful kind of surprise, but the smile remained. The sight drew Michael a step closer. "Thank you."

She stood, and for what seemed an hour, they stared at one another from across the room, both waiting for the other to make the first move.

Finally, she laughed, shaking her head as if to banish the mood. "You look very fine yourself. You clean up well, you know." She took a step toward him, then another. Her dark eyes met his, suddenly serious. "Can I touch you?"

Michael nodded slowly, not trusting himself to speak. His cock was so hard. He could so easily lose control.

Without breaking eye contact, she raised both arms, bringing her hands to his hair. He expected her to draw him close and kiss him, but she didn't. She stayed where she was, arms extended, and raked her hands through his hair, massaging his scalp.

She exhaled loudly. "I've wanted so badly to do this." Her fingers sent a spark down Michael's spine to his belly. His stand, so insistent already, throbbed. "You have such lovely hair."

He closed his eyes, shutting everything else out and allowed the sensation to flow through him. *Control. Control yourself.*

He should pull away—a feeling this good always led to pain of some sort—but he just couldn't. It was too damn good.

So he held himself still, every muscle taut, vibrating with need.

She ran her thumb over his cheek, his chin. Brushed the pad of it lightly along his lips. Her work-roughened fingertip caught against his dry, cracked lips, and there was something so real, so right about the feel of her calloused flesh against his own . . .

Abruptly, her touch fell away. Michael opened his eyes. She was staring at him intently, worrying her bottom lip as if she were considering something. "How shall we do this?" she murmured.

He offered no answer to her question. And she didn't ask again. Instead, she took a step backward, reached for the hem of her chemise, and lifted it over her head.

For the second time that night, Michael stopped breathing.

He'd thought she'd be wiry and sparsely built. Angular. But she wasn't, not at all. Her was that of a goddess—like the statues he'd seen in the plates in Father's books, the ones he'd brought back from his tour in Italy. Diana, Goddess of the Hunt. Lithe and lean. Strong as iron. There was nothing angular about her, just long, gentle curves. Her hips, with a wild bush of black hair nestled between them, her breasts, small and firm, crowned by large, dark nipples. She radiated health and energy.

"Your turn." At her words, he jerked his gaze upward to her face. There was no hint of modesty there, only a pleased smirk. Clearly, she understood that he desired her, and clearly, she'd expected him to.

The doubt resurfaced. Would she desire *him*?

"Well?" Mrs. Blackwell leaned forward and softly touched his shoulder. Her bare nipples grazed the front of his shirt. "If you don't want to, it's all ri—"

Enough. Michael shrugged her off. There was only one way to know. Without giving himself time to think better of it, he pulled his shirt over his head and tossed it aside.

The night air blew cool against his skin. He gazed at the floor, cheeks burning, waiting. She shifted forward, and her fingers stroked his hair once more, then dropped to his shoulder, smoothed down his back, feeling each and every one of his scars.

He could hear her sharp intake of breath. Then her hand was gone, and there was only silence. The ticking of the clock.

At last, he could take it no more. He shifted his eyes to look at her, bracing himself as he did. She was watching him intently—his body, not his face, her lips curved into a frown as if she were judging a piece of art. And finding it wanting.

Of course she did. Who would want this? This . . . shadow of a man.

She seemed to feel his eyes on her and raised her gaze to meet his. Then she smiled. "More."

More.

Cold relief and hot desire flowed equally in his veins. She wanted him. For some unfathomable reason, she wanted him.

But he must take care. He must keep the wild beast in check.

He took a breath before pushing his trousers over his bony hips. They fell into a heap at his feet, and he kicked them away as his cock bobbed forward, finally free of its constraint.

He exhaled, feeling more naked than he'd been in his entire life. He had nothing to give her. No money. No position. Not even a body worth a damn. Nothing.

She extended her hand.

He grasped it, then allowed her to draw him onto the bed.

Fourteen

Dunn stood naked before her, his body aglow in the soft yellow light. He was something behold, his spare frame tensed with lust, his prick straining and hard. He was out of his mind with desire, that was clear. Yet he didn't move toward her. His blue eyes, dark and fathomless, held Caitlin's, as if he were looking for something, or doubting.

He was nervous, wasn't he? So odd for a man. Men were usually quick and demanding. They took what they wanted, then left without another thought.

Was it the scars on his back? Did he fear they would scare her away? Or his looks? He was too thin, it was true, but time would change that. And Caitlin hardly cared. He was all sinew and muscle. Strong and lean. His scars had been earned through noble means—he'd saved a woman from harm. And anyway, they only proved he was human. There was no shame in that. And his cock . . . any bit of hesitation Caitlin had felt disappeared at the sight of it. Indeed, she could hardly keep her eyes off it. It jutted out dark beyond his pale, gaunt hips—long, stiff, and demanding. It probably looked bigger for his scrawniness everywhere else.

Yes, there was fear in his eyes, shame even. But there was also need. Yearning. He'd called her beautiful. *Beautiful*. No man, none of them, had ever called her that.

Her cunt clenched, then throbbed. She knew if she put her hand there, it would be wet.

Perhaps she'd put *his* hand there, instead.

Jesus, she could take no more of this. She reached for him. "Come to bed."

She pulled him onto the bed, and they came to rest on top of the coverlet, both on their sides facing the other. The cotton was cool and soft under her naked body, and Dunn was warm and hard.

She waited for him to touch her, but even now, he didn't. He watched her. Waiting . . .

Bugger. She'd have to do this herself, wouldn't she?

She met his eye, silently asking one more time for permission. He didn't look away. Then, slowly, she leaned in until their bodies were flush. She could feel his cock poking into her belly, his heat spreading through her. She brought her hand up to cradle his cheek, dipped her head forward, and kissed him.

It seemed the right place to start. And it was good, her lips on his. His nervousness seemed to evaporate. Like the previous night, he opened to her in a way he never did during the day. Their mouths yielded to one another—lips rough, tongues smooth—moving together, working as one. He tasted of tobacco and warm breath. But it didn't last long. It wasn't enough. Not for either of them.

Caitlin broke away and rolled onto her back, grasping his hand and bringing it to the aching slit between her legs. She pressed his palm against the little button that lay at the center of that ache. And that was all he needed. That one little bit of encouragement, and he seemed to know exactly what to do. He angled himself toward her, his fingers wrapping around her mound, slipping between her folds.

Sweet Jesus.

She let her head drop back, her arms go limp, and gave herself over to the feeling—the heel of his hand, grinding against her button. His fingers, coarse and calloused, sliding through her smooth wetness. She pushed up with her hips, increasing the pressure just as his middle finger found her opening.

A long, guttural moan spilled from the back of her throat.

As if falling into her, his hand slid forward until his finger was sheathed fully inside. He no longer pressed against her button, but it didn't matter. *Gad.* Caitlin's eyes slid closed with a breath, and she lifted her hips again, bringing him as deep as she could. Moving in small circles until the tip of his finger reached just the right place.

Why had she not thought to have a man before?

But then his hand was gone. The mattress shifted as if he were getting up. "Dunn—" Caitlin's eyes flew open, but her protest died in her throat when she saw what he was doing. He'd pulled himself up, but not off the bed. He had settled himself on his stomach with his head between her splayed legs, and he was gazing at the space between her thighs with glassy, desirous eyes. He slid a finger back into her, then another, sinking deeper, stretching her wide. At the same time, his thumb came back to stroke her button. Back and forth, back and forth.

Caitlin's hips pushed against him. "*Gor.* That's good . . ." she panted.

His eyes flicked to her face. Then, with a soft groan—as if he couldn't help himself—he moved his hands to grasp her open hips, lowered his head, and brought his mouth to her cunt.

He licked the length of her, a glorious sweep of sensation. Then he sucked the pink flesh into his mouth, nibbling it, tasting it as if he really did mean to devour her. He licked her again and plunged his tongue into her depths, fucking her with his mouth. At the same time, his hand found her button once more, pinching, caressing, kneading her . . .

A whirlpool of pleasure swirled around her, and Caitlin was in the center of it. Tumbling. Spiraling.

But she needed more.

She pinched her nipples hard, and a blaze of scorching fire shot straight to her core, where Dunn was working away, all his attention focused on her cunt. More. Deeper. Wider. He was sucking on her button now, his fingers buried deep inside. How many were there?

Did it matter?

She was spinning. Faster. Dizzy. Lost in the cyclone of pleasure. She *was* the pleasure. It was all there was. She was not a wife, not a widow or a farmer or a convict or a whore . . . she was just . . . only . . .

She pinched her nipples again, and a deep, primal roar escaped her throat as the whirlpool sucked her down into its clear blue depths, past all the feelings, all the thoughts, all the cares, until she landed in a place of crystal and light. A place of complete and utter peace.

For a moment she floated.

All was well.

She was safe.

She breathed in. Out. Her body felt heavy, her muscles slack. Every worry evaporated to steam in the heat of their lust.

"Mrs. Blackwell?" Dunn's voice sounded from above.

Caitlin opened her eyes. When had she closed them? He'd moved next to her and was propped on one elbow, facing her.

What had just happened?

A giggle escaped her lips as she rolled toward him. "You must not call me that. Not after—" She didn't finish the sentence. She didn't have to.

"Caitlin." His voice was low and reverent, his eyes bright.

Too overcome to speak, she stared into those eyes as she stroked his cheek, the sharp grit of his day-old whiskers. Then she traced a line from his ear to his shoulder with her finger, smoothing it down his side to his back. At first, he leaned into the touch, but he tensed as she came to the ridges that marked him—the brand of the cat-o'-nine-tails. They were fresh welts, not fully healed. She'd put balm on them later.

But now wasn't the time.

She continued her perusal of him, brushing the back of her hand over his lean stomach. Lower. His breath hitched as she trailed her knuckles over his navel, his jutting hip bones. Then, finally, her fingers wrapped around his cock.

She pulled her gaze back to his face, curious what she'd find there. His eyes were wide, watching her intently, and still dazzlingly bright. He seemed to be barely breathing. She stroked once, firmly, and he gasped, almost as if she'd hurt him, though she knew she hadn't. "And now." She stroked again. "You must fuck me."

Michael's cock had never been so hard. His need had never been so great.

The way she'd come around his fingers, responded to his touch—lost herself entirely. He'd never seen a woman so undone. Didn't know it was possible, really.

She was so damn beautiful it hurt.

And now this goddess desired him, as worthless as he was, to fuck her. She'd said as much—his cock, literally, was in her hands. And no matter how unworthy he might feel, he could at least, follow her command.

In fact, he might die if he didn't.

Her fingers left his shaft, and she rolled onto her back, spreading her thighs wide.

Michael crawled to her, bracing his arms on either side of her shoulders. Her breasts were right there, within reach. Past any kind of rational thought, he acted on pure impulse, lowering his head and taking a nipple in his mouth, suckling hard, nipping just a bit with his teeth. She'd pinched herself as she came. She must like such play.

She uttered a sharp gasp of pain.

Shit. Michael's head flew up. "I'm sorry—"

"Don't you dare stop," she spat out indignantly.

Very well, then.

He suckled each breast in turn while grinding himself against her mound. The feel of her wiry hair against his hard cock would soon drive him mad, but he couldn't enter her just yet. He wouldn't last a minute once he did. And he must keep himself in check. Then she shifted, and the slit of her cunny opened. The sudden slickness almost made him come right there. Just like that.

He stilled. *Control yourself, Michael.*

She lifted her hips, sliding him against her, trying desperately to get them into position.

"Now." She sounded strangled. "*Please*." Just as wrecked as he was.

Her wish. His command. He reached down and guided himself in, sinking inside her until she engulfed all of him.

Michael's eyes rolled up in his head. It was so. Damn. Good. Her perfect cunny spread out around him. Warm and tight and safe.

He stayed there, willing himself to stillness, allowing her time to adjust to him. Then he felt her fingers on his cheek. They threaded through his hair.

Inexplicably, a lump formed in his throat.

"Dunn. Are you all right?" Her voice.

Damn. He hated that name. It was all wrong. Not here. Not now. "Michael," he choked out. "It's—*Michael*."

"Michael." She pushed up her hips, bringing him just a tiny bit deeper.

And the way she said it . . . the way she welcomed him into her body—

He swallowed the fool emotion away. This was just a fuck. Nothing more.

Time to get on with it.

He pushed hard inside her, till his balls were touching her arse.

She gasped, and her hand left his hair to grip the iron bedframe behind her. He thrust again. Harder. Pushing her up against the headboard. He shouldn't like the way her eyes widened in shock or fear, but he did. He came at her again, and she grasped the cold metal, knuckles white, holding her ground. Challenging him with her gaze.

"Michael," she whispered his name again. As if it meant something.

And his control snapped.

He'd show her.

He pushed her. Into the bedframe. Into the wall. Teeth clenched. Muscles pounding. Desperate and violent. She wanted a fuck, he'd give her one. Fast and hard and rough. He'd show her what he really was.

He slammed his body into hers, again and again until finally, *finally*, everything else fell away. The woman he was rutting into ceased to matter. She was faceless. Nameless. A vessel for him to fill. And he filled her. Pounded every bit of his vileness into her.

His balls tightened.

"Michael, you can—" Her voice came from far away, but it was enough to pull him back from the edge. He slipped out of her just in time, and his seed spilled, hot and insistent, splattering on her stomach, her thighs.

Then, silence.

Only the sound of their ragged breathing.

Michael stared down at what he'd done, the shock of it hitting like freezing water. His cock, still in his hand. The woman under him, her dark eyes wide, hair a mess. Her perfect body spattered with his spend and probably bruised by his force.

Goddamn. What had he done?

He opened his mouth to apologize or to somehow, somehow—

But there was nothing to say. No excuse. She'd wanted a lover, and he'd given her—he'd given her the beast.

He couldn't look at her. Couldn't speak to her. Couldn't be in this room for one more bloody second.

He sprang off the bed and bolted for the door.

"Michael—"

But he didn't answer. He pushed the door open, and, stark naked, he fled from the room.

FIFTEEN

MICHAEL WOKE THE NEXT morning to the magpie's singing and his clothes neatly folded outside his door. The house was quiet. The door to Mrs. Blackwell's chamber stood open, the bed made and the woman nowhere to be seen.

Probably in the barn doing the milking.

Glad for a moment of reprieve before he must face her, he ducked outside and headed to the privy. The dew felt cool on his bare feet, and the sun had just cleared the horizon, the sky lit up in soft pinks and purples. He hazarded a glance at the barn. The doors were open, the cow let out to pasture. Chickens pecked in the dust.

She locked those animals up tight at night. She must have already done the chores.

Where was she?

He relieved himself, then poked his nose into the barn, walked the perimeter of the garden. All was empty and eerily still.

A prickling sense of foreboding grew as he drew up a bucket from the well before he made his way back toward the house.

Where the devil could she be? After last night . . . What he'd done . . . She'd probably fled as far from him as she could. To the back fields or her hives. Now that he thought of it, he hadn't seen the horse in the pasture with the cow . . .

His body seemed to grow heavier with each step, as if the shackles were already closing back around his ankles, dragging at him. After his treatment of her, she would, of course, be afraid. How could she keep a man like that in her house? She'd taken the horse, and she'd gone to Windsor, to the magistrate, to report him. And he deserved it—he was a beast, not a man.

He let himself into the empty kitchen, then stood and stared at the cold hearth, not knowing what to do. He didn't dare leave to find her. He could too easily be accused of attempting escape. One way or another, she'd be back. All he could do was wait.

His stomach growled.

Doing his best to ignore the leaden weight in his limbs and the rising roar in his ears, he started the morning's routine. Water poured. *He would be flogged for sure.* Kindling stacked. *Sent to a road gang.* Coals stoked. *He'd die from the heat or the work.* Oats scooped into the pot. *Or worse, he'd live.* Hang it over the fire—

The back door banged open. "Good mornin'!"

Michael wheeled around, the pot still clutched in his hands. Mrs. Blackwell stood on the threshold, her cheeks pink and a smile—too bright to be real—on her face. In one hand, she held the milk pail. The other awkwardly grasped both the egg basket and the handle of a small tin bucket, full to the brim with red raspberries.

Relief pitted his stomach, along with a new kind of dread. She hadn't gone to Windsor, not yet. But she would. And what would he say to her? What excuse could he possibly give for the way he'd behaved—

"Is aught wrong?" Her cheerful look dissolved. He was staring.

"No." He turned back to the hearth and hung the pot on its chain. "G-good morning, Mrs. Blackwell."

"It's Caitlin to you," she reprimanded gently, then added, more briskly, "I got berries for our breakfast." He heard the thud of something being set onto the table, followed by her footfalls as she went to the pantry to put the milk away. "I had to saddle the mare and ride to the far side of the back field, but I found them, and before the birds did, too." A pause. She was near. "Michael?" She sounded concerned, but it must be disguised anger. "You *do* want me to call you that, do you not?"

"Yes." Michael turned slowly, bracing himself for whatever was to come.

But she was smiling. "There you are." She stood beside the table where the pail of berries now sat, and she was smiling, yes, but her eyes were tense, searching him.

Was she sorry for him?

The magpie began to sing again, so loud it might have been in the room with them. Its bubbling glee filled the strained, silent space between them, and Caitlin cocked her head, listening. Then her smile grew even wider. "Such a pretty tune, isn't it?" She grinned. "He's got a nest in the eves." Michael had no idea how to respond, so they stood there just looking at each other as the buoyant sound wound its way around them. "I do so prefer the magpies here to those at home, don't you? They don't steal things." She chuckled. "And their song"—she closed her eyes—"like a bit a' heaven right here on earth." She opened them, fixing him with an expression that was so guileless, so sweet . . . "Don't you think?

Michael forced his head to nod. What was happening? Where was her anger? Was she trying to trick him somehow? Or stall the inevitable unpleasantness?

She chuckled again and popped a berry into her mouth. "Mmh." Her lids fluttered closed once more as she savored the fruit. Then she blinked at him, one brow raised. "Try one?"

Woodenly, Michael crossed the room and reached into the pail. He took out a raspberry. Put it in his mouth. It *was* sweet, and meltingly soft, still warm from the morning sun. But he could hardly taste it. He watched her, barely breathing, waiting for her countenance to change.

Her grin faded as the silence stretched. "You're regretting it, aren't you?" She moved closer but didn't touch him. "I wondered, after how you left so quick. I'm sorry if I forced things. It was wrong of—"

"No." Her eyes widened at his interruption, but the apology in her voice was too much. He couldn't let her go on. Michael swallowed, forcing his tone to soften. "I don't regret anything. Not for my sake. But surely—surely, you're angry with *me*."

Her brows wrinkled. "Me? Angry? Because you left in such a hurry? I'd have liked you to stay and warm me bed, surely, but I understand a man has to—"

"No. Not that. Because of the way I—the way I behaved. Before that. I was so—" He stopped, took a breath. His ears were burning. "I was a brute. I forgot myself."

Her brow smoothed. "The shaggin', you mean? You think I'm angry about *that*?"

"Y-yes. You *should* be. I could have hurt you."

She laughed, rich and throaty, sounding almost like the magpie herself. "You really believe that. That I'd be angry for it?" She stepped closer, bringing her hands to grip his shoulders, then looked him straight in the eye. "I'm no maid, Michael. I can take a good shagging." Then she brought her mouth to his ear and whispered. "*I liked it.*"

A shiver raced down his spine, and his cock twitched, but . . . He drew back, searched her face. Surely, she was lying. There had been women who'd tolerated his base instincts—Lucy in Sydney, whores back in London—but they'd been paid for their trouble, and even Lucy had made it clear in the end that, without money, she abhorred him.

But Caitlin's expression betrayed no hint of doubt nor jest.

And what reason did she have to lie?

"You're not lying." He meant it as a question, but it came out a statement.

"I am not," she answered seriously, almost indignantly. She opened her mouth as if to say more, but it was a few seconds before the words came out. "I was a moll, Michael. I worked the streets of Cork. Then I was dolly to one of the navy men on the ship. Then wife to a good-for-nothing sailor." She ran her palms over his shoulders and down his arms, feeling his biceps through his shirt, his forearms. "None of them—*not one*—shagged me as good as you did last night." She laced her fingers with his. "I went off twice, I did. And it was . . ." She brought their clasped hands to her mouth and kissed his knuckles. "'Twas *glorious*. Just what I needed." She released him, and her open expression turned stern. "But there is one thing that disappointed me."

Michael swallowed. Here it was.

She leaned in again and whispered. "You can spend inside of me. There's no danger in it. I'm barren." Her hot breath went straight to his cock.

He barely registered the meaning of her words as the deeper truth settled in. She'd liked it—liked *him*. She truly had. And she wanted more.

Her hands came around and gripped his arse, drawing him in as he lowered his face to hers, meeting her red-stained, raspberry-flavored lips with his dry, cracked ones.

She wanted this.

It was clear in the way she rubbed herself against him. Clear in the way her lips opened under his, the way her tongue darted out, licking across the roughened surface before slipping inside.

She wanted this.

He sucked the tip of her tongue, then drew it further in until it tangled with his own. Goddamn but she was sweet, like sun-warmed berries and honey. Like everything Michael wasn't.

For a long, frantic moment, he was lost, hands groping for purchase, mouth devouring but wanting more. Body crushed against hers.

She wanted this.

Growling, he stepped forward, and she stumbled, but even still, she urged him on. "That's it. Give it to me, Michael. I can take it." She backed up a step, then another, till he had her pressed against the table. Without breaking the kiss, he lifted her so she was sitting on the table's top, straddling him. Then he—

"Ahem," a voice sounded from the door.

Caitlin's eyes widened as they focused on a point past Michael's shoulder. "Hud."

Damn it to hell. Why did Hud have to show up at that moment? Just when Caitlin had finally pushed past Michael's walls. Had him in the palm of her hand, ready to shag her into the hard wood of the table.

But no, here was Hud, a knowing grin on his face, and his dog dancing at his heels.

How long had he been standing there anyway?

Michael backed away from her, his cheeks darkening to crimson. Caitlin slid from the table, allowing her skirts to fall into place, smoothing them down with what she hoped looked like a no-nonsense flick of her wrists. She set her shoulders, then her jaw. She was a widow, a free woman. There was no shame in taking up with a man—and it was no business of Hud's anyway. But there were appearances to keep up, and she *was* still the master here.

"What do you need, Hud?" She raised a brow.

The convict stepped into the kitchen and lifted an arm, revealing a strung duck, neck bent, eyes closed. Freshly killed, by the looks of it. "We went out on the river this mornin'. Got more than we could eat." His gaze shot to the hearth, and he sniffed and wrinkled his nose, though his eyes twinkled. "I believe your porridge may be burnin', ma'am."

Caitlin heard Michael's footsteps behind her, then a low curse and the clanking of metal. The acrid smell of burnt maize filled the room. How had they not noticed?

"Thank you." She forced a smile and accepted the game. It was a large bird, plump and heavy. "It'll make a fine supper."

Hud nodded. His eyes circled the room one more time, finding Michael who was busy spooning the half-burnt porridge into two bowls—much more slowly and intently than was necessary. Hud watched him for a moment, as if expecting another confrontation or acknowledgment at least. But Michael didn't look up. His face was blazing red.

At last, Hud nodded to her and turned to go. At the sight of his back, Caitlin released a sharp breath of relief. But just inside the threshold, the man stopped and turned. He spoke, loud enough for both Caitlin and Michael to hear him. "Just so's you know, ma'am. Finn and me, we'll steer clear of the house from now on." At that, Michael glanced up in surprise, before quickly looking away again. Hud hesitated, his gaze settling on Caitlin. "What I said the other day—I didna mean no insult. We're glad for you, ma'am. No jokin' about it." Without waiting for a reply, he ducked out of the room.

Caitlin studied the empty space of clear blue sky where Hud had stood. She chuckled. "It seems we've earned their blessing."

In answer, Michael crossed to her and took the dead duck from her hands. He gestured to the table. "I've saved what porridge I could. Not too burned, I don't think."

Sixteen

They shagged again that night, though it still took some urging to convince Michael to let his animal nature run loose. Caitlin did like a good, hard fuck, but truth be told, she'd take him however he came at her: hard and fast or savoringly slow. Either way was pleasurable. And to do it only for herself—not for money, not for gain, but for the pure bodily pleasure of it . . . Perhaps this was a part of her dream, one she'd never considered before. To take control, not only of the farm and her livelihood, but of her own bedroom as well. Her own body.

Afterward, they lay together, naked and panting, listening to the sounds of the night beyond the open window. A wave of feeling rolled through her, propelling her hand to reach out and smooth his hair. Just ten minutes before, he'd put his mouth to her cunt, sending white hot lightning flashing through her entire being and bringing her to heights she'd not known possible. But now his eyes were closed, and a look of pure peace graced his features. He didn't flinch at her touch, so she supposed he was asleep until a soft groan came from deep in his throat.

The sound of contentment.

This was good for him too, wasn't it?

A shiver of unexpected joy raced through her. They had a whole year together.

And she need not worry about the possibility of children.

With John, she'd always felt guilty, knowing he couldn't plant a babe inside her no matter how much he tried. Not that he'd ever spoken of it. Knowing what she did now, it seemed quite possible he hadn't even cared. But with Michael, her barrenness was a liberation of sorts. A small blessing to come from that terrible night in the gaol in Cork when she'd lost the child she hadn't even known she was carrying. There had been so much blood, and then that awful doctor had come with his dirty hands and cold, sneering eyes . . . She'd burned with fever for weeks afterward. The pain had been unbearable. Her courses had been irregular and heavy for a few months, only to disappear completely on the passage to New South Wales.

She turned her attention back to the man beside her. Sleep was calling, but there was something she wanted to do first.

"Roll over." She stood and went to the dresser. "I'll put a salve on your back."

Michael didn't move. He watched her warily, eyes half closed.

"Turn over, then." She spoke more forcefully this time. "I won't hurt you."

"It's not necessary." He glowered at her.

"I know 'tisn't necessary. But I want to." She paused, mellowing her tone and turning the command into a question. "Please?"

Reluctantly, he obeyed, rolling onto his belly and bringing his arms up so that his forehead rested on the backs of his hands.

Caitlin surveyed the ridged landscape of flesh. It could be worse. The wounds were healing, though not what one would call healed. There were some that seemed older and had faded to light pink, thin, puckered lines barely raised above his pale skin. Others were still red and scabbed over. He must have been flogged more than once. Poor man.

"How does this feel?" She opened her hand and placed it, palm down, on the criss-cross of flesh. It felt hot, as if burned by the sun.

He tensed. "Fine."

"Does it hurt you, still?" She ran her hand lightly over the expanse of his injuries.

"Not really. Aches a bit. Itches, mostly," he grunted. "The skin's tight when I move."

"Then this will help." She reached for the little tin of ointment. It was a recipe she made for her own chapped skin—beeswax and wool oil mixed with just a bit of tallow and lavender. "I'll be gentle." She unscrewed the lid, dipped her fingers into the cool, viscous salve, and began to spread it over his back.

At first he held himself so tight he barely seemed to be breathing, but as she kept on, smoothing the ointment in and kneading the muscles below, she could feel him begin to relax.

"They laced you more than once," she observed.

"Yes."

"How many times?"

He was silent for a moment. "Once before I left Sydney—fifty lashes. Then . . ." He trailed off, as if trying to remember. "A few times more. I can't say. Exactly."

"Whatever for?"

He snorted. "The first was part of my sentence. But at Moreton Bay they don't need a reason. The guards are bored and miserable. They just want someone to take it out on."

She scooped a bit more salve out and spread it lower on his back, avoiding the breaks in his skin that were still raw and scabbed. Then—though she knew he probably wouldn't answer—she asked the question that had been on her mind all day. "Is it what you were dreaming of when I woke you? Moreton Bay, I mean."

He didn't answer.

She shouldn't have asked. It was no business of hers. Best let it be.

She focused on the feeling of her cool hands sliding over his skin—

"No." He drew a long breath. "Snakes." His voice had a dull, hollow ring to it, and she suspected he wasn't telling the whole truth. "I was dreaming of snakes."

"*Snakes*?" Caitlin felt her brows raise. "Well then, you should go to Ireland."

"Ireland?" He turned halfway to look up at her.

"Aye, Ireland." Gently, she pushed him back down. "There are no snakes in Ireland, you know. Not since St. Patrick drove them out. They can't abide the smell of Irish earth." Michael didn't answer, so she kept talking, hoping to distract him from whatever dark place her question had sent him to. "Did you know, there was a gentleman near Port Hunter, an Irishman with a large land grant. The poor chap was so plagued by snakes that he had five hundred tons of good Irish bog soil dug up and shipped to him in biscuit barrels."

"Biscuit barrels?" Michael spoke into the mattress, his muffled tone betraying his amusement.

"Aye, biscuit barrels." The corners of Caitlin's mouth twitched up. It was a story she'd heard from one of her assigned men, years ago. Absurd, yet somehow amusing. "They arrived at King's Wharf, safe and sound. Then he dug a trench 'round his farm and filled it with that Irish dirt." The last bit of salve soaked into his skin, and she bent down to press a kiss to his scarred back. "Wouldn't you know it—he never saw a single snake ever again."

Chuckling, she rose, put the tin away, then blew out the candle and lay herself down beside him. He'd rolled onto his side and was looking at her, his features outlined by the silvery moonlight, his eyes indigo blue as the night sky. A smile, a real one—if a disbelieving one—grew from within him.

"What?" she asked. "You don't believe me?"

"Of course I do." He grinned at her. "Why wouldn't I?"

She laughed. Then she leaned in and kissed him. "Goodnight, Michael."

"Goodnight, Caitlin."

The wheat was indeed a record harvest, more than four hundred bushels in all. Michael even found a man in Sydney to buy the extra straw, something Caitlin had always wanted to do, but never managed to convince John the worth of. Summer flowed into fall and the rains came exactly when they should. The pasture stayed lush and green, and there was cream enough from the cows to make butter to sell into the winter. The hogs grew beautifully fat and fetched a king's ransom. Even the bees seemed to be on her side—Caitlin pressed more honey and collected more wax than ever before.

By the time everything was sold, she was closer to settling John's debts than she'd ever dared hope. Only twenty-three pounds remained to be paid.

It was hard work, especially with only two field hands. Caitlin spent most of her hours away from the house, but she always made time to come in for her reading lessons. They were the best part of her days, made even better by the warm, buzzy feeling she got from Michael's encouragement. On one of his trips to Sydney, he bought a child's reader filled with poetry and prose, and one day in early April, she finally reached the end of it.

Simplicity, the last poem inside it was called, and Caitlin would remember it as long as she lived. But it wasn't the words that were important, not really. They were merely the spell that conjured the feeling of that afternoon. The way the autumn sun slanted through the windows. The sight of Michael, sitting across from her, his golden hair shining, his blue eyes—as fathomless as the sky above—fixed on her with rapt attention, urging her on.

Our water is drawn from the clearest of springs,
And our food, nor disease nor satiety brings:
Our mornings are cheerful, our labors are blest,
Our evenings are pleasant, our nights crowned with rest.

She looked up from the page and grinned sideways at him. The corners of his lips curled up in response. Though, as always when he was acting the tutor, he tamped them back down. "Finish it."

She kept reading.

Since such are the joys that Simplicity
yields,
We may well be content with our
woods and our fields,
How useless to us then, ye great, were

your wealth,
When without it we purchase both
pleasure and health.

She closed the book, and Michael allowed his impulse to get the better of him. He grinned, a sudden burst of sunshine as bright as the rays that flooded through the windows. "Well done," was all he said, but the way he said it . . . Caitlin had never felt so proud.

What a wonder it was, to be able to make sense of words on paper.

And this man . . .

At some point—Caitlin could never remember exactly when—there came a day when she woke up and couldn't imagine her life without Michael. He was there when she trudged in, bone weary from the fields, hot food ready on the table. He went to town whenever it was needed, learned to do the laundry and to milk the cow, to skim the cream and churn butter, to press honey and make candles. He even took to packing her pipe and pouring her grog at the end of the day, though he still never drank any himself. And he didn't do any of it simply because she told him to, or because it was his duty. He genuinely seemed to enjoy the rhythms of the farm and the act of caring for her—of giving her the little joys of her daily life.

They converted his room back into a dairy, and every evening after dinner they'd sit on the verandah to smoke and read the paper if they had one. Then they'd retire to Caitlin's room where they'd shag till they were both wrung out. On other nights, they simply held each other as they drifted off to sleep.

Simplicity, indeed.

It was the kind of contented country life she'd imagined for herself when she was a girl on the farm in Goleen. When she'd had time and hope enough to dream, before Father's lease was ended and they'd been forced down that muddy road to Cork.

The simple life seemed to agree with Michael as well. Or at least, she thought it did. Gradually, the gaunt hollows under his eyes filled out. His ribs and hip bones became less stark. She rubbed salve on his scars each night, and over time they faded—though, of course he'd live with them for the rest of his life. He seemed content. But even still, that shell he hid himself away in never quite wore away entirely. She saw long glimpses of the man beneath when they were in bed, or when he didn't think she was looking, but he still spoke sparingly and smiled even less. His nightmares still plagued him. It was as if he were marked not only by the scars on his back but by deeper wounds. Wounds he'd never allow Caitlin to see, much less soothe.

They never spoke of it. All too soon, Michael's year would draw to a close. There was no doubt in Caitlin's mind that he looked forward to leaving, finally a free man, able to set out on his own. Who wouldn't? But did he have a plan? Was he ready? Was she? Whenever the questions arose, Caitlin pushed them away, along with the sense of unease they stirred. It didn't matter. He was here now. No point in worrying about a future she couldn't change.

It was late October, eleven months into Michael's year at Swindale, when the truth of the matter finally became clear to her. It was raining, a steady downpour that seemed like it would never end. Caitlin had planned to plant in the garden, but instead she'd been forced indoors to sit at the kitchen table, cutting candle wicks. There was wax left from the fall, and Mr. Flemming was in need of more tapers. Michael had just finished putting a stew together for supper, and the savory smells of lovage and cooked meat hung like a cloud in the humid air. He came up behind her and put his hands on her shoulders, kneading her muscles the way he knew she liked.

"Mmh." She stretched her head to one side, savoring his touch. "How many did you say Mr. Flemming wanted?"

"Twelve dozen, if you have them." Michael's thumbs found a knot of muscle, and he dug into it, making her squeal. He stopped. "Too much?"

"It is not. Keep going." Obligingly, his fingers came back to her nape. Caitlin let herself go limp, falling into his touch.

Damn, she'd lost count.

She set down the scissors and gave herself over to his ministrations. "That does feel good." So good she never wanted it to end.

And just like that, something inside her shattered into a thousand painful pieces.

She never wanted it to end.

But it would. It *would* end. And soon. He would leave, and she'd be alone in an empty house. Without Michael. In her bed. In her life.

His hands stilled. "You've tensed up again," he said accusingly. "If it's too much, I can—"

"It is *not* too much." She nearly choked on the words. Then she opened her mouth to tell him just how much his leaving would pain her, to ask him what he planned to do—but at the last second, she thought better of it. It was his business, not hers, and anyway, there was no sense in laying her troubles at his feet. "Keep going. Please," was all she could manage.

That night, she came at him with wild abandon. Michael seemed taken aback by the forceful way she rode him, by the tight embrace she wrapped him in afterward, as if she'd never let him go. But he said nothing about it, just fell asleep quickly in her arms. Caitlin lay awake for a long time, listening to his soft snores.

By morning, she was resolved. She would ask him to stay. Not to marry. Just to stay. To keep on as they had been. Such arrangements were common in the colony. It wasn't like in Ireland or England, where unmarried couples were shunned. Even still, he would probably say no. He would make a much better life for himself in Sydney than he could here, and she had so little to offer . . . But it was comfortable on the farm. He was used to the routine, and it was peaceful, something Sydney would never be. Perhaps room and board and part of the farm's profits would tempt him? At least for a time.

She'd just need to find the right time to ask.

SEVENTEEN

THE DISHWATER WAS TOO hot, but Michael didn't care. His hands were so work-roughened by now that he couldn't feel the scald.

He plunged Caitlin's breakfast bowl in, wiped it clean, then set it aside. He always gave her the bowl without the chip in it. Did she notice?

Did it matter?

He'd be leaving soon, and she'd be choosing her own bloody bowl.

He picked up the next dish.

In less than a month's time, he'd be a free man. And he had no idea what he'd do.

He did know that Caitlin would be glad to see the back of him. She'd always made it clear that she didn't want a man, not for keeps. And she'd got what she wanted. She could read as well as anyone of her station and write serviceably. Her debts were nearly paid. Perhaps she'd miss his cooking, but she could employ someone for that, a real house servant. It was only a matter of time before she could afford one, the way things were going.

The only thing that separated Michael from a housemaid was the fucking. And Caitlin was tiring of that too. The way she'd tensed up under his hands the day before, as if his touch repulsed her. Then the way she'd ridden him last night—she'd had to work so hard just to find her pleasure. She'd pulled him close afterward, most likely because she felt sorry for him.

He set the last cup down, clean, then crossed to the table to fetch the porridge pot. The heavy iron was crusted with cooked maize. Better to let it soak a bit before attempting to scrub it out. He poured some of the water inside and began drying the other dishes, putting them away one by one.

His eyes wandered to the back door where she'd disappeared just a half hour before.

What *would* he do?

It was hard to muster the will to even mull the question over. Not with any seriousness. The fact of the matter was, he didn't care what he did or where he went. It didn't matter. But he'd have to go *somewhere*. Take up space in some other town, some other house.

Sydney was the most likely, the only place he could imagine, really. Even if he wanted to stay in the country or one of the smaller towns, finding employment would be next to impossible. Men out here were supposed to work the fields or tend to sheep, and Michael was no good for that kind of job, not the paid type, anyway. He knew his way around a kitchen, and he'd learned plenty of new skills in the last year, but it wasn't as if he could apply for a position as a cook or a dairymaid. No, Sydney was the place to go. He could work at an office or a warehouse, find some hovel to sleep in, lose himself in the stinking crowd, and live out what was left of his life.

Sydney had the grog houses, at least. There would be no reason to avoid the temptation once he was a free man. Davey would try to keep him away from drink, but what did it matter to Davey, really? Michael had kept himself sober this entire year for Davey's sake—and Caitlin's—and what difference had it made? Caitlin knew how to read, but Michael was right back where he'd started. He might as well make himself comfortable there.

He set down the dish towel. Nothing left but the blasted porridge pot and a sinkful of tepid, dirty water. He hated the way the soggy bits of maize polluted the clean water. How they felt on his hands, all moist and slushy.

In the silence, the magpie's song filtered through the half-open window. It was mating time for that bastard again.

He listened for a moment to the trilling, bubbling well of sound as it skipped its way through the silence. Then he huffed a breath. Time to get the scrubbing over with—

A knock sounded at the front door.

Who the devil could that be? Michael stood frozen, thinking. The two field-hands had mostly avoided the house, as promised. But if, for some reason, they needed something, they'd come to the back door, surely. The only person who'd come knocking at the front since Michael had arrived was Mrs. Thatcher, the neighbor, and then only once. She'd said she'd come to call on Caitlin, though Caitlin told him later that she'd really come to spy for her husband, who wanted to purchase the farm and was hoping Caitlin would prove to be inept in her own husband's absence. Thankfully, Michael's presence seemed to scare the old biddy away. One menacing look, and she'd turned white as the linens Michael had just hung out to dry, stammered some excuse, and turned tail.

But this was not the light, fake-friendly knock that Mrs. Thatcher had tapped out. This was more insistent. More presumptuous.

Michael swallowed and brushed his wet hands on his trousers. Whoever it was, he'd have to answer.

The knocking came again, louder.

He strode down the hall and into the sitting room. Without moving the curtain, he angled himself to see as much as he could. A carriage and two well-matched horses stood in the drive, with a bored-looking driver on the perch. Michael couldn't see much of the verandah, but it appeared to be a man standing at the door, neatly dressed in a coat and trousers and a tall hat. No one out here dressed so formally. This caller must be from Sydney. A government official, perhaps here to assess the farm for some reason. Or the men. Or Michael himself.

"Hell," he muttered, as he crossed through the corridor. Then he drew himself up to his full height, trying his best to don the mask of cold authority Father had worked so hard to mold onto his face.

He opened the door.

It was indeed a well-dressed, well-groomed man of perhaps five and twenty. He wore an immaculate black coat, trousers with stirrups, and a somber black waistcoat with a crisply starched cravat. A tall beaver hat sat on his head, and perfectly trimmed side-whiskers framed his thin face. The man didn't even wear boots, but the fine slippers one saw on fops in London. He carried a leather case, like something a solicitor might use to transport papers.

But it wasn't the man's clothing that gave him away for what he was. It was his skin, pale and white. And the scared look in his gray eyes. It was too familiar for Michael not to recognize. He wasn't from Sydney, at least not for long. This man was from England. London most likely.

A creeping sense of foreboding snaked up Michael's spine.

"Can I help you?" Michael allowed the hostility he felt to sound in his voice. He might be in his shirtsleeves, with dishwater staining his trousers and wrinkled, calloused hands, but it would not do to show any kind of deference to this intruder, whoever he was.

The young man stared, clearly not sure what to make of Michael. "I—I've come to see Mrs. Caitlin Blackwell," he stammered. "This is her home?"

"Yes."

The twig's eyes widened at the snarl in Michael's tone. "Is she . . . at home?" He craned his neck to peer beyond Michael into the house.

Michael leaned slightly to the side to block the fop's view. "No."

"Can you tell me when she'll—"

"She's out. In the fields."

"Ah." The lad straightened up. He breathed in through pinched nostrils, then continued in an affected, snobbish tone. "And your position in this house is . . ." He raised a brow.

Michael gritted his teeth. "I'm her secretary."

"I see." The man smiled, as if he'd won something. "Well then, fetch Mrs. Blackwell if you please. I'm here on important business."

Michael stood his ground, scrutinizing his opponent through narrowed eyes. From London. Important business. All his impulses told him to knock this stranger onto his arse, to chase him back into his carriage and then all the way to the other side of the world . . . Still, as intimidating as Michael could make himself look, there was nothing behind it. No real power. As much as he might want to, he could not protect Caitlin from whatever news this man brought.

He grunted and gestured for the lad to follow him into the sitting room. "Wait here." He turned, then raised a brow of his own. "Who shall I tell her is calling?"

"Mr. James. From London."

Michael turned quickly, hiding his surprise. *Mr. James.* That was the name of the solicitor who'd written the letter to tell Caitlin's husband of his inheritance. It had been nearly a year, time enough for a letter to be received in London and to allow for passage back to the colony . . . The sense of foreboding he'd felt earlier settled in, moving from the base of his spine to his gut.

He'd almost reached the door when the man's voice stilled him. "May I ask, sir. Are you a *paid* servant, or . . ."

"A convict?" Michael wheeled around to see that the younger man had opened his bag and was pulling out papers. He didn't look up, and Michael recognized the trick. Show your power by feigning disinterest in your opponent. It was one he'd mastered in his short time as Earl of Banton.

Why did this affected little boy have to remind Michael so much of himself?

He waited, lips pursed, staring at the young man intently until the twig had no choice but to look at him. Ah yes, the fear was returning. Good.

"I'm a convict, sir," Michael growled. He narrowed his eyes and balled his fists. "The worst kind."

The boy's eyes flashed with terror, and he looked quickly back to his papers. Michael left the room.

Caitlin gave the bellows one last squeeze, sending the smoke from the smoldering pile of rags streaming into the hive. Then she set them down carefully, pulled off the lid, and squinted down into the wooden frame.

Her gaze was met by a mass of healthy, smoke-sleepy bees. Beautiful, golden honey filled the top frame. This would be what they'd made from the orchard's blooms—apple, peach, and cherry blossoms. Between the honey and the comb that held it, it would bring in near enough to pay the last of the debts.

"Hello, me lovelies," she murmured.

The low hum of wings was her only reply.

Carefully, she set the lid back on before sitting back on her heels and peeling off her gloves.

A feeling floated up within her like a bubble underwater. It surfaced with a splash, and she wanted to laugh or perhaps screech with delight. What a glorious day. Warm, but not yet hot. The trees that surrounded the hives had set fruit and were well on their way to a beautiful harvest. The wheat was plump and ripening well in the fields. And now this. This was the last hive. She'd inspected all eight of them, and each was ready for the first harvest. Yet it was only November. She'd never seen so much honey so early in the season.

Now she just needed to convince Michael to stay. Then her year of plenty would be complete.

She'd planned to do it this morning over breakfast, but she'd lost her nerve. Not that her world would end if he decided to leave. She'd braced herself for the possibility, but the thought had occurred to her that the last few weeks would feel awkward for both of them if she asked now and he said no.

She'd so enjoyed her time with Michael. To ruin it now seemed a waste.

So she'd hesitated, thinking it better to wait.

But that was daft.

She got up and stamped on the rags to put them out. The jarring motion felt good. Decisive. Michael deserved to know what was on her mind, so he could plan his future—even if it did lead to some temporary discomfort.

And there was always the chance he'd say yes.

A smile spread across her face at the thought, and her eyes wandered across the blue sky, where two magpies soared together over the fields. So free, so happy . . . She could just imagine the two of them here for the rest of their days.

Growing old together, enjoying the fruits of their labors. It was almost like she'd imagined as a girl . . .

No. That had been the dream of a young innocent. She knew better now. Even if he did stay, it wouldn't be forever. Nor did she want it to be. She would still make her own way, independent of any man.

She stooped to pick up the rags and bellows. She'd bring the next set of wooden frames tomorrow morning to set underneath, then collect the top ones the day after that. She'd have to make time to drain and press the honey. Or perhaps Michael could do it.

She straightened and once again scanned the sky. There were no clouds, and the air was already growing heavy and hot. It would be a muggy, thick kind of a day, perhaps with a storm later.

Now on to the garden—

"Caitlin!" Michael's voice called from behind her.

She turned to see him striding quickly through the orchard. Something about the way he walked brought a pang of worry. What had happened?

He reached her, slightly out of breath, eyeing her warily. As if he didn't want to tell her of whatever had brought him here.

"What is it?" she prodded.

"There's a man. Mr. James. Here to see you." At the blank look on her face, he continued. "He's the solicitor from London. The one who wrote that letter."

"*What*?" Caitlin stared at him, trying to understand. "The letter about John's brother?" Michael nodded. "What could he—?" She broke off. There were very few things that would force a man like that to travel from London to this tainted, shameful colony.

Melia murder. She closed her eyes, bit her teeth down hard, and swallowed.

"I don't know why he's here," Michael said gently, touching her arm in reassurance.

Caitlin opened her eyes and forced a smile. Her heart was hammering in her chest. "Best get it over with, then. Where is he?"

EIGHTEEN

THEY CREPT IN QUIETLY through the back door. Caitlin took a moment to peel off her work apron and smooth her hair. The dress she wore was old and stained—she'd not planned for anyone but Michael and the men to see her today—but there was nothing to be done about that now.

Nerves juddered low in her stomach as Michael tucked a strand of hair behind her ear.

"What do I say to him?" She hated how her voice wavered.

"I'll introduce you formally. Simply acknowledge him, then ask him to sit down and hear him out. Perhaps it isn't—" He stopped himself from whatever he'd been about to say, finishing simply, "Anything."

"Perhaps not." But she saw her own doubt reflected in his eyes. A man did not travel from London to New South Wales for nothing. She stepped past Michael. "Very well."

"Whatever happens"—he stopped her with a hand on her arm, drawing her round to face him—"don't show any fear. He's wary already, I've seen to that." He raised his brows ominously. "Best to keep him that way. And"—they were quite alone, but his voice dropped, as though confiding a secret—"I don't know if he suspects, about us. But it's best not to let on. It would reflect poorly on you."

Caitlin's nerves became a prickling heat. This was *her* house. She had the right to do whatever she liked. "I'm not ashamed." She did *not* lower her voice. "And neither should you be."

"Perhaps not." Michael lifted a hand in a placating gesture. "But . . . whatever he's here for, it's best not to let him think you anything other than a respectable widow. Surely you can see that?"

Caitlin drew a long breath. She despised everything about this: the London nob in her sitting room, the deception Michael was insisting she be part of, and the hint of menace in his words. The fear that buzzed about them both, clouding her thoughts. But what Michael said held sense. "Very well." She managed a tight smile. "You're me secretary then. Nothing more." Michael nodded, relief showing on his face. Then another thought struck her, bringing with it a different kind of panic. She grabbed his hand. "You'll stay with me, won't you? You won't leave me alone with him."

"Of course not." He smiled, a small but genuine smile. He leaned down and planted a kiss on her forehead. "I'll be there. Whatever happens."

Something about the press of his lips and the certainty in his voice . . . It was like a gentle smoke to bees. Her nerves calmed to a low hum.

She waited in the darkness of the corridor while Michael announced her. "Mrs. Blackwell will see you now." She could hardly believe that voice was his. All the roughness was gone, replaced by a smooth, sinister kind of snobbery. From anyone else, she'd have loathed it, but given the circumstance, it made her feel just a tiny bit safer. Protected. She took a breath and walked into the sitting room.

It was stiflingly hot. Michael had stationed himself beside the door, and she hazarded a quick glance in his direction as she passed by. He didn't meet her eye, just stared straight ahead, a fierce glower on his face.

"Mrs. Blackwell." Her attention was drawn to the other man in the room, who stood as he said her name. Mr. James was younger than she would have expected, but otherwise the very picture of a London gentleman—or what she supposed a London gentleman might look like. Tall and thin and pale, dressed in an uncomfortable manner with a heavily starched cravat strangling his neck, and perfectly white gloves shrouding his hands. His face was covered in a sheen of sweat.

"Mr. James." She extended her hand, wishing she'd thought to put on gloves to cover her callouses. The man grasped it and inclined his head slightly. "Please, sit down—"

"I've come to—"

They spoke over each other, and Caitlin felt her cheeks heat, though she held her head high. She could sense Michael's presence behind her, bolstering her. She raised a brow and gestured toward the sofa.

Mr. James sat. An unfriendly smile creased his lips. "I've come to speak with you." His eyes swiveled toward Michael. "*Alone*, if I may."

Caitlin remained standing. "Mr. Dunn is me secretary. A trusted servant." Somehow, her voice sounded calm and certain, though she felt strangely disconnected from it. As though someone else were speaking. "He can hear whatever it is you have to say."

Mr. James's gaze was still fixed over her shoulder at Michael. At her words, his eyes flicked nervously back to her face. "Of course." He smiled that strained smile again, a mixture of fear and annoyance.

There was an awkward pause. The young man looked to Michael again as if his attention were drawn there against his will. His brows knitted together, and he swallowed, blinking back at Caitlin. She could only imagine the fearsome look Michael must have conjured.

"What is it you came here for, Mr. James?" Caitlin allowed her voice to rise, making her irritation clear.

The young man took a handkerchief out of his pocket and wiped his brow. "I've come from London. My father wrote to you last year, to inform you of an inheritance of your late husband's."

"I remember." So this was the son. That explained his youth.

"I'll get right to the point, Mrs. Blackwell." Mr. James tucked the cloth back in his pocket, then leaned forward slightly. "In light of your husband's death, we located the next man in line. Another Mr. Blackwell, a cousin. Given the inheritance of this farm, he's interested in developing an investment in New

South Wales. In *sheep*, to be exact, as the prices for merino wool in London are—"

"I believe Mrs. Blackwell made it clear in her letter that this farm would serve as her dower." Michael strode forward as he spoke, his words like steel.

"She did." Mr. James kept his eyes trained on Caitlin. A bead of sweat dripped down the side of his face. "But I'm afraid that won't be possible. You see, Mr. Blackwell—the *new* Mr. Blackwell—has designated a dower portion in Scotland. A large estate in the north that's recently come into the family. Quite nice, I'm sure." He fished the handkerchief back out of his pocket and swiped at his neck, then his brow "I've been directed to provide passage for Mrs. Blackwell and an allowance to be paid annually for expenses."

The air in the room was too thin, her lungs too weak. "But I have the deed to this farm. 'Tis mine, by law."

"Yes, *that*." Mr. James had turned away and was shuffling through some papers he'd laid out on the end table. He selected one and thrust it toward her. "Before I came here, I paid a visit to the land office in Sydney to explain the situation. The men there were quite amenable."

He handed her a document. It only took one glance to see what it was—a land grant, exactly like the one she'd been given after John's death. It had the same official red wax seal, but instead of her name listed as owner, *Mr. Edward Blackwell* was written on the paper.

The words blurred.

She looked up at the man. He was still sweating uncontrollably, but he had a gleam in his eye as he watched her. He knew he had won. He'd won before he'd even arrived—there had never been a contest.

She'd never stood a chance.

The hot air lodged in Caitlin's throat. She couldn't breathe. The world wavered like the far hills on a hot day.

Don't show fear.

Michael's words came to her in the nick of time, along with the memory of his kiss, cool on her brow. Though her lungs rebelled at the motion, she forced a long breath in, then out through her nose, clamping her teeth down hard against the surly words that swarmed in her mouth.

With shaking hands, she passed the paper to Michael. He scrutinized it for a long moment then let it fall to his side. "Mrs. Blackwell has an excellent lawyer in Sydney. We'll take this matter up with him."

Mr. James smirked. "If you insist. I will warn you though, I brought a letter from Lord Bathurst himself in support of Mr. Blackwell's claim."

Caitlin's already labored breath seized completely, the air stuck in her lungs, thick like honey. She and Michael had read about Lord Bathurst in the papers. He was Secretary of the Colonies, one of the most powerful men in England. Even the governor didn't dare stand against him. She gritted her teeth and forced a breath. Another.

Don't show fear.

"May I see that letter?" Somehow, Michael sounded just as composed as he had when they'd stepped into this room.

"Of course." The young man turned to his pile of papers, then handed one to Michael.

Michael scanned the writing. Then he looked up and met Caitlin's eye. He shrugged.

"You have one week to vacate the place." Mr. James's voice faded in and out. She tried to breathe, but there was no air. She would lose everything. The bees. The wheat. The house. And what would become of the men? "I understand you have three convict servants here." It was as if he'd heard her thoughts. "They're to be sent to Sydney for the time being. They're expected at the barracks by Friday."

The garden. The little carrots and turnips that were just now sprouting. The cows . . .

"The livestock?" she choked out. "Surely that's mine?"

Mr. James fidgeted with his hat. "I'm afraid not, ma'am. The letter states that it's to be *everything* on the farm—crops and livestock alike. It's not as if you could take a milk cow with you to Scotland, after all." He smirked, as if they were sharing a joke.

The figure of Mr. James swam before her. She blinked. Blinked again. It did no good. Her legs were trembling, her body weak. "But . . . this land's not suited for sheep," she pleaded, "It's rich farmland—"

"So I've been told." Mr. James nodded, serious again. "Though it's still quite valuable, I understand. I plan to sell it and use the proceeds to set up an operation further inland, past the Blue Mountains." His eyes flicked to Michael, as if he expected an argument. "I've been authorized to make such decisions."

Caitlin shook her head desperately to clear the blur and rubbed her eyes. Her knees would give way any minute—

Then she felt a hand on her arm, steadying her. "I'm sure you can understand, Mr. James, that this news comes as a shock to Mrs. Blackwell. Especially so soon after the death of her beloved husband." Michael's voice was so confident, so solid. Caitlin held to it, grasped at it like a lifeline. "Perhaps you could grant her a month to see to—"

"I'm afraid that's not possible." Mr. James rose and began stuffing papers back into his bag. "I've a schedule to adhere to. I'm sure you understand." He slung the satchel over his shoulder, then addressed Caitlin. "Your passage has been booked, ma'am, on the *Lady Juliana*. She sails next Tuesday. I'll leave a portion of your allowance with the captain, for your expenses. The rest can be collected when you arrive in Liverpool." He held out one last piece of paper toward Caitlin. "The terms of the dower are written here. You may take a maid with you." His brow rose. "*If* you have one. And as I said, your assigned convicts are to report to the barracks within the week." He paused, eyes settling meaningfully on Michael. "They're expected."

Michael stiffened. Obviously, this man didn't know it was bad form to refer to government men as convicts—

Sweet Jesus. *Michael* was to report to the barracks. She'd not even understood when he'd said it earlier. But without Michael, she'd—

"I believe it's time for you to leave, Mr. James." Michael stepped forward, his fists balled tight. Caitlin wavered at the loss of his touch, but somehow her legs held.

Mr. James shrank away. "Of—of course. I'll see myself out." He slunk around the edge of the room, and Michael pivoted to follow him with his eyes. Once he reached the door, the solicitor ducked his head into his hat, then glanced back. "One week, Mrs. Blackwell. I'll have a wagon sent for your trunk. And I've hired a man to look after the place. He's set to arrive on Saturday."

And he turned and fled.

The front door banged shut, leaving a stifling silence behind. The sound of wheels crunching on gravel drifted in, then slowly receded.

The midday sun poured through the front window as a hot rage surged through Michael's veins. He had the overpowering urge to run after that prig, to drag him from his blasted conveyance and beat him to a bloody pulp—

"Michael?" Caitlin's voice, small and scared, pinned though his anger. She was pale as milk, and she was staring at him, blinking slowly.

But before he could find words, her eyes rolled back in her head, and she crumpled.

Shit. He caught her just in time. But she was limp as a rag doll, her eyes closed, her head lolling against his chest. Her breath came light and fast. He hoisted her up, holding her under her arms and knees, but then he hesitated—it was too hot in her bedroom, too hot anywhere in the house. She needed air. He ran through the corridor, through the kitchen and outside, setting her down in the shade of the house. Content that she was as comfortable as he could make her, he strode quickly to the well and filled a bucket with water.

The air was thick as soup. Better than inside, but not by much.

When he returned, she'd already woken and was struggling to sit up.

"You shouldn't—" he started, but it was no use. She ignored him as she pulled herself up to sit against the wall before wrapping her arms tightly around herself. Her face was still white, though it no longer showed that panicked fear. Nor sadness either. Nor emotion of any kind.

"Do you feel any better?" Michael held out a dipperful of water. She gazed up at it and shook her head, her lips pressed tight together—whether it was a rejection of the water or an answer to his question he wasn't sure. Both perhaps. He stood for a minute, looking down at her. Then, not knowing what else to do, he set the bucket on the grass, pressed his back to the wall, and slid down till he was sitting beside her, his knees to his chin, his thigh against hers.

She still didn't acknowledge him. He was just beginning to wonder if he should go—perhaps his presence was an intrusion—when she reached for his hand and threaded their fingers together.

The sounds of the farm wafted around them, the lowing of the cow to her calf and the far-away clank of their bells, the contented cluck of the hens as they gossiped and scratched in the dust. The rustling breeze as it blew the thick air through the gum leaves. The dull clink of the metal pulley as it was blown against the wood of the well cover.

"I—I couldn't breathe." Caitlin's voice joined the chorus of familiar sounds.

Michael brought their clasped hands to his lips and pressed a kiss to her knuckles.

She turned to him, her eyes pleading a desperate hope, as if he might know a way out of this. "That letter from Bathurst . . ."

"It looked real to me." Michael shook his head. He so desperately wanted to give her a reason to hope. But there *was* none, and they both knew it. "You don't have to go away, though, to Scotland, I mean. If you don't want to. You could stay."

She scoffed. "Stay? And do what? Work in some man's house, scrubbing his floors and emptying his chamber pots? Whore myself?"

"No, of course not."

As quickly as it had come, Caitlin's fire died away. Her shoulders sank, and that lost silence settled between them once more. He loosened his hold on her hand so she could get away, but she didn't. She gripped him tighter.

"Do you know anything of Scotland?" She stared blankly into the distance as she spoke.

The question hung in the air for what seemed an eternity as a deep black hole opened inside of Michael. A bottomless well. The weight in his stomach dropped into it, fell and fell into the darkness of the pit . . .

"No," he lied. "My father's family has ties there, but I've never been." He pressed his lips closed.

Caitlin heaved a sigh. "I'd have me own house there, and some money. 'Twould have to be better than . . . Without the farm I've got *nothing* here." She turned her head to look at him. "At least there I'd have me freedom. And a place of me own."

Michael's mouth turned bitter.

He'd be here, and free within the month.

"I just can not believe—" She broke off, and her hand came up to her hair as her eyes searched the landscape before them. "This is mine. It's *mine*. I built it."

Michael swallowed the bitterness away. There was no use for it now. "You did. You deserve better."

She turned to him again, her eyes wide. "And what of you? You'll—"

"I'll be fine."

She searched his face, looking for the truth behind his lie, then looked away.

They sat for a long time, hand in hand, listening to the sounds of the farm.

Finally, Caitlin released her grip and rose, dusting off her apron. "I must go tell the men." Her color had returned, but her lower lip quivered, then pinched tight.

Michael pulled himself up. "I'll come—"

"No. 'Tis me responsibility." She lifted her chin, pivoted away from him and strode toward the fields.

Nineteen

THE SKY BEGAN TO darken as Caitlin walked from the men's huts back to the house. The breeze had stilled, and a mass of bruise-colored clouds gathered on the horizon. The air felt heavy and thick.

A storm was coming.

As if to confirm the thought, a low rumble of thunder echoed in the distance. She quickened her pace.

All things being even, the men had taken the news well. One became used to one's life being upended, she supposed. And if *they* were used to it, surely Caitlin should be. But somehow, the painful ache in her throat refused to be swallowed away.

She was halfway through the last field when the clouds overtook the sun and the rich gold of the ripening wheat dimmed. By pure habit, she reached out a hand and skimmed it over the tops of the stalks, feeling the kiss of the burgeoning kernels beneath her palm. She'd been here so long . . . half her life. She'd grown accustomed to the idea that this would be home forever.

What a sap she'd been.

She jerked her hand away and clenched it into a fist, holding it tight by her side. How had she allowed herself to feel so safe? Had she learned nothing from the story of Esther Abrams? She should have been anticipating this, preparing for it, but no—she'd looked the other way, chosen to forget all about that damn letter and carry on as if nothing could go wrong. Just as she had with Michael. She'd ignored the certainty of his leaving, put off even thinking of it. And now it was too late.

She trained her gaze to the ground, gripping harder till her nails bit into the flesh. With the pain came a flash of memory—that deed, with the stranger's name written where hers should have been. . . This farm might have been her home for the last twenty years, but it no longer was. The sooner she got used to that fact, the better. She didn't own the ripening wheat, nor the fencerow she'd built with her own hands, nor the orchard she'd planted, nor the hives.

The sound of the cow lowing plaintively to her calf drifted through the humid air, and Caitlin's heart ached at the sound. The cow. The calf. Again, that long, haunting sound, then the higher pitched answer. She would check on them to make sure they were secured before the storm. No matter whom they belonged to, they deserved to be safe.

She turned her steps toward the barn, then took a long steeling breath. This was not the first time she'd dealt with adversity. Life must go on. It *would* go on. All she could do was make the best of it.

She'd given Hud and Finn leave to depart whenever they liked. She'd just need to write them a pass, and they'd be on their way. Of course, she hadn't said as much, but she hoped they'd use the extra time to sneak in a few nights of freedom before showing themselves at the barracks.

She would offer the same to Michael, too. There was no sense in prolonging their parting. He could leave whenever he wished—

Without warning, the ach rose in her throat, now a searing burn, and she choked on a sob. At the same time, a sudden gust of wind kicked up the dust, lending a haze to the air. Her hair whipped in every direction; her eyes smarted. She covered them with the heel of her hand.

The barn door gaped open, and she ducked inside. Here, all was still and quiet. The cows had made it in, and the mare stood calmly in her stall, seemingly undisturbed by the rising storm.

Tears streamed down Caitlin's cheeks. She wiped them away. "Be safe, lovies," she murmured, as she closed the sliding doors that led to the pasture. Then she turned and stood in the shelter of the main door, looking out.

It still hadn't started to rain, and the wind had stopped as suddenly as it had begun. The sky had taken on a greenish cast, and the air held a charged, ominous feel.

Her eyes settled on the house. A thin trail of smoke rose from the chimney. A candle shone in the window.

Michael was waiting for her.

A flash of lightning lit the landscape. She didn't see it, but it was close—the skin on the back of her neck tingled, and in the same instant, a crashing boom of thunder shook the air. Another great sob wracked her, and she grasped the wooden doorframe to stay upright.

What would she do without him?

She'd always been alone. Ever since coming here—no, well before that. In that cold gaol in Cork where she'd nearly died, and even before that, on the streets when every day had been a struggle to keep the young ones fed and a roof over their heads. She'd had no one then—not to lean on, nor to talk to. Not since Ma and Pa died . . .

So why did it hurt so much to think of being alone once more?

It was that foolish vision she'd had of the two of them growing old together, living out their days, so peaceful and content. She should never have allowed herself that indulgence. It wasn't what she wanted, not really, and Michael might not have stayed anyway, even if it had been possible.

But it was such a pretty dream . . . Somehow, she just couldn't seem to let it go.

He'd said she could stay, not go to Scotland. Though she couldn't be sure if that was an offer or simply an observation. Even if he *had* been suggesting that they stay together after he was freed, what would they do? He had nothing, and neither did she. Everything she'd earned had gone to paying John's debts. There was no hope of obtaining land of their own. They could settle in Sydney or one of the other towns, but even with Michael, that kind of life would be intolerable.

At least in Scotland she'd have land and quiet. A few jagged pieces of her dream, shattered as it was.

Another bolt of lightning split the dark clouds, and the wind picked up again, roaring through the trees, sending great waves tumbling through the fields. Then a grinding, low growl of thunder that seemed to go on forever, chasing itself around the sky and reverberating in her chest.

If it had been any other day, she'd have worried over the wheat, which was at that fragile stage just before ripening. It could very easily be flattened and ruined by a storm like this. But it didn't matter now.

There was a part of her that hoped it'd be ruined. Good riddance.

She closed her eyes. Balled her fists. Life must go on. It had to.

Then she pulled the barn door shut, hugged herself tight and bolted toward the house as the first few raindrops hit. The smell of newly wet earth flooded her nostrils. Just a dozen paces more and she'd be inside, dry and safe.

But the storm didn't wait. There was another deafening crack of thunder, and the heavens opened up with a great whoosh. Sheets of rain lashed down, soaking her clothes and plastering her hair to her neck. It turned to hail, sharp pebbles of ice stinging her arms and her back. The wind blew hard, thrashing at her skirts and pushing her away from the fields, the orchard, the garden. Away from everything she loved. Everything she'd hoped for. Worked for.

She barreled through the back door—straight into the solid warmth of Michael's arms.

He'd been standing at the door, about to come looking for her.

She should keep running. Past Michael, past the pain, into whatever bleak future awaited her, but goddamn, she was just as fragile as the wheat . . . just as weak. She felt herself sink into him as her whole being wept, her tears soaking into his shirt.

He held her for a long moment, then drew back, his blue eyes clouded with concern. "Caitlin, I—"

She silenced him with her mouth, a bruising, forceful kiss. He grunted in surprise and retreated a step, then two, but she kept pace until she had him pressed against the wall. Even if he left tomorrow, Michael was here. He was safe. He was sureness and care and—and home.

Michael was *home.*

A great sob filtered from her mouth into his. Of course she'd lose him. He was home, and Caitlin didn't have a home. She never had.

Michael struggled beneath her. His breath was a pant. "Caitlin, what's—"

"No—just—" Again, she kissed him, pouring the feelings that had no words into him.

And somehow, he seemed to understand. In an instant, all his protest was gone. His palms came to her face, gripping her and drawing her closer. His tongue swept into her mouth, wrestling with hers.

Caitlin's hands skimmed over his arms and hips; then she frantically worked to undo his falls, hardly noticing when a button came loose and pinged across the room. When at last she'd completed the task, she pushed his trousers down, and he kicked them away.

Michael bucked into her hand. He moaned, the rough, guttural sound reverberating down her own throat.

His breath in her body. His body in her hand.

Her grip on him tightened.

And he understood. Of course he understood.

His mouth never left hers as he reached down and fisted her skirts, jerked them up, handful by handful until he had hold of the hem and she was exposed. She released him for a moment so he could pull the fabric all the way up and out of their way.

Then she leaned in and wrapped one leg around him, pinning him to the wall as she mashed herself against his hard length. She stood on tiptoe and pushed him into her wet slit, moving her hips to bring him closer.

Gor, it wasn't enough. She couldn't—

She stood on tiptoe, gripping him tight with her other leg, searching, frantically trying to fit him inside her, to fill her. A grunt of frustration escaped her lips as she lost her balance and tipped backward.

He caught her, his strong hands digging into her hips—but the pain was so right. In one swift movement, he picked her up, turning them both so Caitlin's back was against the wall. She leaned into its solidity and allowed him to take control, effortlessly lifting her the last few inches and sliding himself deep inside.

At last. Her mind released its hold, and sensation was all there was.

The feel of him inside her. Warm and solid. *Home.*

His eyes, blue as a summer sky. Deep as the sea.

He pulled out and thrust back into her with an animal's snarl, impaling her, pounding her into the wall.

Caitlin's head tipped back, but her eyes never left his. Her hands hung limp at her side, unable to move.

Nothing mattered. None of it. There was just the need—the wanting, then the having. The emptiness, then the fullness. With each thrust the want grew more urgent, more empty and vast, and the fullness more complete, more real, more perfect.

Until it all merged into one, and everything ceased to matter. The wanting, the having, the past, the future, the sorrow, the joy. Michael. Caitlin. None of it mattered. Just this. Here. Now.

She came with a cry—a cry of despair because she didn't want this to end.

But it was. It was ending.

Michael finished with one last, hard thrust. Then he stilled, his cock still buried deep inside her, and his forehead dropped to rest on the top of her head. His ragged breath blew loud in her ear.

The air in the house was close and hot, their skin sticky where it touched. The great gusts of wind had ceased, but the rain still fell, a constant clatter on the roof.

And then it was over. He slipped out of Caitlin, and her skirts fell back into place.

Michael lifted a hand to smooth her wet hair. His gaze settled on her face, and the storm in his eyes was like a knife to Caitlin's gut.

"You're drenched," he murmured.

Caitlin blinked back the tears. Tried and failed to smile. "It's raining."

Michael gave her one last look and bent to pull up his trousers. When he straightened, his expression had hardened back into its usual mask. "You should change into dry clothes." He turned away and walked toward the hearth. "I'll make tea."

She watched as he set two cups on the table, then a plate of bread. The butter dish.

Only a minute ago, they'd been as close as two souls could be. But with each passing second, they would grow farther and farther apart. Tomorrow, he'd leave. Tuesday thereafter, she'd board a ship and sail around the world. She'd never see him again.

Board a ship . . . The idea was like lightning illuminating the darkened sky. Suddenly, she could see what had always been there. Why had she not thought of it before?

Mr. James had said she could bring a maid. And Michael only had a month left on his sentence. He could still say no, but—

A tingling hope spread across Caitlin's chest as her mind whirred, putting the last pieces together.

"Michael—" In her excitement, his name came out more sharply than she'd intended.

He looked up, nearly splashing himself with boiling water from the kettle he was pouring.

"You could come with me."

TWENTY

CAITLIN WASN'T SURE EXACTLY what she'd expected Michael's reaction to be, but she'd thought he'd say *something*, even if it was a refusal. He didn't. He only stared at her for a long moment with a blank, unreadable expression, then looked down and finished pouring the tea. As if she hadn't spoken at all.

She walked around the table toward him. He must not have understood. "Mr. James said I could take a maid. You remember? Well . . ." She laid a hand on his arm, allowing a bit of a coy tease into her voice. "You're me most *trusted* servant. Me secretary. Surely, I could bring you instead?"

He pushed past her to bring the kettle back to the hearth.

Caitlin's hand was still raised, though now she touched only air. She let it drop and turned to watch him, the dull shine of the gray light on his hair, the linen of his shirt, damp and clinging to his skin. "'Tis only a month left on your sentence." She could hear the desperation filtering into her voice, but she had to say it. If there was any chance he'd agree . . . "Surely, Mr. Flemming could use his influence to get your pardon just a bit early."

He stood with his back to her, staring into the fire.

"You needn't stay in Scotland forever." She was pleading now. "Only until I'm settled. It would be such a comfort, and you'd be out of this damn place. You could go to England. *Home*."

Still no response. He crossed his arms.

Caitlin felt her shoulders droop. His silence made it clear—he didn't want to go.

She searched her mind for anything else she could say. But there was nothing. He'd be a free man—his *own* man—in just a few weeks. Why should he want to go to Scotland where he knew no one, as a servant, no less? He'd never spoken of his home or his family. Quite possibly he had none. Or he wouldn't be welcome if he did.

She released a deep sigh. What to say? This heaviness between them was exactly why she hadn't asked him to stay this morning.

How could it be that had only been this morning?

They stood frozen in place for what seemed like hours, the sound of rain tapping on the roof. Michael staring into the hearth. Caitlin staring at Michael's back.

Melia murder. This was ridiculous. She opened her mouth to speak, then quicky closed it to quell her quivering lip. She tried again, this time tightening her jaw and forcing the words out. "Never mind. 'Twas a silly idea. You'll be free soon, And I'll—"

"Enough!" Michael wheeled around. The tendons on his neck stood out in stark relief, his face pinched and white. His eyes narrowed menacingly.

"Michael." Caitlin searched his expression for something familiar, something she understood, but she'd never seen him like this. He was shaking. Livid. What could possibly have him so upset? "'Tisn't a problem. I—"

"I said *enough*." He advanced with long, forceful strides. "Stop. Talking."

For the first time since he'd come to live in her house, Caitlin was afraid. Her stomach lurched, and she backed up a step, then two. Yet he kept coming.

Her heart was hammering. He wouldn't hurt her, would he?

"Michael. *Please*." She held up her hands, creating a barrier between them.

"I'm not. Going. To Scotland." His breath seared her skin, and it was like a flame to a wick, burning his anger into her. How dare he come at her like this? She'd said nothing to provoke him. *Nothing*.

She would not cower.

Her own anger flared red hot, and she drew herself up as tall as she could. Thank God he'd shown himself. This was exactly why she didn't want a man in her life. She took a step forward, bringing them nearly nose to nose. "Leave, then." She spoke softly, but her words were like daggers, and she aimed them at his heart. "Get out." His eyes widened, and she half expected him to strike her. But he didn't. "You've got a week. Go back to town and drink yourself silly or—or—I don't care what you do. Just *get out of me house*."

Then, with the fire still coursing through her veins, she wheeled around and left him.

Michael watched her go. He bloody watched her go.

The door to her bedroom slammed shut.

The tea sat on the table, cold.

A fly buzzed around the bread.

Rain fell, loud on the roof.

His pulse pounded in his ears. His chest.

Scotland. Why did it have to be Scotland? Christ, he'd follow her damn near anywhere, but the one place she wanted him to go was the one place he could never be again. Not after what he'd done.

Goddamn! His fist moved of its own accord, colliding with the wall. Dark blood pooled on his knuckles. An angry gash gaped in the wall. But he felt no pain.

He slammed it again, harder, deepening the hole. The blood poured out of him, dripping to the floor. Still no pain.

He cried out in frustration. He *wanted* the pain. Deserved the pain.

He'd thought he could go on forever in this world of dreams, as if happiness was possible. It wasn't. Underneath it all, he was still Michael Dunn. An evil man. He'd imprisoned an innocent in the depths of hell. He'd wronged his only kin. He'd been selfish and ungrateful to the one man in this blasted country who'd been kind to him, and now . . . now he'd come at Caitlin. He'd shown her once and for all who he truly was.

And he'd lost her.

His eyes fell on the empty space of the doorway where she'd disappeared.

It was better this way. She'd thought him something he wasn't. That damn magpie. Building a nest. A life of peace and beauty. Simplicity.

Horseshit. That's what it was.

Gradually, his pulse slowed. His hand began to throb, and he slumped into a chair. He was tired. So damn tired.

Go back to town and drink yourself silly.

That's what she'd said, what she'd commanded.

His eyes wandered to the door of the pantry, to where the rum was kept. He hadn't touched the stuff in a year—more than that if you counted the months at Moreton Bay—but what good would sobriety do him now?

No good. No good at all.

He held his breath, listening. The house was silent as a tomb. Even the rain had stopped. Caitlin was hiding away in her room. She wouldn't dare come out, not after the beast had attacked her.

As if pulled by an invisible string, he strode to the pantry where the ceramic jug sat on its shelf, cast in shadow. He grasped it, bringing it into the light. It rested cool and welcome in his hand. He uncorked it with his teeth, and the vapors from the alcohol flooded his senses, awakening him from his dream.

Yes. This. This was the way out.

Then, without taking any more time to think, he brought the jug to his lips and took a long draught.

TWENTY-ONE

TRY AS HE MIGHT, Michael could never quite recall the following days. The memories were there, he was sure of it. But as soon as he turned his attention to them, they slipped away, out of focus, then disappeared.

The only thing he could remember with any detail was that first drink. The welcome burn of the rum down his throat. The comfort of it in his stomach. The way, as if by magic, it so quickly wore down all the sharp edges in his mind.

The immense sense of relief.

But after that, everything blurred. He was only able to piece events together from what others told him and the few fragments of memory he retained. He'd written himself a pass and signed it with Caitlin's name, then he'd taken his pipe and two jugs of rum and made his way to Sydney. He must have walked most of the way. He remembered crouching in the dark, hiding in a ditch, the rasp of his own breath overpowering Caitlin's and Hud's shouts of his name. Then there was a jostling wagon, straw sticking in his hair and prickling his skin. Hard boards under his arse. A man shouting angry words.

Somehow, he'd found his way to The Rocks and the familiar dank mustiness of a grog house, a relief after the blistering heat of the streets. The blurred cheer of a drunken man raising a toast. A smear of cheap perfume, mixed with the sour smell of unwashed men.

Hard-packed dirt against his cheek as he spun into the emptiness of sleep.

The broken memories could have made him think it was only one afternoon. But in fact, he wandered the streets of Sydney, drunk, for at least four days before Davey found him.

"How long do you think he'll sleep for?" *A voice.* A dream.

"Your guess is as good as mine. He could barely walk when they came in."

A sigh. A cool hand on his forehead.

"How did he even pay? All that drink, I wonder."

"Davey supposed he sold his clothes. He hadna any coat when he found him or boots or hat."

"He did take those things when he left."

Caitlin. That was Caitlin's voice.

The hand lifted from his head, and Michael wanted to reach out for it, bring it back, but he couldn't move. His body was missing, somehow. There were only his thoughts. And the sound of the two women talking.

"Thank you." Caitlin's voice again. Soft and dear. "I don't know what I'd have done without you."

"You can thank Davey, not me. I wouldna dared go where—where he found him." This voice was Scottish and seemed disapproving. But the woman's tone softened. "What—why would he do this, do you think? After a whole year without drink?"

There was a long pause. Or perhaps Michael had drifted in his sleep, away from the dream.

"I've lost Swindale." The sadness and fatigue was thick in Caitlin's voice. This was no dream.

"What?"

"They found an heir to me husband's estate. A man in England. He wants it—Swindale, I mean." The other woman must have given Caitlin a look because she quickly added, "There's no fighting it. He has Bathurst's backing. We saw proof."

"What's to become of you, then?" The second woman sounded like she still didn't believe it. "If you like, we could find a place. At least for a time . . ."

"I'm going to Scotland. There's a dower portion for me there. An estate." There was a pause. "I asked Michael to go with me, and—he said no. Then he left."

"I see." Emily Flemming. That's who it was.

Another long silence. They were looking at him, most probably. Shaking their heads in pity.

Finally, Mrs. Flemming spoke again. "Whereabouts in Scotland?"

"Somewhere in the North. I'm not sure exactly. With everything else . . . It's written down, but I never looked."

"Most of my friends are near Glasgow, but Lord Banton and his wife have their estate in the North, near Inverness. I've not ever met them, but I know his sister and her husband quite well. And Will—a good friend of mine and Davey's—is a good friend of his. I could write you a letter."

"That would be kind of you."

The Earl of bloody Banton.

A picture appeared in Michael's mind: Caitlin at Darnalay Castle, talking and laughing with Cameron. He'd just told her the story of his evil cousin who'd usurped his title and imprisoned Percy Sommerbell in a dungeon, and she was wide-eyed with shock, unbelieving that any man could be so cruel.

Michael wished he were dead. Why did they have to find him? Why couldn't they have just left him alone with his drink?

He must have made some kind of noise because the conversation stopped. There was a rustle of fabric, a movement of air, the cool palm settling again on his forehead. Then Caitlin's voice, anxious. "Michael? Are you awake?" And, more sternly, "Michael. Look at me."

Bah. He didn't want to open his eyes. Didn't want to see her ever again. Still, her voice, her touch . . . Perhaps he would look. Just one last time.

But it was more difficult than he'd imagined. His eyelids seemed fused. And when he finally did get some light in, it pierced him like a lance straight through the skull.

He shut his eyes again, tight. Everything spun, then stilled. What was he lying on? Not a bed, surely. It was too hard. A floor? A table? He swallowed. His throat was like dry tree bark, and his tongue stuck in his mouth heavy, sore, and bloated.

"Let's get you up, then." Caitlin's hand left his forehead, and her arms came around him from behind, propping him up against a pillow. "Drink this." Cold metal touched his lips. "'Tis only water." The liquid poured down his throat, sweet and pure.

She was kneeling over him. He must be on the ground. But where?

His eyes blinked open again. There was her face, concerned and tired, but he couldn't focus on it. He quickly shifted his gaze to the wall behind her, whitewashed and clean, with crates stacked against it and some bulging grain bags propped beside them. A string of onions hung from the ceiling.

He must be behind Davey's shop, in a storeroom.

"I'll fetch some food." The click of a door shutting told Michael that Mrs. Flemming had left the room.

Caitlin tipped the water cup to give him more—too much. He spluttered, and some of the liquid spilled down his chin. Impulsively, he raised a hand to wipe it away. His stubble felt thick and bristly. How many days had it been since he'd shaved?

Christ. He let his head fall back to the—no, it wasn't a pillow. It was too hard for that. A bag of flour, perhaps?

"Six days," Caitlin said, as if she'd heard his thoughts—though in reality she was scolding him, "six days since you left the farm." She set the cup down. "And what were you *thinking*?"

"I—" What *had* he been thinking? He couldn't remember. "H-how did you find me?"

"*I* didn't. Mr. Flemming did. I looked for you on the road, but you were nowhere. I didn't know what to do or where to go, so I came here, and he went out to look for you." With the last word, the anger in Caitlin's voice broke. She sank to a seated position beside him and took his hand, cradling it in hers. Michael allowed himself to look at her hands, so small against his, yet stronger. So much stronger. "I was so worried." The torment in her voice washed over him, and he wished more than anything that he could take it from her. He deserved that pain. Not Caitlin.

And so, though he dreaded what he might see—*because* he dreaded what he might see—he brought his gaze to rest on her face.

Her skin was pale, her eyes red-rimmed. They looked at him with an anguish that nearly cracked him in two.

No, he couldn't do this. His head dropped back, and his eyes fixed on the ceiling. If only he could have another drink. "I didn't mean to worry you." The words grated against his throat like a knife sawing through thick wood. "But you said I should—"

"I know what I said," she snapped. "And don't you think I've been regretting it every second of every day since?" She tightened her grasp on his hand. "I didn't mean it. Surely you knew I didn't mean it." Her voice shook. "Michael, I—If you don't want to go with me, that's what it is. I'll get by. Emily has friends there, and she—"

"I know. I heard."

Caitlin paused for a moment, and he could feel her looking at him before she continued. "But you can't live like this. You'll drink yourself to death, Michael. Tell me you won't, that you'll find employment or work for Mr. Flemming or *something*. Not this."

Michael stared hard at the ceiling. He couldn't tell her what she wanted to hear because the hard fact was that he *wanted* to drink himself to death. He wanted a bloody drink right now. More than anything in the world.

"Michael, please." She moved her face so it was in his line of sight. Unavoidable. Her cheeks were streaked with tears. "Promise me."

"I can't," he finally managed.

She blinked. "Can't what?"

"Promise. Go with you. I can't—" A sudden, unexpected tightness lodged in his throat. Michael hadn't cried since he was a child. He wasn't about to start now.

"And why can't you?" Her eyes narrowed. "What is it? What's happened to you? Is it what they did to you at Moreton Bay? You were so much better at Swindale. And you never touched a drop. I thought—"

"No." Michael closed his eyes again, blocking the sight of her. And from the blackness, the answer came.

If she knew his true evil, the depravity of who he really was, she would have no choice but to finally leave him to his fate. He'd tell her. Every last despicable act.

"I can't go to Scotland because of what I did there. Because of why I was transported."

"Oh." There was a long silence. "But how could forgery possibly be that—"

"It wasn't forgery." He snapped his eyes back open. "I lied. About that and about never being in Scotland. And a good many other things."

He could practically hear her mind whirring, trying to make sense of his words. "What was it, then? Was it horse thievery or murder or rape or—"

"No. None of those."

"Then what could possibly be so bad to—" Caitlin was cut off by the door swinging open.

"Here we are." Mrs. Flemming bustled in, holding a tray with a teapot, an empty cup, and a bowl filled with some kind of food. "Now, Michael, this is just plain oaten porridge. It'll be good for . . ." Her words trailed off as she took in the pair in front of her. Caitlin, sitting on the floor, her skirts pooled around her. The clasp of their hands. The look passing between them. "Is everything all right?"

Caitlin swallowed and twisted her head toward the other woman. "It is." Her mouth contorted into a false smile. "Just fine."

Mrs. Flemming raised her brows, clearly not believing it. She bent down and set the tray on a crate. Then she straightened back up and dusted her apron. "I've work to attend to." She spoke intently, as if the words held a deeper, invisible meaning. "If you don't mind, Mrs. Blackwell, I'll leave this to you."

"Of course. It's no trouble." Caitlin smiled again, this time more naturally. Clearly the other woman understood that they desired privacy. And she wasn't offended.

"I'll be in the kitchen if you need anything," Mrs. Flemming called over her shoulder as she left the room.

TWENTY-TWO

THE DOOR SNICKED SHUT behind Emily.

Caitlin waited, hoping Michael would speak. What could he possibly have done that was so terrible? But he just lay there, his gaze stubbornly fixed on the ceiling.

Well, if he didn't want to tell her, he didn't have to. She could hardly force it out of him.

Pursing her lips, she turned to the bowl of food Mrs. Flemming had left. Oaten porridge with a generous drizzle of honey—Caitlin's own honey, by the looks of it. Rich and dark, it would have been from last fall's harvest, made from the gum tree's blossoms.

The now familiar heartache drifted in, but at least this bit of the farm's bounty would be useful. It would nourish Michael now, when he most needed it.

She took up the bowl, spooned out a bite, and brought it to his mouth. He grimaced and shook his head, still without looking at her.

"You really should eat," she urged. He probably hadn't had a decent meal since he'd left the house six days ago.

His Adam's apple bobbed as he swallowed. "Not yet." He winced.

She set the bowl aside. "Tea then?"

He stared at the teapot for a moment. Then, as if in defeat, "All right."

She poured him a steaming cup, which he took with a sullen expression . . . and balanced on his chest without drinking. Again, his eyes closed.

Caitlin stared at him, not sure what to do or say. He looked awful, lying there on the hard floor, his head resting on a bag of sugar. He'd not shaved in days, and his beard was growing in, patchy and gray. Dark circles ringed his eyes, and the lines creasing their sides and the corners of his mouth appeared deeper than she remembered.

Then there was the smell: stale rum and days-old sweat.

Who knew what demons haunted this man? Far more of them and fiercer ones than she'd suspected, apparently.

Without thinking, she bent forward and kissed his forehead.

His eyes sprang open. The tea upset, spilling into the saucer and onto his shirt.

"Bah." He put the cup down, then turned to her, glaring.

She pulled back. "I'm sorry, are you burn—"

"I'm fine," he snapped. But as quickly as it had come, his anger drained away. His head dropped. "I'm sorry. I'm . . . I'm not a good man, Caitlin."

What was this about? She'd barely seen him angry in the whole year he'd been with her, but ever since she'd asked him to come with her, he'd been on the sharp edge of a deep rage. He seemed so . . . so *lost* . . . And the drink. Why? What was this monster that had him so firmly in its grip? And if he couldn't speak of it, even to her, what chance did he have of ever freeing himself?

Slowly, softly, she spoke, infusing each word with all the care she felt for him. "What did you do, Michael? Why were you sent here? Tell me."

He was quiet for a long time, his eyes trained on the ceiling. She didn't push. At long last, a pained relief flickered across his face. He lowered his head, closed his eyes, and began to speak in a low, droning tone, as if reading from a book. "I kidnapped an innocent man. I let him rot in a pit with no light, no air, no human company. For weeks." He drew a long breath. "And I usurped my uncle's title. I fought to keep it from my cousin, even when I knew full well it wasn't mine by right. I was cruel to him—my cousin I mean—and his sister. And I planned to—"

"Your uncle's title? He was—"

"The Earl of Banton. The one Mrs. Flemming told you of just now."

Caitlin felt her mouth drop open. "Your uncle is an *earl*?"

"Was," Michael continued in that even, hollow tone. "A Scottish one. He's dead now. It was my uncle's son I wronged, and his sister. And the man I kidnapped, Sommerbell. He was a friend of theirs." He took a long breath. "They only wanted what was right. And I did everything I could to stop them."

Caitlin's head spun as if she were the one who'd had too much grog. But Michael seemed to be done talking. Indeed, he appeared too weary to even lift his head. So, unsure of what else to do, she poured him another cup of now-tepid tea. "Drink this," she commanded.

As if he were a child resigned to his lot, Michael took the cup and drained it. Then, finally, he accepted a spoonful of porridge. She might have imagined it, but it seemed to bring some color back to his cheeks, a bit of life into his eyes. After he'd eaten half the bowl, she spoke again. "Now, what's this about your cousins?"

"My father's brother was the Earl of Banton." Michael set the porridge aside. "He was married to Lady Eleanor, a good friend to my parents in London."

He'd told her he came from London. At least that much was true.

"The earl, my uncle, was seldom in town. He spent his time at Darnalay, the family estate, a castle in the north of Scotland. He only ever came to London when it was absolutely necessary. And even then, he was always busy working. I barely knew him."

"Darnalay. That's the place Mrs. Flemming spoke of."

"Yes." Michael paused, staring at his hands, lost in thought. "Lady Eleanor, my aunt, she never had children, so I was the presumptive heir to the earldom. My father died when I was twenty, but my whole life before that—it was all he ever cared about. That I would inherit the title and restore honor to the family name. And Lady Eleanor wanted it too. Just before she passed, she told me I was the son she'd never had. She hated her husband, and to know that I would become the earl—" Michael stopped again. Swallowed. "It pleased her."

"She hated him? And your father did, too. Why?"

"Good reason." The bluntness in Michael's tone made it clear that he'd held no love for his uncle either. "He had a woman—a mistress who used to be a whore. He had two children by her and kept them at the castle. He spent all his time there, barely saw Eleanor, hardly acknowledged her as his wife. He never had time for Father or for me. It was humiliating."

"I see. He loved this woman, then. His mistress."

"He must have." Michael swallowed, his lips pursed, as if he'd eaten something foul. "When he died, and I inherited, I went to Darnalay to make improvements."

"*Improvements*?" Caitlin knew what that meant. It was the same in Scotland as it had been in Ireland, only worse. "Evictions, you mean?"

Michael nodded, a look of pure misery on his face.

She wanted to understand, truly. But a coldness crept through Caitlin's limbs, and she felt herself drawing away. She'd thought she'd known this man . . .

As if he'd heard her, he repeated, "I told you. I'm not a good man."

His words, so full of pain, brought her back. "Men change."

"Perhaps," he allowed, "but the story's not over yet."

She set her jaw. "Go on."

He brought a hand to his face and scrubbed his eyes, then pinched the bridge of his nose. "It's rather complicated. But what matters is, after I got to Darnalay, I discovered the existence of a letter written by my uncle and his mistress to their children. Lady Eleanor had just passed, and it seems before the dirt had settled on her grave, my uncle married the mistress in Edinburgh. On the way home to Darnalay, they were killed in an accident. He never had time to make things official, but the letter confirmed my uncle's intent that—" Michael broke off, that look of bitter distaste creasing his face once more. "That his son, *Cameron*, inherit the title."

Caitlin's head was spinning. "Your cousin. But he was a bastard by birth. Surely—"

"In Scotland it's permissible for parents to marry *after* the birth of their child. The claim was lawful."

"I see."

"But it seemed so ludicrous. That I would lose the title I'd been promised, that my father and Lady Eleanor had so wanted for me. To a *bastard*."

Caitlin's eyes widened at the force in his words. "Did you destroy this letter, then?"

"If I had, I'd still be the earl. The letter went missing. I extended my stay, searched all the servants' quarters, all the cottages. It had simply . . . disappeared. Then, one day, a man came to the castle. Percy Sommerbell. He was in love with my cousin Jane, and he had the letter—or at least he claimed he did. He demanded I give up the title, or he'd take it to court."

"And where were the cousins in all this?"

"Glasgow. I banished them before I even arrived at Darnalay. They never saw the letter or knew of its existence. Cameron was studying to be a doctor."

"Ah." Caitlin understood what he said, but it all seemed too fanciful to be real. A story from the storybooks. And Michael—Michael was the villain.

"So I put him in the dungeon," Michael continued. "Sommerbell, that is. It was a mad impulse, but I thought—I thought he'd concede quickly and give up the letter. It was so dark down there, and cold. No one could stand it for long. Or so I thought. He did, though. Two weeks he was down there. He nearly went mad. And the longer it lasted, the harder it was to think of freeing him. It was so *wrong*. I was petrified. Cameron came, looking for him, and I claimed I'd never seen him. He shook his head. "I lied. I just—I wanted it all to go away."

She rested a hand on his arm. "And how did it end?"

"Jane, Cameron's sister. I'd never met her before. I didn't know her, so she disguised herself as a servant and—" He hesitated, as if there was some part of the story he was leaving out. "And in the middle of the night, she slipped out of her room, found him, and set him free. They escaped."

"With the letter?"

Michael nodded.

"Did you give chase?"

He snorted. "They took all the horses in the stable. There was nothing I could do. The following day, I left and . . . I ran. I knew I was in the wrong, and after what I'd done to Sommerbell—if I was caught . . . I just . . . I didn't know what else to do. I went to London and tried to disappear. I thought I'd change my name, but they found me. I was tried, convicted, and sent here."

Somehow, a weight seemed to lift from Michael's countenance with the end of the story. He sat himself up a bit and watched her, gauging her reaction.

But Caitlin herself didn't know how she felt. It was so far from anything she'd imagined. He'd done wrong. Truly. The kidnapping and lies were only part of it. If she were honest, it was the evictions that pained her most. It was so close to what had happened to her own people. And Michael had been the landlord . . .

"Are you sorry?" was all she could think to say.

His eyes widened. "Sorry? That's not—of *course* I'm sorry. Looking back . . . I can't even believe I did it. That it was me. That man's face, in the dungeon, looking up at me, half crazed. It never leaves me." He squeezed his eyes tight and shook his head, as if trying to fling the memory away. "He would scream sometimes, about suffocating or being attacked by snakes. He must have seen things in the dark. It was terrible."

"Your nightmares." Of course. *That's* what they were about.

"Yes."

Caitlin steeled herself. "And the people, the tenants. You burned them out, I expect? For sheep?"

He looked at her, eyes shining and so, so sad. He knew what this meant to her. "I meant to, but it all happened before the evictions were scheduled. I'm glad of that now. I don't believe I could live with that on my conscience on top of everything else." He broke off, swallowed. "I—I thought it was the right thing to do. I was so sure." He blinked, then wiped his eyes. "And so bloody wrong."

Caitlin felt her breathing relax. The rest, she could forgive—or understand, at least. He'd been misguided, surely, by his father and aunt. He'd been cruel, yes, but he'd thought his actions were justified somehow. And he'd been too young and too scared to give himself up once he'd realized how deluded and wrong he was. There was no doubt he'd changed. He truly was a different person now than he had been, just as she was different from the night walker who'd nicked that handkerchief all those years ago. But if he'd—if he'd really been the one to burn out the farms of innocent families, even if he regretted it, and even if he'd changed . . . It would haunt her.

She squeezed his arm. "You were young."

His eyes blazed. "It doesn't matter. I'm a villain, Caitlin. They still tell stories of the evil cousin, Michael Dunn. The Flemmings know of me, though somehow they've never connected the tales with the man. My cousins hate me, and that poor devil that I—"

"But you've changed, and you've served your sentence. Surely that counts for something."

Michael let out a long, angry breath, once again refusing to look at her.

Caitlin shifted. It was uncomfortable sitting on the floor. Her back ached. She'd thought knowing would help somehow. But now that she did . . . it only made matters worse. She had to leave, and he'd—he'd *die* here. She knew it, better now than she had before. He'd kill himself with drink and guilt and misery. Mr. Flemming would try to help, but there was a limit to what one man could do for another. And Mr. Flemming had a family to look after.

If only Michael would agree to come with her. She could watch over him, keep him safe. Perhaps someday convince him to forgive himself.

She looked at him, still miserably staring at the ceiling. "I still don't understand why." She spoke slowly, watching his face to be sure she didn't anger him any more than she already had.

His eyes darted to her. "*Why*? I told you. Because I was a damn fool. I thought I was doing right, avenging my aunt and bringing honor to my family name, when in fact—"

"That's not what I meant," she interrupted, before he had the chance to spiral back into that pit. "I mean why you can't come with me to the dower estate." Michael pressed his lips together. "We needn't meet your cousins or their friends. Surely Scotland's a big enough place for us all without bumping into one another."

"No." His tone was as firm as she'd ever heard it. He was terrified, and now she understood why. But even still . . .

"Consider it. You could come as me secretary. Change your name if you like. Once we're there, you'd never even have to leave the estate." His eyes narrowed. "You could, of course," she added quickly. "I wouldn't hold you there. But it would be like when we were at the farm, before. Content. At least I was."

He shook his head, ignoring the pathetic plea in her voice. "But that was only temporary. A year. What would I even do as your secretary? You can read and write now. You've no need of me."

"Of course I've need of you." The words came out louder than she'd intended, but she wanted to shout them, to shake him until he saw sense. "I *like* you, Michael. I was planning to ask you to stay, you know. To stay with me at the farm."

His eyes widened. "Stay with you? After my sentence?"

"Of course. I—I was so content. 'Twas a good life we had." Her voice broke. "But the things I've done. The way I came at you. I don't deserve—"

"Rubbish. I know you, Michael Dunn. You are a good man. Certainly now, and even then . . . you didn't know any better. You loved your aunt. And you wanted to make your father proud. You'd never known any tenant farmers. They were strangers to you." She bit her lip, trying to think of anything more she could say. "And people change Michael. They learn from their mistakes. That's what matters."

His eyes shone in the dim room, like sunlight through cobalt glass. For a moment, Caitlin thought he would relent there and then, agree to go. But instead, he shook his head, broke her gaze, and looked away.

"Please. It would mean so much to me."

Silence.

"What have you got to lose? If it goes poorly, you could go *anywhere* and be a drunk in the gutter. Glasgow. Edinburgh. Manchester. Dublin. There's no end to cities that would welcome you. Why not try?"

His brow lowered, then raised again. "What if my cousin comes?" He spoke to the ceiling. "What if Mrs. Flemming writes to him and tells him of you, and he comes to call? He'd know me."

A smile pushed at Caitlin's lips. She was winning. "Well then, we'd hide you away, wouldn't we. They'd never know. *Please*." She pressed her hands together as if in prayer. "I would feel so much better with you there." For her own sake, but for his too. It would kill her to leave him here like this. To be an ocean away and not know what became of him. To always be fearing the worst.

She could see the muscles of Michael's jaw working. His mind was fighting the idea with everything it had.

But at last, his eyes slid back toward hers. She met his gaze on equal terms, and they looked at one other. Really looked. Through the eyes into the truth of what lay beyond. Then, unsmiling, he spoke. "Very well. If Davey can get me free in time, I'll come with you."

TWENTY-THREE

THE VOYAGE HOME WAS as different from Michael's passage to New South Wales as could be imagined.

Seven years earlier, he'd been confined belowdecks, shackled in irons and only allowed up for air every few days. He'd spent his hours in the dark, crammed up against a hundred other angry, miserable men, playing whist with Davey or lying in his hammock, staring at the low beams of the ceiling and feeling sorry for himself. The food had been meager and tasteless—weevil-infested bread and rotten meat. Stale ale. He'd felt wretched. And he'd been young. So young.

The return trip was far less crowded—with people, that was. Instead of soldiers and men in chains, the stores were packed full of bales of compressed sheep's wool.

And he was a free man. Michael and Caitlin ate their fill with the ship's officers in the gunroom, food that, while neither fresh nor tasteful, was at least sound. There was a daily ration of wine and spirits which Caitlin took gladly, though Michael knew better than to touch. He spent the days at her side, reading or playing chess; on deck when the weather was fine and belowdecks when it wasn't. Though technically, as a manservant accompanying a widow, he claimed a hammock slung between two beams in the forecastle, the captain was a practical and understanding fellow, and he looked the other way when Michael slipped into Caitlin's tiny cabin each night.

The nights were the best of it, rocking gently in the belly of the boat with Caitlin sleeping in his arms, the soft puff of her breath on his neck. He dreaded showing his face in Scotland, but that ordeal was a long way off. Here, in this in-between, he was content.

They sailed west into the sunset, past the Auklands and through the icy seas around Cape Horn. The sailors dreaded the passage around the Cape, predicting all kinds of terror, but besides the bitter cold, no harm came to them. Their only port of call was Perambuco in Brazil, where the captain gave Caitlin and Michael leave to go ashore. Though they were glad to get off the ship, the place turned out to be distasteful—hot and full of the same kind of drunken sailors that infested Sydney, and slave traders, too. After eating at a dirty pub full of rowdy men, Caitlin and Michael strolled the streets arm and arm. They came across a square where people were being put up for sale. Michael's urge was to keep going, not to look, but Caitlin seemed rooted to the spot, her eyes wide as she took in the horrible scene. They watched as a man of Michael's age was auctioned off, followed by a woman with a crying babe in her arms. It was only after they climbed down from the platform and were led away by their new masters that Michael noticed the tortured looks that passed between the adults. The way the child reached toward the man as his mother was dragged through the crowd.

"Sweet heaven. They're a family." Caitlin had drawn the same conclusion. She shuddered, then looked down, blinking away tears.

In a few hours, they were back on the ship.

They reached the equator not long after, and the weather slowly turned cooler. Liverpool was only a week away. Sea birds appeared in the sky, and finally, the call of land rent the air.

The sailors' moods turned joyful as they anticipated all the pleasures of shore while readying the ship for the dock. Caitlin stood at the rail, gazing at the approaching city with wide, expectant eyes, but as the tangle of ships' masts and brown stone warehouses of the Liverpool quay drew closer, all Michael could feel was a looming sense of foreboding.

He shouldn't have come. He didn't belong here.

Once ashore, Caitlin's excitement soon dimmed. She seemed lost in the bustle of the English port city, clinging to his sleeve, and Michael was glad to take on the responsibility of directing their route. Indeed, the distraction and the warmth that came from caring for her were the only two things standing between him and the dread that roiled more and more insistently in his gut. He found the bank Mr. James had directed them to, and she collected the rest of her allowance. Then, ignoring the raised brow of the ticket-seller, Michael booked them passage on a steamer to Port Glasgow. They stayed the night at an inn there—in separate rooms—then took a crowded stage to Edinburgh and finally, a clipper over the choppy North Sea to Inverness.

It was here, on the cold deck of that small ship, after the bustle of travel had subsided and he'd tucked Caitlin into her tiny berth for a much-needed rest, that Michael finally came face to face with the terror that had been stalking him ever since they'd left Sydney.

Her new estate was only a day's ride from Darnalay. He'd known that. He *had*.

So why the devil had he agreed to this? Why was he here?

He gripped the rail, staring into the vast expanse of frigid water. His stomach churned. His head pounded. The wind roared in his ears.

He'd come because she'd asked him to. Because she needed him.

He closed his eyes. Forced a breath.

She *needed* him.

The ship pitched, and he stumbled, losing his grip.

With each turn of the wheel, each snap of the sail, they were getting closer. Closer.

His vision blurred, and he heaved, retching into the sea.

They arrived in Inverness in the early afternoon of a chill, windy March day, spring here, though there was no sign of it. Michael had despised the heat of

New South Wales, but disembarking in this cold northern city, he found himself longing for the sun and the press of hot air.

It didn't help that he kept looking over his shoulder, expecting to see someone from Darnalay staring back at him. It was foolish, really. He'd barely known anyone there, and even those who *had* known him would hardly recognize the man he'd become. Still, he couldn't shake the feeling of being exposed. At risk.

Caitlin shivered and pulled her thin cloak tighter around her. "I suppose we'll need warmer clothes," she murmured.

So they spent the afternoon shopping, spending out of the purse she'd been given at the bank in Liverpool. A greatcoat for Michael and a hat; a woolen cloak and muff for Caitlin, along with a pair of sturdy half boots; stockings and warm gloves for them both.

The shopkeep at the haberdashery studied them curiously, and as they were settling up, he casually asked where they were from.

Michael hesitated. It was a shameful thing to come from New South Wales.

But Caitlin answered straight away. "We've just arrived from Australia, and we're bound for an estate near Croachafearn."

The man's eyes widened at the mention of Australia. Then they narrowed. He knew they were convicts. Michael braced himself for the insult.

But it didn't come.

"Croachafearn you say? In the Monadhliath Hills? Is it Glenoch House, by chance?"

Caitlin nodded. "You know of it?"

"I've a niece works there, in the kitchens." He turned away and continued packing their things, then looked up. "If you don't mind me askin', what will you do there?"

"I—I'm a widow." Caitlin stumbled a bit on her words. "The estate belonged to me husband, and it's been granted to me as a dower."

"Ah." The man's eyes slid to Michael.

"Mr. Dunn is me secretary," Caitlin quickly added, her cheeks turning pink.

If the shopkeep suspected anything, he didn't let on. He only nodded and returned to his work.

Caitlin glanced at Michael, her lips pursed, then she turned her gaze back to the man in front of them. "What do you know of Glenoch House?"

He looked up. "'Tis . . ." He hesitated. "Remote. 'Twas meant for a huntin' lodge, I believe." He shrugged. "I dinna ken. Some fool bought it in recent years, thinkin' to use the land for sheep, but—" He broke off, his eyes widening as he realized what he'd just said about Caitlin's husband. "I mean no offense, ma'am. I'm—"

"It's quite all right." A smile tugged at Caitlin's lips. "You said your niece works there. Are there many servants?"

He shook his head, clearly relieved. "Na." He shrugged. "No one to serve, really. Or—not 'til now, I s'pose."

"I see. And the land?"

"Sir!" Another customer was peering at something on the counter.

"Just a minute now!" the shopkeep barked at the man. Then he looked back to Michael and Caitlin and pushed their package across the counter into Michael's waiting hands. "Good luck to ye. I'm sure you'll be happy at Glenoch. 'Tis a grand house." He smiled politely and strode toward the next customer.

They stepped out into the cold and began walking.

"What do you suppose he meant by *remote*?" Caitlin asked.

Michael tried to sound reassuring, though he felt anything but. "Everywhere here is remote. I'm sure it'll be fine."

Once again, they slept in separate rooms at the inn for the sake of propriety. If it were just her, Caitlin wouldn't have cared a fig for what anyone thought, but Michael kept reminding her that it would do no good for word of her immorality to get back to Mr. James Sr. and his employer.

He'd been like that of late—wary and critical. She'd wanted to argue. Of course she'd lose her dower if she were to marry again, but a widow wasn't at any risk from an affair. What did it matter if Mr. James thought her a lightskirt?

But she'd thought better of it. Just being here was difficult enough for Michael, and provoking him further would do neither of them any good. Things would improve when they arrived at the estate and had some privacy.

Or so she hoped.

Weary beyond belief, Caitlin crawled beneath the cold sheets, but try as she might, sleep wouldn't come. Her thoughts were pulled to that shopkeep—the surprised look on his face when he'd realized where they were going.

What was the estate like? Why had John's brother been a fool to buy it? And what did he mean by remote?

She wracked her mind to remember what Mr. James had said about Glenoch. Not very much. Only that it was a large estate that had recently been acquired by the family. The terms of the dower stated that there was a staff in place, to be paid for out of the allowance she'd been given, but it hadn't specified how many servants, or how big the house was. Certainly nothing about the grounds.

If John's brother had bought it for sheep, surely there must be pasture enough for cows to graze?

Another thought flashed through her mind, bringing with it an unexpected sting. If it had been bought for sheep, did that mean the tenants had been burned out like in so many other places? If that was the case, had John's brother done it, or had the evictions been carried out before he'd owned it? Were there tenants there, still?

Melia murder. These questions had no answers, and she'd find out tomorrow anyway. But even still, it was long past midnight when she finally drifted off.

It seemed only a minute later that Michael was knocking on her door. She glanced at the window. Surely it was still night . . . but true enough, the dull glow of dawn lit up the sky.

After a quick bite in the bar room, Caitlin waited as Michael loaded their battered trunk and the parcels from yesterday's shopping into the dog cart he'd arranged for their transport. The boy driving it, the innkeeper's son, sat on the perch and watched as Michael hoisted himself up, then turned to give her his hand. She gripped him tight, climbed in, and they settled themselves on the trunk. The lad clucked to the nag, and they were off.

They drove south along a winding river. Michael didn't seem to want to talk. He was lost in his own brooding thoughts, and Caitlin wondered suddenly just how close they were to Darnalay. She turned to him to ask, but something about the way he gazed into the distance, that haunted, vacant look . . . the tight set of his jaw . . . She thought better of it.

In the silence, she allowed her attention to be drawn to the passing countryside. The weather was fine, and the fields that lined the glen were newly plowed with rich brown soil. Though she couldn't tell what crops would be planted, it was clearly good farmland. Sheep and cattle dotted the lush pastures that covered the vast slopes rising up from the valley. There were farmers out plowing or planting, and she caught sight of a few thatched cottages tucked into the hillside, all with fenced gardens and laundry flapping in the wind. Children played in the yards. It wasn't Ireland—it was grander somehow, the sky wider, the hills taller—but it was beautiful. She could live here.

Then they left the fields behind and entered a landscape that was the same, yet different. A huge herd of sheep, hundreds or thousands of them, spread across the valley, hungrily devouring the rich grass. A house came into view. No, not a house, the shell of one. Blackened stone and gaping roof. Caitlin's heart hurt at the sight.

They passed by several such houses. Just after midday, the clouds thickened into a cold, spitting drizzle the likes of which Caitlin hadn't known since she was a girl. The cart track diverted from the river they'd been following and led up out of the glen into what must be the Monadhliath Hills the shopkeep had spoken of. The ground turned rocky, covered only by a sparse stubble of heather. The slopes that rose above them were now steep, barren, and craggy. She could see snow speckling the mountains in the distance. There were no fields here, no grass, no livestock, no cottages even. No sign of life at all.

Remote. Was this what the man had meant? Surely, no one would build a grand house up here? As if to emphasize the point, a gust of wind cut right through her and blew the biting rain into her eyes. She shivered, pulling her cloak closer, but it did no good. She was already wet through and chilled to the bone.

Michael put his arm around her, and they huddled together in the back of the cart. His warmth offered some small comfort, though it didn't stop the ominous worry. Caitlin's eyes searched ahead for some kind of change. Surely they'd descend into another green glen. Nothing would grow here. Cows wouldn't find enough to eat. Perhaps sheep or goats, but even they would be hungry.

Just before nightfall, a weathered stone facade swam into view, isolated and alone in the barren landscape.

That couldn't be the place. It couldn't. Caitlin turned to Michael. "You don't think—"

"This here's the place," the boy called over his shoulder.

Caitlin's heart sank. It was a grand house, that was true. Two stories tall, it was a rambling affair made of dingy brown stone with a roof tiled in dark slate. Caitlin counted ten chimneys. If it had been built as a hunting lodge, the hunter in question must have been a wealthy one.

The front entrance protruded like the snout of a dog, with white columns on both sides like its bared teeth. A lantern hung over the door, unlit. All the windows were dark.

The cart came to a stop, and the lad looked back at them expectantly. The rain pelted them harder, and a drop slid from Caitlin's hair down her forehead, dripped from her nose. She wiped it away.

Michael's hand slipped into hers. He squeezed, and her heart warmed just a bit. Brooding or not, she was glad he was here.

She swallowed. "I suppose we should knock."

TWENTY-FOUR

CAITLIN, MICHAEL, AND THEIR driver huddled under the covered entry, the soggy trunk at their feet. Michael pounded on the door, but the hollow banging was swallowed up by the wind. He pounded again. No one came.

Caitlin was just about to suggest they go around to the back when, finally, the door swung open, creaking slightly on its hinges.

"Who is it?" An old man peered out. He was almost bald, with just a few wisps of white hair curling behind his ears. His face, illuminated by the candle he held, was mottled with age.

"Mrs. Caitlin Blackwell, the widow of John Blackwell." Michael spoke with authority, no longer the glowering, distracted man she'd sat next to in the wagon, but the tall, confident servant. "She's come to claim her dower."

The old man's brows raised. "Mrs. Blackwell, eh?" He peered past Michael, raising the candle for more light. "We've been expecting her. Where is she?"

"I'm here." Caitlin stepped into the circle of light. She held her head high but was suddenly conscious of her soggy, unkempt appearance. She hardly looked the part of the well-off widow.

"Stand aside, sir." Michel sounded impatient. "It's been a long day. Mrs. Blackwell is wet and chilled."

"O' course, o' course." The old man stepped back to allow them into the dark entrance hall, turning to light a candelabra that stood on an otherwise empty sideboard. The candles flickered to life, and she could see him more clearly. A stocky build with broad shoulders and a noticeable paunch, he was dressed plainly all in black, with a stiff stock around his neck, slightly askew. A strip of bristly whiskers adorned his chin where he must have missed shaving.

"We'll require hot food and a fire," Michael commanded. "You have a room made up, I assume?" He raised a brow.

"Aye. Of course." The old man sounded almost affronted. "Just need to light the fire, is all. I'll get Jinny to see to it." He shuffled back a step.

Michael didn't let up. He nodded toward their young driver, who was staring at him in awe. "Mr. McCinnis and his horse will need accommodations for the night. He's back to Inverness tomorrow."

The old man nodded to the boy. "And you, sir?" He looked inquiringly at Michael.

Michael hesitated, and Caitlin took the opportunity to speak. She was, after all, the new mistress of this house. "Mr. Dunn is me secretary." She did her best to mimic Michael's decisive tone. "We work closely together. He'll require a chamber near mine."

Both Michael's and the old man's eyes widened and slid to her, and Caitlin got the distinct impression that she'd said something out of turn. But she'd not suggested they would *share* a room. And the house was so big . . . Surely it was acceptable to be near her servant?

Michael glared. Clearly, he wanted to contradict her command, but she glared back, telling him without words that he should not.

"Very well, then." The old man opened a door just past the entry and motioned them through. "Come along into the sitting room. I'll build a fire, then fetch Jinny."

As it turned out, there were only three servants in the vast house: the housekeeper, Mrs. Buchanan, a middle-aged woman who also served as the cook; Jinny, a quiet, sallow-faced girl who was the niece to the shopkeep in Inverness and saw to the cleaning, the dishes, the laundry, and any other tasks Mrs. Buchanan found for her; and Forbes, the steward, who—as far as Caitlin could tell—didn't do anything at all besides avoid Mrs. Buchanan, nap by the fire, and eat the food served to him.

It wasn't his fault. He was as old as the hills. He'd been a cooper at the docks in Inverness, but he'd grown too feeble for that occupation and taken the position of steward for almost no pay. Of all of them, he was the one Caitlin liked most.

And of course there was Michael, but with each passing day, he seemed to sink into a deeper depression. His rare smiles dried up, and nothing she could say—no jest nor kind word—seemed enough to bring them back. He disappeared for hours on end, brooding, and when they spent time together, he snapped at her for no reason, making a show of his disapproval of everything she did. As if he expected her to be someone different now that she was a widow in a dower house.

As if *he* was someone different.

The days, then the weeks dragged on. There was nothing to read in the house, so Caitlin took to spending her mornings outdoors exploring the moor and her afternoons in the kitchen, talking to Forbes and listening to stories from the old man's youth. Not that she was avoiding Michael, not really, but he seemed to prefer to be by himself, and life was dreary enough. She had to cling to any bits of cheer she could find. There was no point in seeking him out if he would only make things worse. Some days she barely saw him, but he did often come to her at night in the cold, draughty room she slept in. She never sent him away—but it wasn't like at Swindale. Their couplings were stiff and pleasureless, and she got no satisfaction from them. Most times, she was left feeling more alone than before they'd shagged. And he always left afterward, afraid that the servants might find them.

Each morning, Caitlin walked farther and farther from the house, hoping to discover that her impression of the land had been wrong. Perhaps she'd find a meadow where grass grew, allowing her to keep a cow or two. But it was no use. There was almost no soil here, nor vegetation. Just a thin layer of life clinging to stone, fighting for survival against the constant bitter wind. Bees could live here, she supposed, but only just. There wouldn't be honey enough to share.

Forbes confirmed her assessment one afternoon over a cup of tea as they sat in the kitchen by the hearth. The gentleman who'd built the house was a laird from an old Highland family, a shifty sort, according to the steward. He'd inherited a vast estate—these square miles in the hills plus an adjoining glen to the southwest. He'd cleared the fertile lands of tenants and given it over to the shepherds, then built this house in the hills as a hunting retreat for himself and his friends, though he visited it only once a year, sometimes less often. Forbes wasn't clear on the details, but he suspected the original owner had come down on his luck and talked Mr. Blackwell—who knew nothing of pasture or sheep—into buying the house and the surrounding land with the idea that he'd be able to use it for wool production.

"Thought he'd make himself a fine feather, he did." Forbes shook his head, chuckling at John's brother's foolishness. "Musta been hot as a red spindle to learn the truth o' it."

"Did he ever come here?" Caitlin asked.

"Na. His man did, once. Didna stay long." Forbes set his cup down and stretched out his legs.

Caitlin stared into the fire. It all made sense now. This land was useless. The perfect place to put an unwanted Irish widow.

But she was stuck, wasn't she? If she left, she'd forfeit her allowance. And there were even fewer options for employment here than there had been in the colony.

The wind howled around the house as her thoughts wandered to those pretty little farms they'd passed on the way from Inverness. They were so very near to this forbidding place, and yet so far away . . .

"On the way here, we passed through some fertile farmland with cottages and fields," she began.

Forbes started. "Eh?"

He must have fallen asleep.

"Farmland," she repeated, more slowly. "On the road from Inverness. There were cottages and fields. It looked as though there were tenants still farming. Do you know the place?"

"On the river there you mean? Before the burnt-out houses?"

"That's right."

The steward nodded, and a far-away smile creased his face. "Aye. I know it."

"Who owns it?"

The old man raised his brows meaningfully. "The farmers do, or most of it. It's their own."

Caitlin wasn't sure she'd heard right. "Their own? What do you mean? Surely, some laird owns it?"

"Nay, lass. It was Banton land before, but the new laird up at Darnalay got the notion to sell the tenants their farms, God bless 'im."

Banton. Darnalay. Caitlin's scalp tightened. "You mean . . . The *Earl* of Banton?" Could they really be so close to Michael's cousin's land? Michael hadn't said a word.

But then, she hadn't asked, had she?

"The very same. He has the castle still, o' course, and a few leases from folks who wanted them. But most of it has gone over to the farmers. Hasna made any of the other lairds too happy, that's the truth of it." The old man grinned at her.

"That's—extraordinary." Caitlin still couldn't quite believe it. It had seemed a paradise, the people happy, the land productive. And it had been Michael's cousin's doing. If only she could have ended up with land like that . . .

She gazed at Forbes, intending to ask more questions, but the steward's head had tipped back, his eyes closed.

Caitlin watched the fire for a long while as the old man snored.

At the end of May, Jinny returned from her day off in Inverness with a letter, the first Caitlin had received since coming to Scotland. It was addressed to Caitlin in Emily Flemming's hand.

Heart racing, Caitlin dashed off to look for Michael. Of course he would want to read it, too. Perhaps it would cheer him.

She'd assumed he was in his chamber, but it stood empty, as did hers. She raced back downstairs. No one was in the sitting room, nor had been recently—the hearth was cold. She stepped back out into the entry hall. Could he have gone for a walk? It didn't seem like him, but it *was* a clear day . . . She strode into the dining room, scanning the moor outside the window. The bleak landscape was as empty as always.

Thunk.

Caitlin froze, listening. That noise—it had come from the small closet that adjoined the room. The serving room, Michael had called the tiny space—a place intended to store dishes and bottles of wine, things that might be needed in the dining room.

She crossed to the paneled door, then pressed her ear to it and listened. A soft, rustling sound drifted through the wood.

A mouse? Had it knocked something over?

She pulled the door open and peered inside.

Other than the creak of the door, all lay quiet and still before her. There were no windows in the cramped space, and only a tiny bit of light filtered through from the dining room. She squinted, assessing the shelves that rose to the ceiling. Everything seemed in order. Her eyes traveled down and scanned the floorboards for anything that might have fallen . . . There. Were those . . . *shoes*?

Heart hammering, she stepped into the room, craning her neck in the darkness as her gaze traveled up a pair of legs and finally landed on—

Sweet Jesus, it was Michael.

His bleak, miserable face stared back at her. He was sitting on the floor in the far corner, pressed up against the wall, his knees drawn to his chin. The shadows wrapped so thick around him he might have been one himself.

"Michael?" She stepped closer. "What are you—" Then she spied the bottle in his hand and the clouded torment in his eyes. Her exhale stuck in her ribs, a shard of sudden, sharp anger. Was this what he'd been doing all those hours she wasn't with him? "*Michael!*" She glared down, hands on her hips, lips pressed together so tight they hurt.

He didn't meet her eye. "I'm sorry," he slurred. "It was just a little, I—"

"How *could* you?"

He didn't answer. He just stared at her skirts with hollow, weary eyes.

Caitlin clenched her jaw and forced a long breath. Her shoulders fell. It would do no good to scold. She should have guessed he'd try to escape in this way, but she'd been too absorbed in avoiding her own misery to think of it.

She sank down beside him, her anger slowly diluted by an empty kind of guilt. As gently as she could, she took the bottle from him and set it aside, thankful for the dark. At least he wouldn't see her hands shaking.

They could not live like this. They couldn't. She must think of a distraction for them both, keep a closer eye on him. Or else . . . Or else she'd lose him for good.

She held up the paper she'd brought, swallowing back the tears. "We've got a letter."

TWENTY-FIVE

MICHAEL WOULDN'T HAVE BELIEVED that things could get any worse, but after Caitlin found him drinking whisky in the serving room, they did.

Life at Glenoch House had proved interminable. Endless hours of nothing. But that wasn't the problem, not really. He'd spent most of his childhood bored stiff in a great, empty house. No, it was the constant gnawing dread that had become unbearable. The unease trimmed with panic that ate away at him, the knowledge of just how bloody close he was to Darnalay. And if that hadn't been enough, now Mrs. Flemming's letter had cheerfully informed them that she'd written the Earl of Banton to tell him of his new neighbor. It was only a matter of time until Cameron came to call.

Michael couldn't shake the agitation, couldn't even find the will to try. Instead he jumped at shadows and snapped at Caitlin for no reason. The nightmares were worse than they'd ever been, so bad that he'd started making excuses to leave Caitlin's bed after their brief and dispassionate encounters. She clearly got no pleasure from them anyway, and Michael found himself wondering more and more what the devil he was doing here. Why would she even want him to stay?

But then again, perhaps it *had been* the boredom that had driven him to drink. Perhaps if he'd had something to *do*, something to distract himself with, he might have been able to forget.

Caitlin had found distraction—in routine, in her walks, in her long conversations with the old steward. But Michael couldn't bring himself to care about either. He'd developed a routine of his own. A game: hide yourself away and drink just enough to quell the dread, but not enough for her to notice.

And it had worked.

Until she'd found him in that damn serving room.

After that, she scoured the house for spirits and made Jinny dump them all out. She wouldn't leave him alone for more than ten minutes, and she was constantly thinking of things for them to do: go for a walk, visit the village, learn to play whist, read from the poetry books she ordered from Inverness. She even half-heartedly suggested they go to the nearby kirk on Sundays—though on that he put his foot down, and she didn't argue. It would have been a disaster. She'd been born a Catholic, he was Church of England, and neither of them had darkened a church door in years.

And so it was with some feeling of freedom that Michael set off alone over the moor on a sunny Monday morning in early June. Caitlin had turned her ankle on their walk the day before, but the weekly mail collection from the small village of Croachafearn would happen on Tuesday, and she wanted to be sure her reply to Mrs. Flemming's letter went out. She'd entrusted Michael with the task reluctantly, admonishing him to deliver the missive and come right home.

As if he were a child.

The two-hour walk passed more pleasantly than he'd imagined. Something about the wild landscape and the exercise seemed to quiet his mind. Spring had turned to summer, and the heather was blooming on the rocky slopes, bringing some warmth and beauty to the craggy, inhospitable hills. Croachafearn was a tiny little hamlet, just a few buildings teetering on the bank of a wide, rushing river. Part of the walk brought him along that torrent and through a forest of scrubby pines. Colorful wildflowers dotted the slopes above, and moss covered the path.

There had been a time when he'd detested the remoteness of the Highlands, but now he found it almost comforting.

If only Darnalay were not so near.

He delivered the letter to the shop where it would be collected on the morrow. As he'd expected, the old woman behind the counter sent him a scornful look. It seemed either Mrs. Buchanan or the girl, Jinny, had spread rumors about his and Caitlin's sleeping arrangements. Either that, or the woman didn't approve of them missing kirk. Michael glowered back at her, daring her to say something. She didn't.

Then he turned back up the road toward Glenoch.

He entered the house the way he'd left—through the front door—and began peeling off his gloves.

A woman's voice he didn't recognize drifted out of the sitting room. "Mrs. Flemming's letter . . . only a half day's ride . . . beautiful country . . ."

He stilled his breath, which was loud from exertion.

"I've brought some fresh scones for ye. Mayhap ye have yer own cook here, but just in case." Another woman's voice, this one a thick brogue. "I can send somethin' for that ankle too. A comfrey salve. I'll have one of the lads bring it up for ye."

"Thank you. That's very kind." Caitlin's voice, polite, yet strained.

Michael crept closer to the half-open door. His lungs felt tight, urging him to draw more air, but he daren't be too loud.

Caitlin continued, "Me steward tells me that your husband has sold land to his tenants. Their farms, I mean. That's very good of him. We passed through the glen on our way. 'Twas beautiful."

A prickling started at the base of Michael's neck, and his head felt light. What was she talking about? Whose husband? What glen? She'd never spoken to him of this.

"They're no longer his tenants," the first woman said, her tone surprisingly stern. He couldn't place her accent. Neither Scottish nor English . . . nor American either. "They're landholders in their own right." There was a pause, and Michael imagined them all uncomfortably sipping their tea. "Are you a farmer, Mrs. Blackwell?"

"I was," Caitlin answered wistfully. "I was born on a farm in County Cork, a dairy, but we—left when I was a girl."

"Evicted?" the other woman asked softly.

"Just so. Enclosing the common lands wasn't enough. The landlord wanted all the pastures for himself. Then . . . in New South Wales I had a farm. For twenty years."

There was another pause. Michael drew in a breath. Slow. Controlled. Silent.

"You should come to Darnalay." The exhale caught in his throat, and he nearly choked. It was the woman with the odd accent who'd spoken, and forcefully, as if it were a command. "That's why we've come, to invite you. The whole family is there. My husband Cameron and I, his sister Jane and her family, and a few others. You could meet Will—Mr. Flemming's friend from Glasgow. I'm sure you've heard of him."

Michael's pulse was pounding so hard it was a wonder they didn't hear it through the walls.

This was Cameron's wife?

"I have." Caitlin's tone was tight.

He had to go. Hide. But he'd have to pass by the half-open door to get further into the house—

"Anyway, I do hope you'll call at the castle." Lady Banton again. "We are neighbors, after all."

He could run past. Hope they didn't see—

"I . . . I'm afraid I can not. Me ankle, you see . . ."

Or go back out the front door and around. Yes, that was it.

"Well, if you change your mind, you're always welcome. We'll be there through the end of the month. Oh no, don't get up. We'll see ourselves out."

It was too late. The visitors had risen and started toward the door. There was no time. They'd see him.

They didn't know him, though. Did they?

Without stopping to think, he clasped his shaking hands behind his back and acted as if he'd just arrived at the door. "Mrs. Blackwell"—he raised his voice, willing it to the smooth deference of a servant—"I've delivered the letter—*oh*." He feigned surprise as the visitors came into view. "I apologize. I didn't know you had guests."

The countess was slim and pretty, with dark hair and tanned skin. She was dressed modestly for her station, and there was a sternness to her look, as if she'd examined the world and found it to be wanting. Indeed, she examined him now and most certainly found him wanting. Michael's heart raced as her dark eyes bored into him. His ears grew hot. It made no sense, but he was sure as anything that this woman could see right through him. She knew—

"Michael." Caitlin's strained voice came from inside the room. "This is the Countess of Banton. And Mrs. Brodie, the cook from Darnalay Castle."

The cook? All thoughts of the countess flew from his mind. Was it the same—? His gaze darted to the older woman, who was tying on a bonnet. The dark hair, the creased face.

Shit.

"Ladies," Caitlin continued, "this is—" She stopped, clearly thinking better of using Michael's name. "Me secretary."

The old woman's eyes settled on Michael for a moment. She nodded politely, then looked away.

The rush of relief nearly knocked him over. She hadn't recognized him.

Not daring to breathe, he turned away from Mrs. Brodie and bowed stiffly to the countess. "An honor, my lady," he choked out. Then he stepped aside, praying they would leave.

Not giving him a second glance, the countess strode past him. The cook followed.

The door closed behind them, and Michael slumped against the wall, closing his eyes and gasping for breath.

It shouldn't be a surprise that the cook hadn't placed him. They'd known each other years ago, and Lord knew Michael had changed since then. He wouldn't have known *her* if he hadn't learned who she was, but now he remembered only too clearly. That day in the library at Darnalay. The older woman and a younger one, the girl she'd introduced as her niece Janie—in truth, his cousin Jane come to rescue Sommerbell. The girl with the dark blue eyes, staring right through him . . . He pressed a hand to his face, trying to force the scene from his mind, trying to forget what had come after, but it wouldn't go . . .

"Michael." Caitlin's hand brushed his cheek. She must have hobbled over to him. "They're gone. It's all right." He opened his eyes just as she rested her palm on his cheek. "You needn't worry. I won't go there." She lifted her chin. "I don't even want to."

She'd schooled her voice to sound sure, but he could see in her eyes that she very much wanted to go. And why wouldn't she? Those people could be friends to her. Something to break up the monotony of her days.

If he were a good man, he'd tell her to go. Or better still, he'd leave this place and allow her to build a life of her own, free of the burden of him. And yet . . . the feel of her hand on his cheek . . . He leaned into it as a painful lump formed in his throat. He *wasn't* a good man. Or a strong one.

"There now," she murmured. Then she shifted toward him, only to draw back quickly, stumbling and yelping with pain.

Damn it. Her ankle. How had he forgotten?

Still unable to speak, and perhaps with more force than was necessary, he scooped her up and carried her back into the sitting room.

TWENTY-SIX

THEY SPENT THE REST of the afternoon in silence, Michael sitting in the armchair by the window, staring blankly at the moor; Caitlin trying to read one of the books she'd got from Inverness, a novel. She gave up when she'd read the same passage five times over and couldn't for the life of her remember anything about it. Her thoughts were elsewhere.

Clearly, this arrangement was not working. Michael was miserable, and there was nothing she could do to make it better. Indeed, the events of this afternoon proved it could only get worse. He didn't believe her when she said she didn't want to go to Darnalay, and why should he? It was a lie. A visit to a castle, meeting new people—*friends* . . . Oh, it sounded lovely. But it was also true that she'd give a hundred such visits for one day with Michael as he used to be. The caring lover. The understanding friend. The man she'd fallen in love with.

For it was love, what she'd felt for him. She couldn't deny it.

She blinked, and the words on the page blurred as she realized what her own thoughts had just betrayed.

Felt. In the past.

The Michael she'd loved was gone, wasn't he? He'd vanished the moment they set foot on Scottish soil. And now it was simply a matter of time before he would leave in body as he already had in spirit. He would find some dark hole to climb into and booze his life away, and she'd be alone in this vast, empty house on this vast, empty moor. Such a bleak existence . . . The more she tried to imagine it, the less real it seemed. It wasn't her. She couldn't do it. Could not live the rest of her life like that. She'd go cracked, she would.

She'd thought she'd find pieces of her dream here, that it would be enough. But she'd been wrong.

Her dream. It had been ages since she'd allowed herself to think of it, to picture it . . . but now that she did, even *that* seemed empty. A farm, independence, wealth of her own. It would be better than *this*, surely, but it didn't shine in her imagination as it once had. Something was missing.

Her eyes fell on Michael who sat so forlornly at the window, the sunlight reflecting off his skin, lighting up his hair like spun gold.

It was *him*. Michael. Michael was missing.

Her stomach clenched as she watched him. But it was the Michael of the past she wanted, not this stranger before her. And she'd tried everything she could think of to help him. *Everything*. Why couldn't he just move on? He'd served his sentence, done his time. Surely he deserved to live. What more could she do or say to convince him?

He must have sensed her looking, for he turned and met her gaze. His blue eyes, sharp and angry, pierced through her like needles through cloth. She shook her head and returned to her book, once more blinking away tears.

Nothing she could say would convince him to let go of the past. He was too jaded, too lost in his own misery.

Her heart ached at the thought of losing him, yet in the cut of that pain lay a truth she must face. She might well have lost him already. And that was *his* choice, not hers.

Now the only question was if she would lose herself as well.

Caitlin wasn't at all sure he would come to her bed that night, but he did. Just after she'd slid beneath the blankets, Michael padded in on bare feet, then climbed in beside her. He kept a distance between them, lying on his side, facing away from her. Not touching.

But he'd come. Somewhere deep down, under that thick shell of his, he must still want to be close.

Caitlin stared at the shadows on the ceiling and took several long breaths, summoning all her resolve.

"I can't stay here." Her words hung like cold fog in the air above them. She waited for him to respond, but he didn't. "I must get away. I thought perhaps America . . . somewhere where I can make a new start." Michael rolled over and stared at her with hard, cynical eyes. "It wouldn't be easy, but there's folks that have less than us. And—'twould be better than *this*."

He was silent for a long, terrible moment. "*Us?*"

Such a caustic look he had. Caitlin gritted her teeth, then forced the words out. She must try. Even if it did no good. She must try, one last time. "I do hope you'll come with me. I can't force you to, though I do so want you to—" She swallowed, inhaled. "But even if you don't, *I* will go. I can't live like this Michael. *We* can't live like this."

"You'd lose your allowance. You'd have nothing."

"I know that. But it isn't *me* money anyway. Or me house. I hate it here. I'll take on wage work if need be. Save enough to buy a bit of land. I could do it alone, but . . . we could do it together."

Something seemed to soften in him, and he stared at her for a few long breaths. Then his expression hardened again. "Go, then. I can take care of myself."

Caitlin's jaw clenched. "Is that really what you want?"

"What does it matter what I want?" He was still looking at her, but he no longer saw her. He was retreating into that shell. She was losing him.

"It matters a great deal." She reached out to touch him, to bring him back to her, but he rolled away, and she was once more staring at his back.

She couldn't let him go. Not like this. Not without making him hear the truth first.

"I love you, Michael."

They were the most difficult words she'd ever spoken. Words that peeled off all the layers she'd built up, words that exposed her, raw and naked and needy. Words that carried the admittance of the end of the dream she'd once had and the beginning of a new one—or the rebirth of a very old one. It was the dream she'd allowed herself as a girl. The silly, starry-eyed dream of a peaceful, simple life with the man she loved.

The dream of her heart that might very well never come true.

"All I want in this world is you and a farm and a life like—like we had . . . I'll do it alone if I have to, but I don't *want* to. I don't. I want you there. To grow old with you to be—to *be* together." She reached for him again, and her hand landed in his hair, his fine, yellow hair. "But I can't decide for you. And I can't always be there, watchin' over you. That's no way to live. For either of us. You know it as well as I. You have to choose. You have to *want* life."

Michael lay on his side, staring at the blank wall. The window. The stars beyond. Caitlin's hand, gentle as a feather, stroked his hair, but he could hardly feel it. He was lost. Lost in the darkness of the sky. In the night. In the bottomless confines of his own mind.

You have to want life.

Did he? Did he want life?

Not this life, surely. Never this. With the guilt of what he'd done chaining him to the rock of his misery so much more effectively than any of the irons he'd worn in New South Wales.

He'd come to her tonight to tell her that it was time to give up. That he'd resolved to go, leave her to her happiness.

But she loved him. And life as she described it, simple and easy, caring for her and being cared for in return. Living together, day in and day out. For better or for worse. That was love, wasn't it?

He loved her.

The truth of it pulled at him. A chain of a different sort, one that connected him to the world, and drew him up, up, out of the dark . . .

But it hadn't been perfect, had it? Yes, they'd found peace together, even love, but there had always been a shadow looming, weighing him down. The nightmares hadn't gone away. And they never would, no matter how far or close he was to Darnalay. That's what had come clear to him today. The worst had happened, or nearly. He'd confronted Cameron's wife, come face to face with the cook—a woman he'd wronged just as he'd wronged everyone at Darnalay. It was so near to the fate he'd been dreading, he'd expected something terrible to happen, for his wretchedness to increase somehow. But it hadn't. The countess had left and nothing had changed. Because the fact was, it didn't matter where in the world he was. Didn't matter if he ran away or froze in place. The guilt of what he'd done would never leave him. It would always be there. Always. It was inside him. Part of him. It was irredeemable.

Which was why he'd resolved to leave. But . . .

You have to choose.

Could he? Could he choose? Was it possible to rid himself of this weight rather than be crushed by it? To break his chains once and for all?

What if he went to Darnalay? Apologized, and asked forgiveness?

He pushed the idea away before it could take shape. Just a spectral mist, banished with a breath. No. He couldn't. What he'd done was unforgivable. And to go there, it would—

It would what?

Kill him? Surely not. Embarrass him? Perhaps, but what did that matter?

It was quite possible it wouldn't change a thing. But it could hardly make things worse.

And what if it *did* change things? What if he could be with Caitlin, in a life of their own, without the guilt?

What if he could be happy?

The idea was dizzying, like standing on a bridge high over a swiftly moving river and looking down. His stomach flipped. No. He didn't have the resolve for such a thing, and even if he could bring himself to try, he'd muck it up somehow.

It would be better to let Caitlin go alone and find a new life for herself. She'd be happier that way in the end, even if she couldn't see it now. Then he could go to London or some other city. Live out what was left of his life without anyone else's happiness to worry about—

"Are you still awake?" Caitlin's voice brought him back into his body. Into the bed. Her fingers trailed over his shoulder.

He grunted, trying desperately to ignore the draw of her touch.

"What are you thinking?"

To wake up with her. To walk with her, arm in arm. To drink tea each afternoon. To sit and smoke together each night. To fall asleep in her arms. To rejoice with her in the good times and comfort her in the bad . . .

"Michael? Please. Say something."

If he *could* choose. He would choose that. Life. With her.

You must choose.

"Michael, please."

The pain in her voice was too much to bear. He rolled over and met her eyes. They were bright with unshed tears, her expression gripped with worry. She'd had the courage to lay herself bare. She deserved the same from him.

"I love you." It was just a stream of air through his lips, but it took every shred of will he possessed. A single tear welled in her eye, overflowed, rolled down her cheek. She smiled and brushed it away. Then he leaned in and kissed her.

He poured everything he couldn't say into that kiss. Love and despair. Defeat and hope. Guilt and freedom. He loved her. Beyond all doubt. Beyond all fear. He had no idea what would come, if the choice was really even within his power, but it didn't matter. He would take the risk. Somehow, he would find the strength to try.

For her. For himself. For them.

She kissed him back in equal measure. Desperate, not for body to be closer to body, but for soul to meet soul. Her cheek was wet against his, and he pulled her closer, wrapping his arms around her and bringing her into his heart, where she would be for the rest of his days. No matter if they were twined together in passion, or separated by fathomless oceans.

From one breath to the next, the clothes between them were too much. He needed her skin on his. He moved back and peeled off his shirt, helped her rid herself of her night rail, and then they were together again. Mouth on mouth. Breath in breath.

She was on top of him, rising up, his goddess, fitting herself around him, sinking down onto him. Accepting every naked, miserable part of him. Loving him. Choosing him.

Michael.

Michael Dunn.

The imposter. The kidnapper. The beast. The lover. The man.

She lifted up and slowly lowered herself back down, savoring each inch of their joining. His hands came to her breasts, cupping them and pinching the nipples just how she liked. Caitlin groaned. Her eyes lost their focus, and her head tipped back, her unbound hair floating behind her in a whirling black cloud.

Goddamn, she was beautiful.

She rose off him again, then slammed back down, and all his thoughts and worries disintegrated as he lost himself to the pleasure. She rode him faster and harder and mindless until she lost her rhythm and fell upon him, gripping him tight, begging for something beyond words. Something only he could give. He held on for dear life and thrust up into her, giving her everything he had. Everything he could ever be. The hero and the villain. The man and the beast. It was all hers. *He* was all hers.

Then Michael's vision blurred and Caitlin cried out, and they came together in an explosion of tears and shouts and love. He spilled inside her, each thrust taking him deeper, bringing him closer they'd ever been.

Until finally, wrung out, bodies entwined, hearts joined, they stilled.

They lay together, panting, for a long while. Eventually, Caitlin pulled herself up and went to the wash basin. "I suppose I have me answer, then." There was such relief in her voice, such happiness, that Michael couldn't bring himself to tell her what he planned to do.

TWENTY-SEVEN

FOR THE FIRST TIME since he'd come to Glenoch, Michael allowed himself the luxury of holding Caitlin as she slept.

It was peaceful, with the soft puff of her breath on his chest, her skin warm against his, her hair tickling his cheek. He didn't intend to drop off himself, but he must have because at some point in the middle of the night he surfaced from mindlessness into a kind of clarity he hadn't known in years.

This hope of forgiveness was not new. There had been a time, after the panic of his departure from Darnalay and before he'd been apprehended in London—when the guilt was still fresh—that he'd resolved to find his cousins and Sommerbell and apologize, explain everything and beg for absolution. But that idea had died the minute he'd been clapped into irons. It had been buried deep in the hull of that cursed ship to New South Wales, right beside the rigid, vainglorious view of the world he'd inherited from Father. Michael had cast aside both impulses—the pathetic apology and the pompous pride—deeming them naive, two sides of the same coin. Then he'd enclosed himself in the tough, cynical armor he'd worn ever since.

But now, with the perspective of time, in the arms of the woman he loved—the woman who loved him in return—he could see how foolish he'd been. That soft youth who'd inherited the earldom, who'd only wanted to make his father proud, and ended up on a ship to Botany Bay . . . he hadn't been wrong, or—not *all* wrong. He'd been unwise, to be sure, and gullible to all sorts of terrible ideas, cruel even, but he hadn't been wrong in his softness, in his impulse to do right by the people he loved or to make amends to those he'd hurt.

It wasn't callow to apologize for one's wrongdoings. It was brave.

At least it must be, because the prospect was terrifying.

It might be too late. Certainly, after the blundering way he'd tried to seduce Jane while she was disguised as a maid he'd not be at all shocked if she refused his apology. He'd only met Cameron once, and then briefly. He had no idea what kind of man he was. And Sommerbell . . . Would he be at the castle as well? The countess had said Cameron's sister and her family were staying there, but Michael had no way of knowing if that meant only their children or the husband, too.

Michael shuddered at the thought of coming face to face with the pale, haunted visage of his nightmares.

Still, after what he'd done to the man, he deserved whatever came from the meeting. Certainly, it would be nothing compared to what Sommerbell had been through at Michael's hands.

What would happen afterward? What would he do? Two scenes kept playing in his head. One in which he strode over the Darnalay drawbridge, victorious and proud, mounted his horse, and rode back to Caitlin, sweeping her into his arms and carrying her off to a beautiful little farm in America where they would live happily ever after. In the other, himself running and running, head down through a dark world. Just as he had the first time.

The moon still shone through the window when he gently extricated himself from Caitlin's arms, rose from the bed, and tiptoed to his own chamber where he dressed hurriedly and scribbled a quick note. Then he stole back into her room and put the paper on the pillow that still held the impression of his head. She was sleeping soundly, curled up on her side, her hands tucked beneath her head. Soft snores escaped her parted lips, which seemed to be smiling.

He wanted so badly to kiss her, but he daren't. Instead, he turned and left the room.

The shining sun projected a patch of warm, yellow-white light onto the bed when Caitlin woke. She rolled into it, stretching from her fingers to her toes, and allowed the warmth to soak into her skin.

She was naked under the sheets, and she felt lithe and sensual against them—oh *yes*. A different kind of warmth flowed through her as she remembered the night that had just passed. She'd laid herself bare; then he'd declared his love. He *had*. They would go to America together, and—

Something brushed against her cheek. Paper?

She grasped at it. A note, in Michael's hand.

Dearest,

I've gone to Darnalay. I must attempt to make amends. I've taken the horse but will see that it's returned to you.

Please understand. I love you, but I can't live with the guilt hanging over me. It will only lead to sorrow, for both of us. I hope to return to you, but if I do not, please don't look for me. It's for the best.

You have, and will forever keep my heart.

Michael

The note dropped to the pillow as her panic rose. *Darnalay?* Of course, it was a noble thought, but . . . Michael was defenseless in the face of his demons. If he tried to fight them and failed . . .

She flung the coverlet aside. She had to get up, get dressed. How long ago had he left? If she could make it to the village and find someone willing to hire her a horse, if she rode like the wind, she might get there before he—

She caught her own eye in the mirror and froze. Her hair was a disheveled mess, black streaked with gray. Her body was pale, her nipples taut in the chill air. Her chest heaved. Her hand rose to her mouth, the same lips that had kissed him so deeply. Then it trailed down her throat, settled above her heart. Her heartbeat pounded beneath her palm. She'd surrendered this heart, this body to him mere hours ago, given him all of herself.

What had she told him? She'd told him he had to choose.

And he had.

If it were anyone other than Michael—the man she loved—she would have cheered his impulse to seek forgiveness. It was the right thing to do. A brave thing to do, but . . . but if it broke him . . . If she lost him . . .

She forced a long, slow breath through parted lips. She could almost see it, a cloud of fear and acceptance blown out into the world. Then she let her hand fall to her side.

It would kill her to sit here and wait, but that's what she must do.

TWENTY-EIGHT

PERHAPS IF MICHAEL HAD a better horse, he could have accomplished the ride to Darnalay in the half day the countess had described. But the old mare from the stables at Glenoch was not to be rushed.

They plodded down the road to Inverness, into the glen, past the burnt-out houses and great flocks of sheep until they came to the smattering of farms on the riverbank that he now knew were part of the Banton estate—or, used to be.

From there he asked directions, grateful for both his change in appearance and the distance he'd kept from the tenants in his brief time as laird here. He got plenty of curious looks, but no one seemed to recognize him for the man who had come so close to evicting them eight years before.

As he rode through the fields of rippling oats and hay, past the tidy cottages that were nearly hidden by the gardens surrounding them, he wondered how on earth he could have ever seen this land as a wasteland, needing improvement of any kind.

He swerved to avoid a flock of fat hens scratching in the dirt, and the sound of children's laughter floated on the breeze.

This was Eden. And he'd almost destroyed it.

Looking out over that lush landscape, for the first time in his life he was glad of what had transpired. Glad that Sommerbell had found the letter and held the secret of it through all those days in the dungeon. Glad, even, that Michael himself had been caught. His years in New South Wales had been nothing compared to the misery that might have transpired if he had succeeded in his plans here.

The sun was well past its zenith when he finally made it to the village of Darnalay. Here, he had no doubt he could be recognized so he pulled down his hat and rode through without stopping. It wasn't until he came to the stone bridge—that same bridge where Sommerbell had hidden the letter, and where Michael had confronted his cousins for the last time—that he allowed himself to breathe.

It felt unreal somehow, this place. So familiar, yet entirely altered. Probably, it was the same, and it was Michael who had changed.

He rounded the bend, and the castle came into view.

It looked exactly as it had when he'd first arrived after his uncle's death, and before he'd allowed everything to fall into disrepair. A bright red flag flew high over the tower, stretching and snapping in the breeze. Below it, the grand stone facade shone golden in the afternoon light, surrounded by sprawling orchards dappled with shadow. Towering trees flanked the drawbridge, and the portcullis was raised, opening up a view into the courtyard where two large urns overflowed with flowers.

Above the clopping of his horse's feet, the piercing, gleeful shriek of a child sounded. A lad appeared in the archway—a little boy of six or seven—dashing in and out of sight from one courtyard to the next. His small hands reached for a dog that was darting ahead of him.

"James. Come back!" An older girl, almost a woman, followed close in pursuit, her blonde braids streaming behind her.

Neither of them noticed him.

It wasn't cold. The sun was shining on his back. Still, Michael shivered.

He started to dismount, but before his foot touched the ground, the same dog—a squat, fat bulldog with an ugly, scarred face—galloped over the drawbridge, its tongue lolling. Clearly, it was enjoying the chase. The children followed hard on its heels.

Halfway over the bridge, the dog seemed to register the man and horse. Its errant path gained purpose, and it stiffened and ran straight at them, barking wildly. Michael's horse shied. He took his seat again, fighting to hold the mare steady.

As soon as he noticed Michael, the little boy scampered back into the castle, but the girl forged on, darting forward to grab hold of the bully. "I'm sorry, sir," she called to Michael. "He's a good boy, just not used to strangers."

A footman emerged, passing by the girl as she dragged the dog back into the courtyard. "G'day Miss Rose." He smiled with evident amusement. Then he bowed to Michael and flashed an unaffected grin. "G'day sir. May I be of help?"

Michael stared at him. He could still change his mind.

No.

He swung down from his horse, handed the man the reins, forced the air into his lungs, then spoke. "I am here to see the earl."

"And who should I say is callin'?"

There was a buzzing in Michael's ears, his feet felt unsteady all of a sudden, as if the ground were shifting beneath him. "I'm Michael Dunn. His cousin."

The servant's eyes widened. Obviously, he'd heard the story of Michael Dunn. "H-his cousin, ye say?" His eyes darted back the way he'd come, but he made no move to lead Michael there.

"Yes."

"I—" Clearly, the man wasn't sure if he should allow Michael entry. And for good reason.

"Please." Michael put his hands up, trying hard to sound as harmless as he could. "You can tell him I come bearing no ill will."

The servant's wary gaze skipped from Michael to Michael's horse "Very well, sir." Then he shouted toward the stables. "Niall, there's a—"

Before he could finish, a stable boy appeared. Niall, evidently. He took the mare's reins and began to lead her away. The footman followed the lad for a few paces before leaning in and murmuring something in his ear. The boy's eyes flew to Michael. They exchanged a few more words. Then the boy nodded and continued on his way.

The footman returned. The open friendliness of his greeting had vanished, replaced by a suspicious sense of responsibility. "Follow me, sir."

They went over the wooden drawbridge, under the portcullis, then down the steps and through the courtyard. Michael barely recognized the place. It looked so different from the barren, cold fortress he had briefly been master of. There were flowers everywhere, and wooden benches lined the stone walls. One had a shawl draped across it, an open book carelessly left behind on the seat.

They came to the thick, wooden door that led into the castle itself. This door had not changed. It was the same red cedar with the same black iron hinges, the same handle, and the same lantern hanging above. The thick buzzing in Michael's ears returned, and his knees threatened to give way. He almost stumbled as he crossed the threshold. But somehow he forced himself to walk, as if his body were made of wood and he, its puppeteer.

The great room, too, was as Michael remembered. High ceilings, fine furniture. A huge hearth towered at one end, and portraits of the family lined the walls. It was clean, much cleaner than Michael had ever kept it, and it held an air of peace. A room well loved.

The door behind them opened. Michael held his breath, but it wasn't Cameron who came through. This man had black hair, not ginger like his cousin. He strode toward him, and Michael met his glowering stare. He knew who this was. It was the stablemaster, one of the servants who had helped his cousins on that fateful night.

What was his name? Damn. He couldn't remember.

The man stared at Michael for a long time. Then he nodded to the footman. "Wait here. I'll tell 'im." He turned and strode toward the stairs that led deeper into the castle. Just before the dark-haired man disappeared from view, he turned, once again addressing the servant. "Search 'im, will ye?"

Then he was gone.

The footman awkwardly crossed to Michael and proceeded to follow the stablemaster's orders. His hands shook during the task, but he did a thorough job—as good as any guard in New South Wales—first patting Michael down, then examining his coat and shaking out his boots. He even looked inside Michael's hat. When no weapons were forthcoming, they began their wait.

Michael stood. The footman stood. They didn't say anything, didn't look at each other. There wasn't even a clock to break the silence. The late afternoon sun streamed in through the windows. The shadows lengthened.

Finally, the stablemaster returned. He addressed the footman first. "You searched 'im?"

"Aye, sir," the servant answered. "There's nothin' on 'im."

The stable master's eyes settled on Michael. "He'll see you." His expression was hard as granite. He turned to the footman. "He's in the library."

If the wait in the great room had felt endless, then it had been a mercy, because the walk to the library seemed far too short. It was as if each step were a beat of the drum leading to Michael's execution. He was guilty. A man already condemned.

They reached the top of the stairs, and the panic flared. This was a fool's errand. Why had he come?

He froze. Every impulse urged him to turn around. To flee.

In the shadow of the corridor ahead, Caitlin's face appeared, beckoning him. Warm sunlight and fields of ripe wheat reflected in her eyes, her lips red with raspberries, sweet with honey . . .

Somehow, inexplicably, the magpie's lilting song echoed off the stone. It cut through the roar in his ears and urged him on.

For her. For them.

Then they turned a corner, and another door loomed. The footman opened it and stepped inside. "Mr. Michael Dunn," he announced.

The buzzing in Michael's head rushed back to the fore. It was deafening now, his heartbeat pounding through him so hard he shook with it. Slowly, he forced one foot forward, then another.

The smell was the first thing that hit him. Wood smoke and old books. One inhalation, and the memories came crashing down . . . This was the room where he'd planned the cruel-hearted improvements to the estate. The room where he'd argued with Sommerbell and given in to the mad urge to send the man tumbling into the pit. The room where he'd sat, frozen in place as his victim's horrible screams filtered up through the floor. And where he'd ogled his own cousin, only feigning kindness because he imagined himself in her bed . . . This room had seen him at his most vile, his most evil. And now he was back—

"Thank you, Gregor." A voice jolted Michael from his daze. Cameron—it was unmistakably Cameron as he looked just like his father—was sitting behind the great desk, his chin resting on steepled fingers. He gazed at Michael with an unreadable expression, and Michael stared back. He'd rehearsed this conversation, over and over on the way, but now, standing here, the words he'd planned seemed absurd. Meaningless. How had this seemed like a good idea?

The door snicked shut.

He swallowed. Absurd or not, they were the only words he had.

"I—I came to apologize." It was his own voice, but he heard it from a distance, barely audible over the roaring in his head. "I should have sooner, but I—" He swayed slightly, then caught himself and continued, "I have no excuse. I am so very, very sorry." The words shook as they left his mouth and hung in the air, empty and pathetic. "I was unconscionably cruel to you and your sister both." He hesitated. "And to—to Sommerbell—" His voice cracked, and before he could stop it, a shuddering sob escaped his lips. His body convulsed, and he reached up to cover his eyes, pressing hard to stop the tears.

When he dared to let his hand drop, he found Cameron staring at him. His cousin opened his mouth, closed it again, then chuckled mirthlessly under his breath. "I wasna prepared for this." He looked past Michael, out of the window at the gathering dusk. "You're right. What you did all those years ago . . . 'Twas cruel beyond anything." His brown eyes focused on Michael. "I dinna so much blame you for my part. Your father drilled it into you that you were to be the earl, I suppose. And fathers—well, they have an effect on one, dinna they? In truth, I had no wish for the title." He shrugged. "But what you did to Sommerbell"—he shook his head, his tone grinding into anger—"and what you *almost* did to the tenants. 'Twas—"

"Unconscionable," Michael repeated. "I know. I've regretted it every day since."

"It was *unforgivable*," Cameron corrected him. He glared at Michael, and when he spoke again, the words were slow and labored, as if it took a great deal of effort to get them out. "I dinna ken if you fully understand. What you did to Sommerbell . . . It's taken *years* for him to recover. I dinna ken if he ever truly will. He still can't abide small rooms, you know, or closed carriages."

Unforgivable. The word ricocheted off the inside of Michael's skull.

Cameron's eyes narrowed, and his voice rose. "What do you want me to say to you, cousin?" He shrugged. "I dinna wish you ill. You've served your time. But I canna sit here and tell you all is well. That everything's forgiven. I *canna*. It's simply not true."

There was a long silence as Michael struggled to think, to find the right thing to say next. But everywhere he looked there was just one word, looming, blocking his path.

Unforgivable.

Surely, there was more he could say. Something to convince Cameron, to *show* him just how much he'd suffered. How sorry he was.

Unforgivable.

What did it matter how sorry he was? What difference did it make? It wasn't as if a few paltry words of apology or any suffering on his part would be enough to smooth over the enormity of what he'd done. Nothing could make it better. Of course it couldn't. How had he even thought that?

Unforgivable.

It was over. He'd failed. He'd been a fool to even try.

"I understand." He blinked at the stinging in his eyes. "I'm—I'm sorry for bothering you. Thank you for seeing me."

Something softened in Cameron's gaze. "I *do* mean it, you know. I wish you well. Truly. I hope you find happiness. Just not— here."

Michael nodded. The buzzing had gone, replaced by a desperate, ringing silence and the sudden urge to flee. He must leave. Get out. Now.

Cameron rose. "I'll call Gregor to see you out—"

But he couldn't wait. Michael turned, wrenched open the door, and tore out of the room. He fled down the stairs, through the great hall, past the heavy cedar door, into the courtyard.

Cool air enveloped him, along with music. Guitar music.

The sky spread above the stone walls, indigo blue studded with the first few pale stars. A man sat on a bench on the far side of the courtyard, bent over an instrument. A group of children crowded around him. Michael recognized the boy he'd seen earlier, James, as well as the older girl, who now had her dog on her lap and was absently stroking its head. They evidently hadn't noticed Michael's entrance.

The man was playing a jaunty, happy tune, and the children were watching, the light of a single lantern dancing over them. Clearly, they were entranced. One young girl was whirling around in circles, her skirts ballooning around her.

It didn't dawn on Michael who the man was until he ended the song with a grand flourish and looked up at his adoring audience. "And now, 'tis time for bed." He grinned.

It was Sommerbell.

Michael stumbled backward as if he'd been struck.

"Just one more, *pleeease*," the tiny dancing girl begged.

Michael backed up another step into the shadows. He must leave. He shouldn't be here. But somehow, he couldn't look away.

Sommerbell cocked a brow and laughed. "I already played one more. *Three* times. To bed with you all. Come along." He stood, brought his guitar back into position, started to play again, and led the children like the Pied Piper toward the door Michael had just come through. They'd almost reached it when it opened and a woman's head poked out.

"There you are." There was a note of anxiety in her voice. She stepped into the courtyard and craned her neck, as if looking for something. "Is all well?"

She was looking for Michael. Of course she was. He'd run out of the library like a mad man. They were probably searching the castle for him.

But Sommerbell seemed oblivious. Without stopping the music, he leaned forward and kissed her deeply. "All is well, my love. We were just going to bed."

"I see." Her tone changed. His kiss had assured her. She chuckled, a low, joyous sound. "Come along, then."

The group disappeared. The door closed. The lantern flickered.

All was silent save for the rusty chirping of crickets outside the castle walls. Michael stood in the shadows and stared at the heavy cedar door.

And finally, he understood.

Forgiveness wasn't the point. Cameron was right, Michael's actions truly *were* unforgivable. To pretend otherwise would be a lie, a lie that didn't serve anyone. What Michael sought, what he *needed*, was grace. The strength to wrest himself away from his past, to step out of the black shadow cast by the man he used to be and allow himself to move into the light.

That face, that grinning joyous face surrounded by children and music and life—it was so different from the pale, terrified visage of Michael's nightmares. Sommerbell might never truly recover, but he'd learned to live with his pain. To move past it and to be happy.

And so could Michael.

The weight lifted. The chain broke.

Just as he had when his fetters had been cleaved off in Sydney, Michael felt unstable. Teetering at the shock of freedom.

The door flew open again, and the same footman who'd escorted him into the library stalked out, a lantern raised before him.

"I'm here." Michael stepped out of the shadows, showing himself. "I was just going to collect my horse."

TWENTY-NINE

THE FIRST DAY MICHAEL was gone was easier. There was no chance he'd be back so soon.

But the second . . . it went on forever. After a fitful night of sleep, Caitlin rose early and spent the morning outdoors, walking the now familiar paths through the hills, trying to find some distraction in the beauty of the moor in bloom, in the way the shadows of the clouds raced across the land. Of course, unless he'd ridden all night, she couldn't expect him home this early, but even still, when she reached the heights far above the house, she couldn't help but look for him, a lone horseman emerging over the distant rise, following the ribbon of road that stretched from Inverness.

She took her midday meal in the kitchen, then retired to the sitting room where she tried to read. After an hour, she gave up and surrendered to the urge to drag her chair to the window and stare out at the road.

Time seemed to slow even more. The wind blew the heather, the birds swooped overhead, the sun tracked from its zenith, lower, then lower still, until the light poured through the pane, dazzling her and nearly obscuring the view.

At some point, Jinny poked her head in, reminding Caitlin that tea was waiting.

"I'll take it in here," Caitlin murmured.

"Of course, ma'am." The maid gave her a curious look. Caitlin had not explained things to any of the servants. There was nothing to explain.

The girl left.

Caitlin's eyes were drawn to the road once more. Perhaps in the few moments she hadn't been watching he—

No. The road was as empty as it had been all day.

She exhaled and craned her neck to the side, massaging the tense muscles. There was a chance he would never return. She should be prepared for that. He could be drunk right now, wandering his way south, giving up on life entirely.

After all, she'd told him she'd leave alone if need be, that he'd have to choose. But if it came down to it, and he chose to run away, could she really go without him? Make her home in some far-off land, knowing that he was here, somewhere. That he might be suffering alone—

Was that movement?

She squinted. The slanting sun made it hard to see clearly, but . . .

There. There *was* something on the road. A horse and a rider.

She flew out of the house, not bothering with a bonnet or cloak.

"Michael!" She strode toward the figure on the horse, shading her eyes with her hand. It was the right horse, surely. The old mare's gray coat was easy to spot. But the rider was hard to make out, a hat pulled low over his face. Was it him?

He lifted a hand in greeting.

Caitlin broke into a run.

As she approached, his features came into focus, and a wash of relief spilled though her when she saw he was smiling—an unaffected, unreserved, ear-to-ear grin. She'd never seen anything like it.

Michael swung down from the saddle just in time to catch her in his arms.

Their mouths found each other, but Caitlin was too out of breath for a long kiss. She pulled back and looked at him, framing his face with her hands. That wondrous smile . . . She couldn't help but laugh. His whiskers were bristly under her palms, his clothes a bit rumpled, but it was *him*. The man she loved. She drew him to her and kissed him again. Held him as tight as she'd ever held anything in all her life.

When she finally withdrew once more, his hat had tumbled to the ground, and they were both breathless. "And how did it go, then?"

"It went . . . *well*. Not at all how I expected." He beamed at her and bent down to retrieve his hat.

"Tell me."

"I will, but let's walk. I haven't eaten since yesterday. I'm ravenous." He put the hat back on, then shifted the horse's reins to his other hand and offered his arm. She looped hers through, and they started toward the house.

"It took all day to get there," Michael began. "Cameron received me in the library at the castle yesterday evening."

"And you . . . apologized?"

"Yes. It felt bloody foolish by the time I got there, but I apologized as I'd planned. Said I was sorry for everything." He fell silent.

"And?"

Michael shrugged. "He didn't accept. He said what I did was unforgivable." Caitlin's heart sank. Had she mistaken his happiness somehow? "He didn't wish me ill either. But he said he couldn't simply take my apology and act as if all were well. And he was right not to. It isn't." A shiver ran through her, and she suddenly wished she's brought a shawl. "Do you know, Sommerbell still can't ride in closed carriages, or be in small rooms . . . " Again, Michael stopped talking. He seemed to be lost in thought.

Caitlin trained her eyes on the brown stone of the house, doing her best to keep the impatience and worry out of her tone. "What happened then? Did he turn you out?"

"I left before he could, or ran away is more like it. I felt . . . wretched. I couldn't stand to be there for a second longer." As he spoke, that joyous grin flooded back onto his face, as mismatched with his words as could be.

"I don't understand," Caitlin stilled, pulled Michael to a halt, and planted herself in front of him, forcing him to look her in the eye. "If it went so poorly, why are you smiling?"

Michael's grin widened further. "Well, on my way out of the castle I happened upon Sommerbell." Caitlin felt her eyes go wide. "He didn't see me,"

Michael added quickly. "But I saw him. And he was—he was *happy*. As happy as a man can be. And Jane, my other cousin. She's happy too. Despite it all. Everything I did. They've moved on."

Understanding began to slide into place, and a warmth spread in Caitlin's chest. "Have they, now?"

"Yes. I think so." Michael nodded solemnly, all mirth gone from his face, replaced by an innocent kind of wonder she'd never seen there. "Do you know, I don't think it matters that Cameron didn't forgive me. I mean—like I said, what I did was unforgivable. I don't blame him at all. I don't know that I'll ever be able to forgive myself, if I'm honest. But that doesn't mean I can't change, does it? Be happy as the man I am now?" He shook his head. "I'm not making any sense, am I?"

Caitlin gazed into the clear blue of his eyes, her lips spreading into a wide smile. "Oh, but you are. You're making all the sense in the world."

Half an hour later they were in the sitting room, where Michael was devouring a plate of bread, boiled eggs, and cheese. He hadn't been exaggerating about not eating. When Caitlin asked where he'd slept, he shrugged and said he hadn't wanted to intrude on the innkeeper at Darnalay Village—he'd apparently had doings with the woman while he'd lived there—so he'd tethered his horse and laid himself down on the heather by the road.

"Did you sleep?" she asked, incredulously.

"A bit." He grinned and swallowed the large mouthful he was chewing. "But I really just wanted to be here, so I was up as soon as there was light enough to see."

Caitlin bent over and kissed his cheek. "That explains this, then." She plucked a heather blossom from his tousled hair. Then she rose. "I'll just call Jinny to draw you a bath."

When she returned, his plate was empty, and Michael was sitting back comfortably on the sofa, his eyes half closed. A rush of memory blew through her, of the day they'd first met. He'd been in need of a bath then, too, but that was the only resemblance she could find between this man and the lost soul who'd arrived on her doorstep all those months ago.

He opened his eyes as she approached and smiled a lazy, contented grin. "Is that bath ready?"

"Not quite." Caitlin sank down beside him, and he drew her close till she was half sitting on his lap, his arms encircling her. He smelled of pipe smoke and heather and the windswept moor.

She rested her head on his chest. "Michael?"

"Hmm?" She felt his voice as much as heard it. The rumble in his chest, the warmth of his breath on her scalp.

"You'll come with me, then, won't you? To America?"

His arms tightened around her, and he pressed a kiss to her neck. "Of course. Was there any doubt?"

"No. I suppose not."

Silence fell between them as Caitlin rode the waves of Michael's breath. The sun had just set, and the sky outside the window was awash with vibrant colors.

"Michael?" Caitlin spoke again, barely whispering. She wasn't at all sure he was awake, and she didn't want to wake him, but she also needed to ask. Somehow, she couldn't wait.

"Yes, love?"

"I wonder. Would you like to get married?"

He was silent for a long time. Then, almost as if he hadn't understood the meaning of the word, "Married?"

"Married. Wed." She turned so she could see his face and was relieved to find a gentle smile there. "If we're to live together in America, share a bedroom, I mean, and on the boat over . . . It does seem . . . the proper thing, does it not?"

His look darkened a bit. "You'd lose your dower. There'd be no going back."

"I know that." She kissed him lightly on the lips. "I love you, Michael Dunn. I don't want to go back."

His smile grew—first on his lips, then in his eyes, a sunburst as bright as the colors outside the window. "You really want to? I mean—I would live with you without it, you know. I don't mind."

She grinned up at him. "I've never been more certain of anything in me life."

"Well then, let's get married." He gazed at her, his eyes soft with love, and pulled her in for a kiss. A long, deep, forever kind of kiss. A promise. A vow.

They sat together, lost in their love, as the bright colors of sunset dissolved into the gentle hush of twilight. A swallow swooped low, finding dinner for his family. The clouds blew by. And the end of one day became the beginning of another.

EPILOGUE

14 MONTHS LATER

MICHAEL PUSHED THE DOOR open and stepped out into the moonlight.

Caitlin sat on the front step, her chin resting in her hands, a silhouette gazing at the rising moon. The yellow circle of light hung low in the sky as the rhythmic chime of insects lulled the still, humid air.

She turned at the sound of the door and sent him a tired but satisfied smile. "We'll need some chairs out here, I think."

"In time." He offered her the glass he carried, fished their pipes out of his pocket, then sank down beside her, glad to put an end to this long day at last. The music of the crickets soaked into him along with the gentle babble of the creek that ran behind the house. A sudden breeze blew sweet with the aroma of fresh cut hay, ruffling his hair and cutting through the heat of the day—so different from the fetid air of the city. "This'll certainly do for now."

Her head sank onto his shoulder, and her body relaxed against him. "Indeed."

Their day had begun well before dawn when they'd woken in the cramped tenement that had been their home for the last ten months. They'd crossed the city to collect the second-hand wagon and gelding they'd purchased, then driven it back, loaded everything in, and set out for the new farm—first boarding the ferry to Staten Island, then turning north and driving through the farm country of New Jersey.

They'd arrived before sunset, with just enough time for Caitlin to settle the horse and for Michael to set up the bedstead before darkness set in.

"Gor, but it's pretty here." Caitlin sighed. She lifted her head and took a sip of her rum. "There's so much to do, though."

"In time," Michael repeated. He snaked his arm around her and drew her closer.

Ever since they'd left Scotland, he'd been moving—rolling over the choppy waves of the Atlantic, forcing his way through the crowds of Manhattan, jostling down that long dirt road, working as hard as he ever had in his life while worrying for the future and all that might go wrong. But as he lit his pipe and brought the smoke into his mouth, then exhaled, long and slow, the months of drudgery in that dirty city of New York faded away, along with all the anxiety and tension . . .

They'd arrived.

Yes, there was a lot to do. The kitchen was filthy, the rooms empty of furniture, the garden overgrown.

But they were home.

When Caitlin had shown him the notice in the *Evening Post*, he'd assumed they'd never get this place. The family who'd lived here were moving further west, leaving behind a farmhouse, a barn, and thirty acres of cleared pasture and fields. They'd answered the advertisement right away, offering all that they'd managed to keep from Caitlin's dower allowance, plus what they'd saved from Michael's clerking and Caitlin's piecework. He'd been astounded when the answer had come posthaste.

The farm was theirs if they could get there within the month.

And not only that, but Michael had found a position teaching at the school in Minisink, just to the east. His wages would feed them over the winter and help them set up the farm properly in the spring.

"There's room for at least five cows in that barn, and with the pasture and hayfields . . . we'll be able to send milk and butter to the city for certain." Caitlin pulled from her pipe, then exhaled, and the smoke floated up, disappearing into the stars. "I'll order hives in the spring. This land'll be perfect for bees." She rested her head on his shoulder again. "'Tis perfect," she murmured.

Michael could hear the excitement in her voice, her joy at the future that stretched before them. He shared it, truly. It was everything they'd ever wanted. Yet all he could think of was now. The settled stillness, the deep-rooted feeling of contentment, of knowing that this was what he'd been born for.

This moment.

Right now.

He pressed a kiss into his wife's hair, savoring the smell of her, the tickle of her curls against his nose. "The bed's all set up."

"Is it, now?" She turned to face him, a knowing smile on her lips.

For a moment, Michael was lost in the sparkle of her eyes. He could hardly believe their luck. But no. It wasn't luck. It was damn hard work that had got them here. And that was better than luck, better by far.

In a world so full of injustice, they had found their reward.

He leaned forward, joining his lips with hers, and in the fullness of that moment under the rising moon, there was peace.

A Note at the End

Dearest Reader,

Thank you for reading this book.

I wrote The Song of the Magpie at a particularly difficult time for my family. I'd anticipated writing through the winter and publishing in the spring of 2024. But then Mr. Mayberry (the main breadwinner for our family of five), was laid off just before Christmas, and all of our plans went out the window.

It was an incredibly stressful time—an *impossibly* stressful time—as nearly all our energy went to keeping our family afloat and simply getting by.

But you know what? We *did* get by. We picked up gig work and side work, reduced our bills as much as we could, and together, we not only survived our year of challenge, but we thrived. By the time he landed a new (and much better) job in the late summer of 2024, our family had forged a sense of closeness and resilience that we never would have come to in any other way.

And somehow, in the small cracks and crevices of time in between cooking dinner, freelance writing, driving Uber and getting my kids where they needed to go, I managed to write The Song of the Magpie. It was published in late September, six months after I'd originally planned, but I did it.

So you see, Magpie was born of real-life resilience, determination, and grit... and a whole lot of heart-wrenching angst and anxiety. I hope you've come to the end of it with a heart as full as mine was when I finally typed The End.

After completing this book (which I'd intended as the final installment in the series), I found I wasn't quite ready to say goodbye to the Darnalay Castle world, or these characters... so I wrote a conclusory novella: A Portrait of a Highlander.

'Portrait' is Tavish, the stablemaster's, story. But it's more than that. It's an ode to the castle itself, and to the Highlands... to both the past and the future. I hope you'll decide to keep reading!

But whether you do or not, I hope you'll stay in touch. Visit my website (www.louisemayberry.com) to sign up for my newsletter. My email is louise @louisemayberry.com. I'd love to hear from you.

All my very best,

Louise

HISTORICAL NOTES

Australia in the nineteenth century was a place unlike any other in history—a colony intended to serve as a solution to the overcrowded gaols and prison hulks of Britain, and separated from the mother country by an arduous four-month journey.

It's very difficult for us, in this age of instant communication, to fully grasp what this distance meant to the convicts of the time. How traumatic it would have been to be forcibly separated from all friends and family, with no real hope of ever seeing them again. Even if a convict did manage to correspond with loved ones, it could easily be a year or more between sending a letter and receiving a reply.

There are instances, however, of husbands and wives following their convict spouses to Australia to start a new life. In fact, Sarah McCullogh, the wife of one of the political radicals who was transported after the 1820 Radical War in Glasgow, did just that. In a letter home, her husband Thomas wrote:

"The whole of our party is much respected here by the most respectable people in this country, and if you will only come out, a steady man and woman can do well, as they are very rare articles to be found here."

Sarah arrived, along with their two sons, in 1823. Shortly afterward, Thomas, still under his sentence, was assigned to her as an indentured servant, and like Davey and Emily they began to build a new life in Sydney.

But such reunifications were rare—out of the financial reach of the vast majority of the convict population.

Though its easy to envision the convicts of New South Wales as a violent lot—and of course, some of them were—most were non-violent petty thieves. This was because British law in the eighteenth and early nineteenth centuries was much more concerned with property rights than it is today. Prostitution was legal, and while crimes such as physical assault were largely ignored, people were transported for offenses as small as stealing a yard of cloth, a single spoon or (as in Caitlin's case), a handkerchief.

Once in the colony, a convict's experience could vary dramatically based on their sex, the skills they brought with them, and luck. Many were assigned as indentured servants to free settlers, while others worked for the government in a variety of positions.

White women comprised only fifteen percent of the English population, and consequently, their company was highly sought after as prostitutes, mistresses and wives. When Caitlin mentions that she was "picked out of a lineup" by her first husband, she's not exaggerating. Women convicts were literally lined up and put on display for any lucky man who was granted permission by the government to marry. The man would examine each woman in turn, perhaps ask them a question or two, then make his decision. This was the extent of the courtship.

There are several documented instances of women successfully managing farms in the colony, the most prominent of them being Esther Johnstone (née Abrams), who's story, as told in his novel, is very much real. In fact, the newspaper article about Esther's trial, and subsequent loss of her farm, is taken verbatim from *The Australian*, one of the leading newspapers of the time.

The fortunes of a male convict were largely prescribed by whatever trade (or lack thereof) he brought with him from Britain. The crime he'd been convicted of wasn't considered. Tradesmen such as blacksmiths and bricklayers were in demand in the growing colony, so it would not have been unusual to find a blacksmith who'd committed murder plying his trade and enjoying relative freedom, while a simple London pickpocket did grueling manual labor under heavy guard.

A convict like Michael, with a good education and upper class manners, was a rarity, and would very likely have been placed in a position of relative power and freedom such as a teacher, a clerk, or a manager.

While the government was happy to ignore the convict's original sentences, misbehavior and crime in the colony was harshly dealt with. Flogging was very common, and convicts who committed new crimes while serving their sentences were routinely imprisoned in secondary penal settlements such as Moreton Bay (near current day Brisbane), Norfolk Island and Port Macquarie. By all accounts, these were bleak, terrible places, where men were worked for long hours, given starvation rations and punished cruelly for any small infraction. For many, it was a fate worse than death, and there are indeed records of men who murdered their fellow inmates only for the opportunity to be shipped back to Sydney, tried and hung for their crime.

There are so many tragic stories within this unique and fascinating history. It was a great pleasure to write one with a happy ending.

A well deserved peace, indeed.

ACKNOWLEDGEMENTS

I am deeply indebted to my many writer friends who provided not only technical help and advice as I was writing The Song of the Magpie, but also moral support and encouragement when I needed it most.

Thank you to Alivia Fleur for her expertise in Australian history, her insistence on impeccable craft and her beautiful, generous friendship. To Jane Hadley, for helping me find Caitlin and Michael's happily-ever-after, and for always demanding to *feel* everything right along with my characters. To Amber Night, for her long, introspective emails and for the magic she worked with my words. Amber's editing transformed this book from a rather dusty rock (with potential) into a glittering diamond. And to Heather Hallman, for her support and honest conversation.

Thank you also to Brendon, who's been with me from the beginning. His critiques of plot and character have helped shape me into the writer I am today.

And of course, thank you to my family. To my children for putting up with a mom who's as distracted and angsty as any of my heroines. And to my dear, dear husband, Mr. Mayberry. I've said it before, and I'll say it again and again and again: *He makes it all possible.*

THE DARNALAY CASTLE SERIES

The Darnalay Castle Series

From the smoke-filled alleys of early-industrial Glasgow and the wild glens of the Highlands, to the far reaches of the British empire—these evocative historical romances will sweep you away, capture your heart, and transport you to a different time.

Book 1: Roses in Red Wax
Book 2: Swept Into the Storm
Book 3: A Radical Affair
Book 4: The Song of the Magpie
Book 4.5: A Portrait of a Highlander

Available from all major book retailers, or purchase directly from Louise's website: **www.louisemayberry.com**

ABOUT THE AUTHOR

LOUISE MAYBERRY LIVES WITH her family in the Upper Midwest, where she savors the summers and survives the winters. When not writing, she can be found wandering in her garden, attempting to talk her her kids into eating healthy food, or curled up in a pool of sunshine with a cup of tea and a good book.